--- ★ ---

THE SOUNDS OF CHRISTMAS

The zing of the bullet seemed even closer. Molly waved her orange muffler in the air. "Don't fire! I'm over here!" she screamed. Whoever it was would have to be both blind and deaf not to see or hear her. Surely no one had mistaken her for a deer! Had Joy talked Myrtis into shooting down some mistletoe, she wondered; but the tree was on the other side of the pasture.

Molly crawled to her knees and shouted, "Myrtis? It's Molly! Where are you?"

An answer came sooner than she expected as a shell hit the ground somewhere behind her. Someone was deliberately shooting at her!

--- ★ ---

Also available from Worldwide Mystery by
MIGNON F. BALLARD

CRY AT DUSK

DEADLY PROMISE

MIGNON F. BALLARD

W🌐RLDWIDE.

TORONTO • NEW YORK • LONDON • PARIS
AMSTERDAM • STOCKHOLM • HAMBURG
ATHENS • MILAN • TOKYO • SYDNEY

Special thanks to York County Coroner,
Jim Chapman

DEADLY PROMISE

A Worldwide Mystery/December 1991

First published by Carroll & Graf Publishers, Inc.

ISBN 0-373-26086-5

For the Charlotte Wednesday Writers Workshop,
and for my editor, Margaret Norton

ONE

SHE AWOKE to a still, gray dawn and a sense of something not quite right. At first she thought he was Father Christmas, an illustration from an antique greeting card, the tall figure in the scarlet cape. He stood at the far corner of the house in the frosty luster of a December morning with something—a basket?—in his hand and a garland of holly around his head.

Shivering, Molly Stonehouse leaned on the windowsill. Except for the slight fluttering of his cape caught by the wind, he was as motionless as a statue. It was too dark to see his face, but his shoes, she noticed, were a bright green. He seemed to be waiting for something to happen, standing there with his basket held in front of him. But what? It was too early—or too late—for a costume party.

Molly crawled back into bed and pulled the covers to her chin, reluctant to leave this rumpled island of security. She watched the quiet light loiter over dark oak floors and creep up the marble-topped dresser, where someone had placed a small white pitcher of holly: a festive token of Christmas, her first without Ethan.

The wallpaper was the same: fading lavender flowers on a background of green, just as her husband had described it. Molly stretched in the big walnut bed that had been his in the room that had been his and felt the heavy awareness descend upon her as it had every morning since Ethan had died. With the weight of stone it pressed down on her, this daily awakening of her loneliness without him.

Molly placed cold fingers over her burning eyes and counted to ten. It always calmed her. She was warm beneath the quilts, but her hands were cold. The touch of them shocked her into reality. She blinked. The flowers still zigzagged across the walls as they had when Ethan was twelve, the Christmas he and his friends had discovered a hidden message and buried it in a harmless childhood game—or so they had thought. Now, twenty-three years later, two of them were dead.

Sitting up in bed, Molly looked again for the strange figure in red, but he was gone. That portion of the back yard was bare except for a thick row of dark green holly trees screening a garage that had once been white. Closer to the house, the huge oak where Ethan had built his tree house reached out dark limbs against a slate sky.

I must be hallucinating from eating all that chocolate, Molly thought, padding across the cold floor in search of her suitcase. It was a five-hour drive from Charlotte to the small Georgia town of Harmony where her husband's aunts lived, and her thirteen-year-old daughter, Joy, had complained all the way. It had been a two-Hershey trip.

Molly swore under her breath as she stubbed her toe on a rocking chair, then hobbled about groping for her shoes. What am I doing in this place? she thought. Maybe her daughter was right. Maybe she shouldn't have insisted they spend the Christmas holidays in this rambling old house with relatives they hardly knew.

It had been years since she came here with Ethan, but she remembered the deep, rich redness of the soil; the gray stone columns that marked the edge of town; winding streets and generous lawns reminiscent of days of croquet games and ice cream socials. The "teacup" town, Ethan had called the little village nestled in the foothills of the north Georgia mountains.

She sniffed, afraid to hope. The real thing, the smell of coffee, drifted from the kitchen below along with the spicy aroma of something sweet and warm—and probably fattening, but Molly didn't care. She could afford to put on some of the weight she had lost in the nine months since Ethan's death.

Someone shuffled down the hall outside her door trying not to make any noise. She heard a door softly open and close; a heavy pan clanged on the stove, and the radiator beneath her window banged to life with blessed heat. The house was awake and so was she.

Molly dressed quietly, trying not to wake Joy, who slept on a roll-away bed in the corner. Looking at her sleeping daughter, at the fluff of light brown hair around her face, Molly wanted to gather her into her arms as she had so many times before, but she knew the child who seemed so peaceful in her sleep would, at her mother's touch, draw into a cold, resentful shell. For the last few months, Molly had conditioned herself not to touch her own daughter because the rejection was more than she could bear.

Joy slept soundly, looking even younger than her thirteen years, with one arm hugging Marjorie, the stuffed bear her father had given her when she was three. "Let's name it after your mother," Ethan had suggested, laughing. "She's always a bear in the morning." Molly smiled at her namesake. At least one of us is getting some affection, she thought. Joy clung to the bear as if it were a part of her father, and Molly knew she was almost as guilty. She gave her short blond hair a few strokes with a brush and pulled on the faded blue sweatsuit that had been her husband's. She told herself she wore it because it was soft and warm, but she liked the familiar touch of it on her skin and the small comfort it gave.

A door slammed across the hall, and someone clomped down the stairs.

"Emma Beth, for God's sake, you sound like a herd of buffalo. Do you want to wake the dead?" A male voice spoke in bored tones as if he had said this many times before. It was probably Asa Brown, Emma Beth's father and Ethan's first cousin, Molly thought.

She followed the sound of voices to the dining room, leaving Joy to find her own way downstairs, and was immediately whisked into a seat at the table by a short, plump woman with curling gray hair who patted her shoulder with one hand and poured coffee with the other. The smell of bacon lingered about her, and Molly realized how hungry she was.

"Afraid I woke you with all my clattering about down here! Hope you slept all right in that relic of a bed. I just can't abide a soft mattress myself." Ethan's Aunt Ivalee bustled into the kitchen through a swinging door, calling to her granddaughter at the table. "Emma Beth, come in here, honey, and give me a hand with these grits before they stick." She paused to meet Molly's sleepy gaze. "You do eat grits, don't you?

"Asa, holler up and tell your Aunt Iris to come on down now." The door flapped shut behind her.

Molly watched mutely as a large girl with her auburn hair in hot curlers crammed a biscuit oozing peach preserves into her mouth and followed her grandmother without a word.

Asa Brown sat across from her. He merely grinned and took a swallow of coffee. "Aunt Iris will come down when she'd good and ready," he said. "It won't do to rush her." He unfolded the thick newspaper beside him and offered her a section, and Molly remembered with a shock that it was Sunday. She worked in the registrar's office of a small community college, and since they were closed for the holidays, she had lost track of the days of the week.

Asa, munching a sticky bun while glancing through the entertainment section, wore a coat and tie, and the other two seemed to be in varying stages of Sunday dress. Almost as an afterthought, he passed the pastries to her. "Sorry. Guess I'm not used to having company. Have one—Mother's a wizard in the kitchen."

When he smiled he looked a little like Ethan, Molly thought. There was something about the corners of his mouth and the way his eyes were set, although Ethan had dark hair and Asa's was reddish-brown; and he looked handsome in a brown tweed jacket and bronze silk tie. Though he and Ethan were about the same age, they had never been very close, but the two cousins shared expensive tastes in clothes, Molly noticed. She wondered if Asa Brown helped with the household expenses in the home he and Emma Beth shared with his mother and aunt. After his Grandmother Stonehouse died, Ethan had told her, the property was left to his aunt Iris, the youngest, who had remained single and stayed to care for her mother. Her sister, Ivalee Brown, had come home to share the house after her husband died. Asa, her son, had moved in when Emma Beth was small after the child's mother ran off with a rock group in Atlanta.

"I'm afraid I forgot what day it was," Molly confessed, accepting the gooey pastry. "Do you think I should wake Joy for church?"

"Nonsense. Let the child sleep; you both need the rest." Aunt Iris stood in the doorway, a tall, slender woman in a tailored green suit that matched her eyes. Molly thought she would have been stunning if her dark hair had not been so obviously dyed; and the bright pink lipstick she wore was not at all becoming to her. "With all the running around we do, it's a wonder we aren't all sick," she added with a faint little sniff. "Especially with the flu going around."

Iris Stonehouse took the chair beside Molly's just as Ivalee and her granddaughter brought in steaming bowls from the kitchen. "We're so glad you and Joy could be with us for Christmas," she said with a smile. "I hope you slept well after that long drive." She spoke in a warm, cheerful voice, yet her eyes were serious, almost solemn, and her hand lingered briefly on Molly's as she passed the platter of eggs.

Why, the woman feels guilty, Molly thought as Asa asked a tardy blessing. Iris must feel responsible for Ethan's death because he was on his way home from Harmony when he was killed.

"I don't remember a thing after I closed my eyes last night," Molly told her. "But I did see something peculiar this morning—or I think I did." And she told them about the figure in the red cape.

"Oh, that's just Sonny Earl Dinsmore," Asa said. "He lives next door with his mother. Let's just say he wasn't bit by Solomon's dog."

"Now, that's not true, Asa!" Iris said. "Sonny Earl had as fine a mind as anyone in this room until he came down with that fever. Why, he could out-spell everybody in our class."

"Poor Miss Eula," Ivalee said. "She's getting too old to keep up with him—even had to give up driving last year. Sonny Earl could wander off and get hurt; anything could happen. Where was he when you saw him?"

"Standing out back." Molly smiled. "I thought I was having a vision."

"That's his costume for the season," Asa said. "Probably found it in the attic. Last month he dressed like an Indian: went around wrapped in a blanket!"

Iris cut her bacon into pieces. "Mama tried to tell Miss Eula he needed some kind of training, but she wouldn't listen. She never listens."

Her sister laughed. "Eula Dinsmore quit speaking to Mama after they got into that argument about peeling tomatoes."

Molly glanced up to see Asa smiling at her. "What about peeling tomatoes?" she asked.

"Oh, they were slicing some for a picnic," Ivalee said, "and Mama told Miss Eula even a pig wouldn't eat tomato peel." She poured cream into her coffee. "She was right, of course, but Miss Eula's been distant ever since."

Emma Beth stirred a generous portion of butter into her grits. "Daddy, do I have to go to church today?" she whined.

"Do we have to go through this every Sunday?" Asa Brown spoke evenly, never taking his eyes from his plate. "Yes, you have to go; and if you don't hurry, we'll be late. Forget second helpings, Emma Beth; you don't need them anyway."

The girl's flush was darker than the sprinkle of freckles across her face. She threw down her napkin and ran from the room. Molly supressed an impulse to run after her. She stared at her plate, her appetite gone. She and Joy should fit in just fine here.

"High strung," Ivalee whispered aside to Molly.

"Umm," Iris grunted, looking as if she wished she were somewhere else.

Molly wished she were somewhere else, too, but she was here for a purpose and was determined to make the best of it. She had promised herself she would try to find out the reason for Ethan's death. Ignoring their protests, she insisted on washing the dishes while the others got ready for church. It would give her time to be alone, time to think, and maybe she and Joy could agree to some kind of acceptable truce to get them through the holidays.

Molly knew that in some irrational way Joy blamed her for her father's death. The child had worshipped Ethan—and why not? He had given her everything she asked for and left the discipline to Molly. A few days before he was killed, he and Molly had argued loudly, emotionally, and she had accused him of being selfish and impractical. Ethan had put a lot of money down on a pleasure boat without even consulting her. It was a luxury they couldn't afford, and she had been furious. She was tired of being the tight-fisted money manager while the family bank account stayed drained and anemic from her husband's extravagances. But what did it matter now?

The house was quiet after the others left for church, and still Joy slept, or pretended to sleep, upstairs. Molly filled the kitchen sink with hot sudsy water. The simple task of washing the breakfast dishes was relaxing in its dullness, and she was glad to delay the disagreeable chore of waking her daughter. What an awful way to feel about your own offspring, she thought, swishing a rose-patterned plate in the foam. If ever they needed one another, it was now.

Last year the three of them had spent Christmas skiing in Colorado, and Molly had shut her eyes to the expense and had a wonderful time. Now she scraped the egg from a fork and stared out the window at brown leaves skidding across the floor of the deserted summerhouse at the far end of the yard. It looked as bleak as she felt. Her happiness of the year before seemed distant, unreachable, as if it had happened to someone else. Then Harmony had been just a pleasant place in Ethan's childhood and the secret message had made a fascinating story about a game of "buried treasure."

Although he grew up in Florida, Ethan had spent part of each holiday at his grandparents' home in Harmony. The Christmas he was twelve, his best friend Neil Fry had come with him, and they, along with a third child, Gus Duncan, had discovered to their delight a secret "mailbox" for love letters in a hollow tree on the back path to town.

"We had been to the Saturday morning movie," Ethan told her, "and were ambling along the back way home when we saw this paper sticking out of a tree." Her husband had laughed. "Of course we read it," he admitted. "It was written to a girl named Rowena Sterling, who lived just outside of town. She was a pretty girl, home from college for the holidays, and Grandma said she was 'fast,' so of course that made it all the more interesting."

Ethan never said who had written the letters, or if he did, Molly had forgotten, but the three intercepted several messages after that, always putting them back where they found them before Rowena came along.

"We decided they were left there in the early mornings and picked up after dark," he explained. "Rowena had a part-time job at Murphy's drugstore about a block from where the letters were hidden."

But one morning the envelope had contained airline tickets as well as a curious message. "Fly away with me," the note read. "Meet me tonight at the usual place and time." The three weren't familiar with the names on the tickets.

"Well, you never saw any kids more excited than we were!" Ethan's eyes had sparkled as he told her the story, and Molly felt a little jealous that she hadn't been there, too. "We were planning to follow Rowena that night and discover the facts of life—or so we hoped. But before we could put the envelope back, Grandpa came along on his way back from town and insisted we ride home with him."

The children's families had other plans for them that afternoon, so they didn't get back to the tree. "The next day," Ethan continued, "we learned that Rowena had run away with some drifter her father had hired to work on his farm. He had fired the guy after an argument that day, and the night Rowena left, the Sterlings' stable burned. Everybody thought this man had done it for spite."

"What did you do with the tickets?" Molly asked.

"We really felt guilty about that," Ethan confessed. "We were afraid somebody would find out what we'd done, so Gus suggested we bury them. And we all made a promise we'd never tell a soul."

"But bury them? Why?"

Her husband grinned. "We were twelve years old, remember? We made a game out of it—a time capsule—and buried the tickets, message, and all out in the yard somewhere. Heck, we even drew a treasure map, planning to come back the next summer and dig it up."

"Well, did you?" Molly asked.

Ethan shook his head. "No. Gus moved away, and Neil and I went to camp; then Grandma died when I was about fourteen or fifteen, and I never went back much after that.

"You know, I worried about that for the longest time," he admitted, "about that silly letter and those tickets. I wonder if they're still there." He shrugged. "I guess everybody has forgotten about it now."

But everyone hadn't. Molly let the water drain from the sink and sprinkled cleanser on the enamel, rubbing it in widening circles. Her husband had shared this childhood story soon after they were married, and aside from an occasional reference, he had never discussed it again. If she had not run across a hasty note from Neil while sorting Ethan's papers the month before, she might never have suspected her husband's death was anything but an accident.

The two men had remained in touch throughout the years, but Molly had been so overcome with grief when Ethan died that she had neglected to get in touch with Neil. It was not until she received a Christmas card from Neil's family that she learned of his death from a hit-and-run accident in April. He had been jogging early one morning on a sparsely traveled road, and the police had never apprehended the driver. Still, Molly didn't connect the two deaths until she remembered Neil's warning note:

There's discord in Harmony, and I think it has something to do with the name on the message we found. Call me pronto. It's important! I'll try to warn Gus.

The letter was dated a week before Ethan's fatal accident. Had Gus been warned, or had he been murdered, too? Molly didn't know how to get in touch with him.

She dried her wrinkled hands and rewarded herself with another cup of coffee. Steaming cup in hand, she strolled through the downstairs rooms. The dining room was elegant-threadbare; the oval mahogany table and chairs that had belonged to Ethan's great-grandmother shone with years of polish, but the needlepoint cushions were faded. A hand-carved whatnot stand in the corner was filled with fragile china figurines. Molly felt sorry for whoever had to dust them.

The half-filled coffee cup sat on the living-room end table; *The Atlanta Constitution*, carelessly folded, awaited the family's return. Molly noted a scattering of Christmas cards displayed on the mantel, and there were candles in the windows. A few blocks away church bells chimed "Oh Come, All Ye Faithful."

Molly held the warm mug in both hands. She was among relatives her husband had loved in the town where he had spent his happiest times, but something was wrong—horribly wrong—and it had begun right here in Harmony.

TWO

"Is the house on fire? What is that ghastly smell?" Asa Brown paused in the hallway and poked his head around the living-room door. He had changed into a sweater and slacks and was obviously in a hurry to escape the Sunday afternoon doldrums that had settled upon the rest of the family.

Iris added another envelope to her stack of neatly addressed Christmas cards. "Emma Beth's making cookies. Says she's going to give them to her friends."

"Good lord, I hope not!" Asa rolled his eyes at Molly. "I thought I'd browse around some, maybe do a little Christmas shopping. Care to come?"

Molly tossed her magazine aside. "Are the stores open today?" She had made her major purchases but was considering adding a couple of stocking-stuffers for Joy.

"Just plain greedy!" Iris muttered, not bothering to look up. "Afraid they'll miss a dollar. Why, I remember when we couldn't even go to a picture show on Sunday."

Molly grinned at Asa's secret wink. She felt sluggish after the heavy noon meal and would welcome an excuse to get away for a while. Through an archway into the dining room, she saw Joy sitting alone at the far end of the table diligently writing letters to her friends back home. She could imagine her daughter's pitiful messages deploring her plight: "There's nothing to do here... I'm bored to death....Nobody cares what I think!" The longest one went, no doubt, to the straw-haired boy down the street who seemed to have established residence in their kitchen.

His name was Dwayne; he wore his hair in a rat tail, spoke in monosyllables, and had a skateboard permanently attached to his foot. Joy was experiencing her first case of lovesickness, and Molly prayed nightly that medical science would come up with a vaccine.

Asa glanced at his watch. "Stores close at six," he said, edging toward the door.

Molly looked from Aunt Iris to the magazine featuring "Ten Creative Ways to Make Ornaments from Egg Cartons" and decided to go with Asa and take her chances. Then something metallic crashed to the floor in the kitchen. "Ouch! Damn it all!" Emma Beth screamed. Molly threw the magazine aside and raced for the scene of the calamity with Asa and Iris close behind her.

Red-faced and teary-eyed, Emma Beth stood amid a clutter of black crumbs while sucking on a finger. "I burned my hand," she explained, "and I've already ruined two batches."

"Sugar doesn't grow on trees," Iris said, shaking her head. "And be sure and turn off that oven when you're through. Our gas bill was sky high last month."

Molly pressed an ice cube into the girl's hand and a broom into Asa's. "That should soothe it," she said. She hoped her look told Asa Brown that if he dared to walk out now, he'd have to answer to her. The shopping trip could wait.

Later, Molly was glad she stayed. Until now she and Joy had suffered the afternoon in silence. It was a relief to hear her daughter laugh as Asa put silver-dotted spectacles on a Santa cookie. Iris Stonehouse had gone quietly back to her Christmas cards, and her sister napped upstairs.

Molly felt some of the day's strain ease away as the four of them decorated pastries in tolerant silence. They were almost like a normal family except that Ethan wasn't there.

In spite of their obvious annoyance with one another, it was hard to believe that someone in this house could have anything to do with murder. But just how innocent was the unfortunate man next door who seemed to roam at will?

Molly finished off the rest of the chocolate bits left in the bag—not enough to save—and added a final glittering sprinkle to a tray full of bells before sliding them into the oven. "A masterpiece if I do say so," she bragged. "Who's getting all these goodies, Emma Beth?"

Emma Beth shrugged. "Oh, you know—some of my girlfriends, and my art teacher, Mrs. Gillespie. And there's this cute boy, Max, who sits across from me in history..."

"What about Miss Curtis?" her father asked. "The poor soul had to put up with you for algebra every day. Doesn't old Myrt warrant at least a cookie or two?"

"Yuck! Don't remind me!" Emma Beth made a face. "I'd like to give her a cookie, all right—a poison cookie, the bossy old witch!"

"Come on now, that's not funny." Asa looked almost stern. "I've always liked our Myrtis. It's not her fault you can't add two and two."

Emma Beth bit the head off an angel cookie, looking as if she wished it were her father's.

"Who in the world is Myrtis Curtis?" Molly asked.

Emma Beth groaned. "Our choir director, and she just loves to tell everyone else what to do!"

Asa washed the sugar from his hands. "She and Jud Horne have directed the pageant together for twenty years or more." He flicked water at his daughter. "And this year Em here painted the scenery."

"Quit it!" Emma Beth giggled. "Daddy's a shepherd, Gram's in charge of costumes, and Aunt Iris sings in the choir. They'll put you in there, too, if you don't watch out.''

Molly laughed. "Who sits in the congregation?"

"The what?" Asa scratched his head and frowned. "No kidding," he added, "we could use another stagehand." He shrugged. "After all, you're going to be there anyway, aren't you? And Jud can fill you in at rehearsal tonight."

Molly looked at Joy. The child had a clear soprano voice, but she knew her daughter would resist anything she suggested. "Why not?" she agreed.

"What about Joy?" Emma Beth asked. "We need another angel since Myrt threw Louann Dobson out of the cast for missing practice." She frowned. "But you'd have to be able to sing, and you'd probably never learn the music in time."

Joy sat up straighter. "I sang first soprano with the junior high chorus last year."

"Yeah? Well, this music's kinda hard," Emma Beth insisted. "At least Aunt Iris says it is, and she's been practicing for weeks."

"Really?" Joy's eyes brightened.

Asa took his young cousin by the arm. "Come on! Your Aunt Iris loves a challenge."

Molly smiled. Her daughter liked a challenge, too. She pretended not to notice as Emma Beth distributed the cookies among several red cardboard containers, eating at least two out of every batch she packed.

"I think I'll give this one to Max," Emma Beth said, carefully placing a chocolate-studded reindeer in the last carton. She poked the cookie with a purple fingernail and sighed. "I don't know—maybe not!"

After a pause, Emma Beth scribbled a name on a label and slapped it on the box. "I just know he's gonna ask me to Allison Whittemore's New Year's party! Allison practically told me." She darted a look at Molly. "No big deal. The worst he can do is not eat 'em."

"I guess you're right." Molly smiled. Yet she knew that not eating the cookies was not the worst thing Max could do; she hoped Emma Beth wouldn't find out the hard way.

But in a way the girl was right. Sometimes you had to take chances. Wasn't that why she was here? And she might as well start with Asa Brown.

She found him slouched on the den sofa watching a football game on television. From the living room she heard Joy's sweet young voice accompanied by her aunt at the piano: "Glory to God in the highest, and on earth peace, good will to men."

I am not going to cry, Molly told herself, hesitating in the doorway. Joy had inherited her musical ability from her father, who had loved singing the old carols in his hearty bass voice, especially after a few drinks.

Asa looked up expectantly as she sat down beside him. How could she go about this without arousing his suspicions? A picture of the two boys when they were small hung on the wall. Molly studied it in silence. "Tell me about you and Ethan growing up together," she began finally. "I've heard some wild tales about his adventures here in Harmony."

Asa laced his fingers together and stared intently at his shoelaces. "Well, you know we lived in Gainesville then. I didn't get down here as often as Ethan did." He grinned. "But I remember one time we just about set the woods on fire smoking rabbit tobacco behind that field where they're building the new mall. We didn't have any water, so Ethan suggested we wet it down the only way we knew how."

Molly laughed. "And did you put it out?"

"Yeah." Asa shook his head. "That Ethan! He could get by with anything." He smiled when he said it, but Molly thought there was a hint of resentment in his voice.

"Do you remember the time capsule?" she asked.

"Time capsule?" Asa frowned. "We weren't always here at the same time," he reminded her. "But that sounds like something Ethan would do."

"It was the Christmas he was twelve," Molly told him. "He and Neil Fry and some boy called Gus found a letter addressed to a girl named Rowena. It had plane tickets in it."

"Rowena Sterling?" Asa grinned. "I remember her, all right! Harmony's answer to Marilyn Monroe, except she had dark hair. They said she ran off with a hippie."

Molly nodded. "The same day the boys found those tickets. They were so scared, they buried them so nobody would find out what they'd done." She tried to sound casual. "I wonder if they're still there."

Asa shrugged. "Don't know. I wasn't in on that one. Must have been the year Mother made me take piano lessons. Wouldn't let me go anywhere!" He grinned. "Even the teacher finally admitted I had a tin ear."

"Do you remember his name?" Molly asked. "The guy she ran away with. Was it someone from around here?"

Asa shook his head. "Some drifter her dad hired to pick peaches and who ended up staying awhile. Old man Sterling had let him go after an argument—probably about Rowena—and there was a stable fire that night. They say he set it for spite. Rowena's stepmother died soon after that, and her dad never did hear from her—left her out of his will altogether. Myrtis Curtis lives in the old Sterling place now," he said. "She was the only heir. She and Rowena were stepsisters, you know—used to run around together."

Asa stretched and walked to the window, where he stood with his hands in his pockets watching a ballerinalike spruce dipping and swaying in the strong wind. "Cold out there," he announced, scanning the darkening street. "What about a drink before we brave the elements?"

Molly, who would have liked nothing better after a very long day, declined. It would never do for Ethan's young widow to appear at the church pageant rehearsal with liquor on her breath, especially in the company of her husband's handsome cousin. Besides, she needed all her wits about her if she was going to find out where Rowena's letter was hidden.

Since his parents were both dead, Ethan had been due to inherit the Stonehouse property after Iris died. Now it would go to Asa. She wondered what Asa was holding back. For someone who claimed to have been away when Rowena Sterling disappeared, he certainly knew a lot about what happened that night.

THREE

THE ORGAN WHEEZED, then came to an abrupt stop. Hurrying into the twilight of the sanctuary, Molly heard the woman's voice, a mixture of bawdy burlesque and girls' gym coach. "Is there a snake in here? Stop hissing those esses! This measure hasn't changed since we rehearsed it last week. Sing it softly now, softly! This isn't reveille!" There was laughter from the choir, and the great instrument bellowed to life again behind the canvas backdrop of Emma Beth's biblical street scene.

Molly dropped her coat and bag into a pew piled with wraps and followed Asa and Emma Beth down the aisle. Only a dim light shone on the temporary platform that served as a stage, but she could make out a graceful swag of balsam draped over the choir loft and magnolia leaves and pine at each stained-glass window. The church smelled of evergreens and candlewax, musty hymnals and mice. Ethan had been baptized in this church; his grandparents had been married here and were buried in the cemetery out back.

The minister, a large red-bearded man in a voluminous black robe, fiddled with the sound equipment, his dogeared script under his arm. His enormous hand swallowed Molly's small one as Asa introduced them and she noticed a guitar to one side.

"Our Reuben is a man of many talents," Asa explained. "Aunt Iris tells me he played first string football in high school and was a member of one of those wild rock bands back in college."

Reuben Anthony laughed, and his big voice echoed throughout the sanctuary. "Well, I did when they let me! The Metamorphics, our group was called—that's a genuine rock group if you're into geology."

Asa led Molly through a door to one side of the stage, where throngs of robed and sandaled Nazarenes waited with baskets and jugs. An imposing man with brilliant blue eyes and thinning sandy hair clamped a hand on Asa's shoulder. "Good, you're here! Hurry into your costume. We begin in fifteen minutes." He snatched a hard roll from a muslin-swathed preschooler. "Sally Jean, that bread's a prop! Put it back in Mama's basket." With a frantic moan he glanced at his watch. "Has anybody seen the prophet Isaiah? It takes forever to put on that beard."

"Oh, he's here. He's ready," said an elderly angel in a flowing gown.

"Good! Good!" The man's smile changed his whole appearance, Molly thought. He took both of her hands in his as Asa introduced him as Judson Horne, the pageant's director. She wasn't surprised to learn that he also played Santa Claus at the lighting of the town tree.

"I've brought you an extra stagehand," Asa told him as his mother tossed him a long striped garment. "And now, like fine wine, I have to go through the aging process," he added as she hurried him into the crowded makeup room.

"I hope you don't mind filling in. As you can see, we need all the help we can get," Jud Horne said as they waded through a narrow hall lined with bearded shepherds. They stepped over three small angels, a coloring book, and a pack of crayons into a tiny room to one side of the stage. "You can be our fog-maker," he said. "We only use it three times, but you have to be careful not to get it too thick. Last year it looked like the church was on fire, and the angel Gabriel tripped over one of the shepherds trying to get offstage!'' When Jud Horne laughed, he didn't exactly go ''Ho, ho, ho!'' but his large belly quivered, Molly noticed.

He showed her how to scoop dry ice from a cooler into a dishpan. ''When the script calls for fog, just pour hot water on it from one of these percolators and blow it onstage with a fan. Myrtis will give you your cues. Here, I'll show you.'' Presenting her with a well-worn script, he herded her into the choir loft.

Molly felt a sharp elbow in her side and was shoved against Jud's bulky stomach as someone pushed past them through the door. A small Pekingese of a woman in heavy gold jewelry marched in, bracelets jangling.

''My daughter came home crying yesterday after you told her she couldn't sing in the pageant!'' the woman said, glaring at the organist. ''And now I hear you're going to replace her after all the work she's done!''

''I'm sorry, Mildred.'' Myrtis Curtis stiffened. ''But Louann has missed all but two rehearsals, and she was late for those. She just doesn't know the music.''

Louann's mother looked at the flustered choir members about her, and Molly sensed that if the woman could shoot bullets from her eyes, they would all be dead.

''Who in the world is that?'' Molly whispered to Jud as the woman stalked away.

''Mildred Dobson, our church secretary—unfortunately.'' Judson Horne took her by the arm. ''Ignore her if you can. Come on, I want you to meet Myrt.''

''So you're Ethan's Molly?'' The woman sitting at the organ smiled warmly as she rose to greet her. ''Thanks for letting us borrow your Joy. As you can see, we're an angel short this year.'' Myrtis enfolded Molly in sturdy, beige-sweatered arms. ''I'm so sorry about Ethan,'' she whispered. "I remember when he used to sing in the junior choir."

Molly almost smiled. Ethan a choirboy! Well, life certainly was full of surprises—and Myrtis was due for a surprise, too, if she expected to make an angel out of Joy. She glanced at her white-robed daughter sitting demurely in the front row of the soprano section looking every bit the part.

A stocky, robust woman with a ruddy complexion, Myrtis's ample figure strained at the confines of a pullover that should have been baggy but wasn't. Her short-cropped brown hair stood in peculiar spikes as if she had just seen an electrifying horror movie. Molly soon discovered why.

"Enunciate! Enunciate!" The organist's hands flew from the keyboard to tug at her unruly locks as the choir sang of the prophecy of Isaiah. "Do you see a crescendo there? I don't." She shook a stubby finger at the sopranos. "And you—the chainsaw sisters—tone it down a little, okay?"

Molly laughed along with the rest of them as they prepared for Isaiah's smoggy entrance, but Judson Horne was not amused. "All right, let's take it from the top," he said in commanding tones. "This time, no stopping. I'd like to get through here before midnight."

"So would I!" groaned Asa, who stood in the wings looking on. He peered at his wrist, which was bare. "What time is it getting to be? They won't let us wear our watches."

Molly glanced at hers. "About eight forty-five. What's your rush?"

"Dinner date," he explained. "Just a little late supper, but I told her we'd be through here by nine."

"It's Daddy's Sunday-night girlfriend, Corrine Harris," Emma Beth whispered, grinning. "She feeds him spaghetti. That's all she knows how to make."

"Now Em, that's not true," her father protested.

"Never mind—I'm sure she has other talents." Emma Beth rolled her eyes at Molly as she hurried to reset the stage for the opening scene, leaving Asa with a red face that had nothing to do with makeup.

Molly marveled at the girl's artistic ability as the play progressed and the village street was replaced by rolling hills dotted with blobs of grazing sheep. The manger was a cleverly thatched shed concealed by dark curtains until the final scene.

"I hope you're planning to do something with this talent of yours," Molly told Emma Beth. "Your sets are wonderful!"

"Gotta do something. I can't sing. Used to before I had my tonsils out a couple of years ago, but the doctor messed up." Emma Beth shrugged. "Myrt says I sound like a frog!"

"You know how Myrtis jokes," Molly said. "I'll bet she can't paint, either—as a matter of fact, neither can I!" She made a face. "I'm still waiting to find out what my talent is."

Emma Beth looked at her for a minute and gave her a quick smile. "Well, you make pretty good fog," she said, and hurried to collect her props.

Molly wished for as much regard from her own daughter, but Joy breezed past her wearing her familiar resentful expression. "I'm riding back with Aunt Ivalee," she said, stepping out of her robe after rehearsal. "Don't wait for me."

Molly whirled as someone stepped up behind her in the shadows. "Sh! It's me," Asa whispered close to her face.

"I'm cutting out of here. If Jud has any notes for me, pass them along, okay?"

"Sure, but don't you need a ride? How are you going to get there?"

"Oh, it's only a few blocks from here." Asa gave her a quick salute as he hurried away. "Walking will give me an appetite for the inevitable spaghetti."

While the cast filed in and found seats, Jud introduced Molly to his wife Zebina and her housekeeper-companion Undine Larsen, who sat in a pew at the back. The delicate, dark-haired Zebina was dwarfed by the robust woman in white beside her. Except for the flush on her cheeks, the companion's skin was almost as colorless as her charge's, and her pale blue eyes seemed to study everyone keenly from behind gold-rimmed glasses. Zebina, a docile, pleasant woman, appeared to be in no hurry to leave, but her housekeeper bundled her away with surprising gentleness. Molly noticed that she spoke with a slight Scandinavian accent.

Molly sat next to Iris in the sanctuary as Jud Horne went over the pageant notes, pointing out strengths and weaknesses in the evening's performance. She wondered what kind of girl Asa was seeing. Was Corrine Harris pretty? Was Asa serious about her? Of course she was only mildly curious, Molly told herself. After all, she hardly knew Asa Brown.

"Good rehearsal, folks," Jud said, winding up his talk. "We got a late start tonight, but it's shaping up well." He beamed at them from the stage. "Thanks for all your hard work, and I'll see you here for dress rehearsal Friday."

Iris dug into a pile of wraps for her coat. "It's bed and aspirin for me. My head is splitting! Are you about ready to leave?"

"In a few minutes," Molly said. "I want to be sure those percolators are unplugged, and I think I left my script in the choir room. You go on; I'll be there in a minute."

Iris frowned impatiently. "I'm not going to leave you here alone. I'll wait until you're through, and you can follow me." And she crossed her arms in front of her.

"With a sick headache? You'll do no such thing! Besides, I know the way. I drove over here, didn't I? I'll be fine," Molly insisted.

"Well, if you're sure." Iris tossed Emma Beth her jacket. "Come on, Em, you'd better ride with us. You still have homework to do."

"I'll be right behind you," Molly said as the girl started to protest. She tried to sound positive, but she let her shoulders sag as she watched them leave together. The church was dim and silent, and except for a few people tidying up backstage, she was alone.

Leaving her coat and purse on the pew, she hurried to the room behind the stage and unplugged the two electric percolators, then fumbled about in the choir room for her script. She found it on top of the organ, where she had left it after going over the cues again with Myrtis. As she left the choir loft, Molly heard the minister and someone else exchange "good nights" as the side door clicked shut. The lights went off in the back rooms that served as dressing areas, and only a low light burned at the back of the church. She was alone.

Throwing her coat over her shoulders, Molly scrambled in her bag for her car keys. Church or no church, she felt uneasy in the dark empty building and was in a hurry to be gone.

Possibly in too much of a hurry, as she couldn't seem to find the elusive keys. Sighing with impatience, Molly dumped the contents of her bag onto the pew beside her, groping in the poor light to sort them out. But it was no use. The keys weren't there. She checked her coat pockets; not there, either. Molly tried to remember: Had she taken the keys backstage with her when Asa introduced her to Judson Horne?

Where else could they be? Aggravated with herself for being so absent-minded, she flicked on the light switch in the small prop room and looked about. The narrow table held assorted baskets and jugs, a couple of cardboard swords, an ornate wine cup for Herod, and of course the three gifts of the Magi, but no car keys. She fared no better in the choir loft.

Molly stood at the edge of the stage looking out into the gray-lit sanctuary. She would just have to call Aunt Iris and have someone come and get her, or else walk the several blocks home. Molly shivered thinking about it. It was cold and windy, and she remembered the steep climb to the aunts' house on Muscadine Hill. It would be wiser to call. She was almost sure she had seen a telephone in the conference room at the end of the hall.

She was on her way to find it when all the lights went out.

Something soft and filmy brushed her face. Reaching out, Molly grabbed a handful of cloth. She remembered the gauzy black material that hung at each end of the platform to keep the congregation from seeing backstage. And weren't there stairs there? Molly carefully felt around with one foot and eased down two shallow steps into what she remembered was the narrow hallway where she had first met Judson Horne.

She leaned against the wall listening to her own heartbeat. All she could see was darkness. This was what it must be like to be blind, she thought.

Wasn't there a door to the outside from this hall? Molly maneuvered sideways along the wall and bumped into something metallic and square. A water cooler.

Blindly she felt for the doorframe and found it. She was just inside the prop room. From here she could feel her way into the sanctuary and up the aisle to the main door. She heard a sigh. It was her own.

It couldn't have been more than five minutes since the lights went off, she thought, yet it seemed she had been trapped in this darkness for hours. But why had the lights gone off in the first place? Had there been an electrical failure? Or possibly the lights were controlled by a timer.

Of course! That must be it. Moving more confidently now, she walked across the room to the door that led to the sanctuary. Her hand was on the knob when she heard it— a soft but distinctive thump from the other side of the platform. It sounded as if someone had bumped into a doorframe or a wall.

The noise could result from old timbers creaking, settling at the end of a busy day, the furnace clattering as it cooled, she told herself. Or was someone else left behind in the darkness, as she was?

Molly hesitated at the edge of the stage. "Is anyone there?" she called to the other side.

There was no answer but silence. "It's Molly Stonehouse!" she shouted again. "Who's there?" She waited with one hand on the door to the sanctuary. It was a straight shot up the aisle—if only the heavy front door was unlocked. "Answer me!" Molly demanded.

But there was only the faint echo of a rustle in the dark passageway. Molly shut her eyes as if by doing so she would become invisible. Why would anyone want to frighten her? Maybe someone had guessed why she came to spend Christmas in Harmony—that she was suspicious about her husband's death.

Molly listened over the sound of her own breathing as she made her way slowly up the aisle, lightly touching the back of each pew. Was that a bulky shape behind her beneath the gray light of the window? Did it move?

The cooler air of the narthex rushed to meet her, and with two great steps she threw herself against the massive front door and felt it move beneath her hands. Freedom blasted her in the face with a gust of cold air.

Molly raced down the steps and over the winding brick walk to where a solitary light kept vigil over the street. She ran with long, quick strides as she had in her high school basketball-playing days, her feet soundless on the cold, hard surface.

A clump of berry-laden nandina bushes screened the church parking lot, but she knew her car was there...waiting.

"Let it wait," Molly said as she vaulted past. She felt she could run all the way on pure adrenaline—if she could just remember how to get there!

She stiffened at the sound of approaching footsteps parallel to her own. The leaves on an evergreen trembled as a tall figure stepped out from behind it. Too late, Molly plunged into his outstretched arms.

FOUR

"LET ME GO! Get away from me!" Molly shoved his chest with both hands and stumbled backward into low, prickly shrubbery as the man did exactly as she demanded. "Just leave me alone!" She waved away his offer of a helping hand and looked up into the concerned face of a stranger. "What do you want?"

He smiled. "I'm sorry. I didn't mean to frighten you. I hope you're not hurt." When he spoke, he didn't sound sorry at all—in fact, he seemed to be having trouble keeping a straight face.

Molly brushed herself off and moved closer to the streetlight, where she could be seen by passing motorists if any ever came along. The tall man followed with long, gangling strides.

"If you didn't mean to frighten me, why were you sneaking around behind me in that pitch-black church?" Molly shivered.

"What?" He almost smiled. "Are you serious?"

"No, I do this for exercise. Of course I'm serious! Why do you think I was running?"

He sat on the low brick wall and rubbed his hands together for warmth. "Well, it wasn't me, I promise, although I did come here to find you—that is, if you're Molly Stonehouse." Again he offered his hand, standing.

"Who are you? How did you know where I was?" She ignored his outstretched hand.

"My name's Duncan. I'm an old friend of Ethan's, and your aunt said I might find you here." He smiled. "You are Molly Stonehouse, aren't you? Because if you're not, I've made an awful fool of myself."

Molly smiled back. "No worse than I have, I'm afraid," she said, finally accepting his hand. "Duncan. You're the third one. You're Ethan's friend Gus, aren't you? Neil tried to find you. I guess you heard what happened."

He nodded. "That's why I'm here. We need to talk. By the way, I wish you'd call me Tyrus—for a while, at least." He looked back toward the parking lot. "My car's just over there. Where are you parked?"

Molly told him about her missing keys and the experience that followed. "It won't hurt my car to stay here overnight," she added. "Tomorrow when it's good and light, I'll come back and look for the keys—that is, if I can get four or five armed guards to come with me."

"Where are they? I'll be glad to get them for you," he offered.

"No, please!" Molly gripped his arm. "Maybe I imagined it, but if I didn't, whoever was in there might still be inside. Besides, I don't want to be left out here alone."

He put a steady hand on her arm. "You're shivering. Come on, my car's still warm. Is there somewhere nearby we can go for coffee?"

"YOU DON'T suppose it was some kid playing a prank, do you?" he asked later as they sat in the Cherokee Grill sipping hot coffee from thick white mugs.

Molly had telephoned the aunts and explained that Tyrus Duncan was a friend of hers and Ethan's who was passing through on his way to visit relatives in Atlanta. She held stiff fingers over the steam from her cup and shook her head. "Maybe, or no one at all. I've been a little jumpy lately." Molly leaned back in her seat. "Ethan and Neil were killed last spring," she said, watching his face. "Why all the sudden concern?"

He took a quick swallow of coffee. "I didn't know until now, or at least until a week or so ago." He shrugged. "I did get Neil's letter—something about a warning, but I didn't take it seriously. He and Ethan were always clowning around, at least when I knew them."

Tyrus Duncan pushed his empty cup aside. "I kept Neil's address, though, because we'd lost touch, and I wanted to send a Christmas card, which I did. I got a note from his father last week telling me what happened." He looked across the table at Molly and forced her to meet his gaze. "Look, I'm on your side. I want to find out what's going on, too. That's why I'm here, and except for you, I'd rather no one know who I am."

Molly felt some of the tension ease from her. She needed someone she could trust. "Is that why it's Tyrus now instead of Gus? Won't people remember you anyway?"

"I don't think so. We only lived here a little less than a year while Dad was a Fort McPherson." He smiled. "I was an army brat."

"But *Tyrus*?"

"It really is my first name. Most people call me Ty." He stripped off his heavy jacket to reveal a glaring red sweater and snatched up the empty mugs, clanking them together. "Refill?"

Molly nodded. She would have to be blind not to notice how gray his eyes were and how they grew brighter when he laughed. She felt her face getting hotter. Ethan had been dead for nine months and here she was inspecting every good-looking man she met.

Well, not every man—just Asa and Tyrus, a silent voice argued in her defense. For months after her husband's death, Molly had been oblivious to everything except the necessities of living. Now she was feeling again, and she wasn't sure she was ready for it.

"Here we are." Ty set two brimming mugs on the table and slid into the seat across from her. "Now. Tell me from the beginning what you think led to Ethan's accident last March."

Molly looked past him to the dark street beyond the window. "It started back in the early spring," she said. "Sometime around the first of March." She thought back to that night. It all seemed so long ago. Molly tasted her coffee. It was strong and hot.

"We had been gone all day," she said, "and we checked for phone messages as soon as we came in. There was one from Neil—something about a time capsule, and he wanted to know what happened to the map."

Ty leaned forward. "And then what?"

"And then Ethan called him and they talked," Molly said. "I didn't pay much attention. I wish now that I had, but I know they were trying to remember who had the map to show where the capsule was buried."

"Didn't you think it was rather odd for two grown men to be talking about digging up an old tin can full of junk?" Ty asked.

"Ordinarily it would have been, but not for these two," Molly admitted. "I thought they were probably plotting a big joke. Ethan and Neil were both unpredictable—like their friendship. We wouldn't hear from Neil for years, and then he would just show up out of the blue! Nothing they did would have surprised me." Molly blotted a coffee spill with a paper napkin. "But I do remember this much: Neil said he had run into somebody from Harmony at a convention or something, and this person seemed more than interested in whatever the three of you found that Christmas when Ethan was twelve."

Ty frowned. "But you don't know who it was or why it was important?"

"That's why I'm here," Molly reminded him. "I know they were trying to get in touch with you to see if you might have the map. Do you?"

"Are you kidding? And I gave away my G.I. Joe and my comic books, too." He shifted in his seat. "What happened after that?"

"Neil came here to Harmony about a week later on the pretext of a business trip, but I think he wanted to find out what was really going on."

"Do you think he did?" Ty looked at her over his cup.

Molly nodded. "He must have learned something. That's when he wrote that warning note I found the other day. He said something was wrong and it had to do with that old letter you found. He was going to try to warn you." She wove her fingers together, gripped them tightly. "If I hadn't read that, I might never have guessed anything was wrong."

"But if it was that urgent, why would he write instead of call?"

"Maybe he did try to call, but Joy's school was on spring break and the three of us went off for a long weekend—our last one, as it turned out." Molly paused, finding it hard to speak. "Ethan called Neil as soon as we got home, and then left a few days later for Harmony." Her throat felt tight, and someone in the next booth was chain smoking. "I could use some air," she said.

"I know it's hard for you to revive all this," Ty said as they stood in the parking lot, "but it's the only way I know to go about it."

"It's all right." Molly leaned against the car. "You said you received a warning from Neil. Where was it mailed? Do you remember what it said?"

Tyrus looked behind him before answering. "Something like, 'Be careful—you're in danger,' and it had a number to call. The letter was postmarked in Harmony."

Molly looked up at a clear, bright sky. The wind had diminished, and the exhaust from the Grill belched the smell of hamburgers. Somewhere down the empty street a dog barked. "You didn't call the number?" she asked, getting into the car.

Tyrus Duncan paused with his hand on the door. "I thought it was just one of Neil's little jokes and I'd get an obscene recording or something. I had no idea he was serious. Obviously, whoever is doing this hasn't found out about me yet."

Slowly he drove through the dark quiet streets, where Christmas lights winked from almost every window. At a brightly lit house on the corner, plastic reindeer pranced across the roof while carols played over a loudspeaker. Molly wondered if the neighbors were out of town for the season. She hoped so.

"The accident." Ty glanced at her as he stopped for a traffic light. "Do you think you could tell me about it?"

"There's not much to tell. Ethan was on his way home from Harmony. I thought he'd gone there to spend a few days with his aunts; now I know it was more than that."

She leaned her head against the cool window glass. "Of course he never reached home. His car went off the side of a mountain. I think somebody ran him off the road."

Dry leaves crunched as they turned into the driveway of the old Stonehouse place on Muscadine Hill. She could imagine the aunts peering from the window.

"What makes you think that?" Tyrus asked. She couldn't see his face in the darkness.

"There were tire marks, and the police thought he had swerved to avoid an animal. It's the worst curve on the road; there've been a lot of accidents there. Ethan went right through the guard rail.'' Her voice rose in anger and grief at the idea that someone had deliberately caused her husband's death.

"Did anyone know he was coming here then, or when he planned to leave Harmony?" Tyrus Duncan touched her shoulder as if gently apologizing for his questions.

"Well, of course he told the aunts; they were expecting him," Molly began, and then admitted the obvious. "Which means everyone in Harmony knew."

FIVE

"YOU SHOULD HAVE TIME for a ride before dark if you don't go too far," Myrtis Curtis said, watching with apparent approval as Joy saddled the handsome red bay. "Shortcake here will be glad for the exercise. I haven't been able to ride her much except on weekends," she added. "It gets dark so early now."

Joy mounted the horse in one quick, light motion and reached down to stroke its neck. Her face looked as if someone had turned on a light inside it. Molly heard her laugh as the horse broke into a gallop.

"Don't worry. She's a natural; she'll be fine." Myrtis assured her as they started back to the house, where smoke curled from a huge stone chimney. A tan and white mixed collie trotted at her heels. "You stay outside, Colonel," she said to the dog. "You've been baptized in the creek again." Her pet was named for Colonel Sanders, Myrt explained, because of an affinity for chicken: an unfortunate trait, according to his first master, who owned a hen house.

"Come on," she said, "let's have a cup of coffee and some of this good fruitcake you've brought me. Iris makes the best in the world, and she knows how much I love it; sends me one every Christmas, God love'er!"

Molly had been happy to deliver the aunts' annual Christmas gift to their friend. Not only did it give Joy a chance to ride (and one less reason to complain), but it also would allow Molly an excuse to talk with the woman who, according to Asa, had inherited Rowena Sterling's family home.

"Just throw your coat anywhere," Myrtis said, stamping her feet at the kitchen door. "I'll get the cups, and we'll have our coffee by the fire." She eased the top from the cake tin Molly had brought and inhaled with glee. "Ah, smell that rum! This will make your taste buds sit up and take notice."

Molly sniffed the rich, fruity aroma and watched as Myrtis carefully lifted the liquor-soaked cheesecloth and cut two thick slices of cake. Iris had placed half an apple in the center of the ring to keep the fruit cake moist.

"That Emma Beth found an excuse not to come, I guess." Myrtis sprawled in a faded green swivel rocker by the fire and motioned for Molly to take the sofa. "She doesn't like me, you know. She's not good in math, which I teach, and can't carry a tune in a bucket. Seems to blame it on me." She took a forkful of cake and chewed it with pleasure.

Molly nodded between bites. "Too bad about that doctor messing up her vocal cords," she said.

Myrt leaned forward. "What?"

"When he took her tonsils out. She said it ruined her voice."

"I've known that child all her life," Myrt said, "and as far as I know, she's never had her tonsils out."

"Then why would she say that? Lie to me like that?"

Myrt shook her head. "To get attention, I guess. This has been going on for a while."

"I guess I ought to quit trying to figure out what makes any of them do what they do," Molly said. She found it a relief to confide in someone who could be objective. "Today is the first time I've heard Joy laugh in months, and that was because of a horse. She loves riding." She nibbled a pungent raisin. "Sometimes I wonder if she'd like me a little more if I whinnied, barked, or clawed the furniture. Ethan and I didn't always see eye to eye," she admitted. "We argued the night before he left to come here—just before he was killed—and Joy hasn't forgiven me for that."

Myrtis cracked a pecan from a bowl on the table and threw the shells into the fire. "I wouldn't let her go on like this too long," she said.

Molly leaned back against plump cushions and felt the flames warm on her face. "Easier said than done." She spoke with a trace of testiness in her voice.

"You'll think of something. You're her mother." Myrtis's voice was as comforting as the large pine-paneled room, where nothing really matched but the colors all seemed to get along well enough together. The low table was marred with water rings, the braided rugs worn and faded. The only piece of furniture that shone with polish was the grand piano by the window. A framed poem written by Myrt as a child hung on the wall above it.

"I like your house," Molly said. "Have you lived here all your life?" A deceitful question, as she knew the property had been inherited.

"Almost. This was my stepfather's place; I called him Daddy Clyde. Mother and I came here when they married. I was only four at the time, and he was a good father to me—left me this farm when he died." She looked at Molly with a direct brown-eyed gaze that made her want to squirm. "I imagine you've heard about Rowena?"

"Ethan told me something." Molly held the cup to her face as if it could hide her discomfort. "I think he had a crush on her."

Myrtis smiled. "Most men did, even the very young ones. Rowena was beautiful, and she enjoyed it to the hilt." She laughed. "My sister developed flirting into a fine art."

Molly watched as the older woman stood to add a log to the fire. The glow from the blaze softened her imposing features and firm, square jaw, making her almost pretty. "I guess I was a little jealous of 'Ena," Myrtis admitted, dusting off her hands. "She had every boy in town after her, and I—well..." She smiled. "But we had a good time growing up. We'd get together with Jud and your Aunt Iris and put on plays for the other kids. Rowena had a good imagination."

"Asa said Rowena eloped with some guy working on the farm," Molly said. "I don't suppose you ever heard from her?"

Myrtis walked to the window and stood with one hand resting on the piano. Molly couldn't see her face. "No, I didn't," she said finally, "and that's always bothered me, because in spite of our differences, Rowena and I got along well together. She used to tell me almost everything, but I never imagined she was serious about this Jones fellow."

"Jones?"

Myrtis nodded and moved back to her chair. "Barlow Jones he *said* his name was; wrote poetry and played the guitar. 'Ena though he had 'depth.' He was sensitive, she said." Myrtis laughed. "Rowena always managed to dream up at least one redeeming characteristic—it made it easier for her to fall in love." The last words were spoken with an edge to them, as if she meant them in jest.

"It just about killed Daddy Clyde when she left," she went on. "He only lived a few years after that. Rowena was his only child, and her leaving like that made him bitter. When she didn't come back, he burned everything that belonged to her—even her photographs; never mentioned her name again."

Myrtis opened a drawer in an end table and drew out a large flat book. "Our high school annual," she said, flipping through the pages. She passed the book to Molly, tapping her finger on the photograph of a smiling girl in sweater and pearls. "There. That's Rowena," she said.

The sex appeal was apparent even in the photograph, Molly thought. Rowena Sterling's dark curly hair framed her face with softness. Her mouth was wide and sensuous; dark eyes promised fun and games. If anyone was made for love, this girl was, Molly decided. "Why?" she asked.

"I don't know, unless this guy got her on drugs," Myrtis said. "And they say he set fire to the stable the night they left. There weren't any animals in there at the time, but still, I never understood the reason for it. Rowena wouldn't have allowed it."

"Maybe she didn't know what he'd done until it was too late." Molly was relieved to hear Shortcake's hoofbeats and went to the window to watch her daughter dismount. "Didn't her father try to find her?" she asked.

"Frantically for a while, but how do you look for a drifter named Jones? We had no idea where he was from or where they went from here." Myrtis rocked back and forth. "Sometimes I still think about her, wonder where she is, how she is. I'm not even sure she's alive."

"You and Rowena and Jud and Iris," Molly began. "You went all through school together. You must have been close."

Myrtis sighed. "Well, yes, most of the time. Except for the Christmas Rowena left, she and—" Myrt stood suddenly as they heard Joy playing with the Colonel outside. "Isn't that...I believe I hear Joy?"

Molly was glad Joy was back. It was almost dark outside. "Do you still have the orchards?" she asked as they took their plates to the kitchen.

"Oh, I still get a shirttail full of peaches now and then, but I don't keep them up anymore—too much trouble." Myrtis pointed to a far hill through the kitchen window. "This farm used to be close to six hundred acres, but I sold off some last year for a new shopping center." She reached into a cabinet and brought down two pint jars filled with rosy peaches. "I figured I might as well make some money out of it; not gonna get rich teaching!"

"By the way, I want to thank you for letting Joy sing in the pageant," Molly said, accepting the spiced peaches for the aunts. "I was going to say something last night, but you got away before I could find you."

"Had a zillion papers to grade, two-thirds of them disgraceful!" Myrtis said as they stepped outside. "When it gets this close to Christmas, they might as well close down the school."

Molly fished her car keys out of her pocket and let the motor run while Joy said good-bye to Myrt. She and Ivalee had gone back to the church that morning and found her car keys on the pew where she'd been sitting.

"I just had a feeling you'd find them here," Ivalee said. "The sanctuary was so dark last night, it was impossible to see."

But the keys were on a pew that Molly was almost sure she had searched the night before. She had said nothing about her experience in the church to anyone but Tyrus Duncan. She didn't want to frighten the girls or the aunts, and she had no idea who her pursuer might have been, or even if there had been one.

Now, Myrtis leaned in the window on the driver's side as Joy walked slowly back to the car. The girl was obviously having trouble looking unhappy. "Remember what I said now," Myrtis whispered with a meaningful look at

Joy. "And when you're ready for your Christmas tree, come out and take your pick."

Molly felt she was breaking a tie with security as she drove away from the Curtis farm. She liked the friendly, plain-spoken woman, liked her comfortable just-me disposition and unassuming home. She wished they could stay longer. For some reason, she felt safer there.

Joy was quiet but apparently serene as they drove back to Muscadine Hill, and Molly, deciding to let well enough alone, didn't try to make conversation. Tomorrow when Ty returned from his sister's home in Atlanta, they would put together some kind of plan. That morning after breakfast, while Ivalee and Joy lingered in the kitchen and the others had left for the day, Molly had searched her room, the room that had always been Ethan's, hoping to discover the childish map; but she really hadn't expected to find it. The aunts had probably thrown it out long ago— if it had been left there in the first place.

"Can't you remember where you buried that thing?" Molly had asked Tyrus before he left.

And Tyrus, obviously noticing the edge to her voice, had given her a martyred look. "Did you ever hide anything when you were little?" he asked.

"Sure, when I was ten I hid the hideous mittens my Aunt Pauline gave me in the roots of a big oak tree on the school ground."

He laughed. "Didn't care much for them, I take it?"

"I couldn't stand them," Molly said. "And to tell the truth, I couldn't stand Aunt Pauline, either!"

"Which tree did you hide them in?" Ty persisted. "Do you think you could find it today?"

Molly shrugged. "Maybe; I'm not sure." She smiled. "I see what you mean. But don't you know the general area where you buried the can?"

"Somewhere in your aunts' back yard, but it would be a lot easier if we could find the map. You don't suppose Ethan found it, do you, when he went back to Harmony?"

Molly turned away. "He didn't have it with him, or at least they didn't find anything like it." She watched the light go off in Iris's room and wondered what had happened to the aspirin and early bedtime. "What do you suppose is in that old tin can that's important enough to kill for?" she asked.

"It has to be the name on the message," Ty answered, shrugging.

"Which you can't remember," she said.

"Which I can't remember," he admitted. "I'll spend the next day or so with my sister in Atlanta, in case anyone bothers to check on my story," he said. "See what you can find out while I'm gone, and when I come back, we'll take it from there."

Molly now drove through the small downtown business district, where garlands of fresh greenery tied with bright crimson ribbons decorated every lamppost, and glowing red Christmas lanterns swung at intervals across the wide street. A big spruce tree in the town square awaited the magic moment when the mayor would turn on its lights for Santa's arrival.

Her husband and his friend Neil had been killed because of something that happened in this little town twenty-three years before. Someone wanted the two men out of the way because of what they knew. Was that same person now trying to frighten her—or worse?

Molly turned into the driveway and parked beneath a tall oak, where a few brown leaves still clung; masses of mistletoe hung in clumps from the highest branches. Lights shone from the kitchen window, and she was eager to get inside. Was she making someone uncomfortable? Someone here in Harmony? Molly sighed. She wished she knew who, and why.

SIX

JOY SLOUCHED in the bedroom doorway as Molly smoothed the covers on her bed. "Why not?" Joy demanded for the fourth time. "Why can't I call Dwayne?"

Like the whine of a large, annoying horsefly, her words had pestered Molly all morning as she followed her about. "Because I say so!" Molly snapped, gripping the spread with both hands. "Dwayne knows where you are. Let him call you."

"He's not the one who left town." Her daughter leaned against the doorframe as if she were just too exhausted to stand.

"For heaven's sake, Joy, you're thirteen years old! You'll live, believe me." Molly plopped a pillow into place. "Come on, I'll help you spread up your bed."

But Joy threw herself violently across the cot. "Never mind! I'll just stay in it. There's nothing else to do!"

"Suit yourself!" Molly muttered, managing by extreme self-control not to slam the door on the way out.

"Sarah Bernhardt is upstairs behaving like a royal pain," Molly told Ivalee, who was stirring up yeast biscuits at the round oak table. "How many more years does this last?"

Ivalee smiled. "Maybe it's just girls. I don't remember Asa being this emotional. Emma Beth told me this morning she was going to give her little friend his Christmas cookies incognito, leave them on his desk or something. I think she's afraid the others will laugh at her, bless her heart."

Molly was relieved at the girl's foresight. "Maybe that's best," she said. She watched her aunt drape a dish towel over the dough and sighed. "I know Joy misses her father, and this first Christmas is especially hard; hard for both of us." She leaned forward. "Aunt Ivalee, did you and Aunt Iris keep any of Ethan's things? You know, letters, pictures, things he did as a child. I'd like to have them if you did."

"Well, of course you would, and I'm sure Iris must have saved some little keepsakes of Ethan's, just as she did of Asa's." She pulled out a kitchen chair and sat down, crossing her freckled arms on the table. "You see, I only came to share the homeplace with Iris after my dear Beckworth passed away."

Molly nodded. "Of course. Somehow I always pictured your being here during the holidays when Ethan was growing up."

"We were in and out, being a little over fifty miles away, but Asa was raised in Gainesville, you see; he had his own activities—piano lessons, things like that. He has an ear for music, you know."

Molly smiled. "Myrtis was telling me about her sister Rowena. Were you here the Christmas she ran away?"

"With the hippie?" Ivalee frowned, drumming her fingers on the table. "I can't remember for sure. We heard about it of course. Everyone was shocked, but Mama said she wasn't a bit surprised. She always claimed Rowena Sterling was as fast as greased lightning. She was in the same class as Iris, you know. They grew up together; ran around with the same crowd—much to Mama's dismay!"

"I can't imagine Iris having too much in common with the seductive Rowena," Molly said.

"My sister wasn't always as prim and proper as she'd like you to believe. Oh, she wasn't anything like Rowena by a long shot, but she enjoyed a good time as much as the next person. They were always having parties, that bunch!'' Ivalee smiled. ''And they were cute when they were little, dressing up and acting out the movies they'd seen. Why they were there every time the feature changed! That was before poor Sonny Earl got so sick. He and Jud would take turns being the hero.''

Ivalee rearranged a bowl of fruit on the table, switching an apple and a tangerine, then putting them back again. ''That was an interesting crowd: Iris, Rowena, Judson, Myrtis—and later Reuben Anthony, too. They were all so different, yet they got along well together.'' She frowned. ''They were so close; downright clannish! Sometimes I couldn't help but be a little jealous of them. They didn't seem to need anyone else.''

''It is unusual,'' Molly said. ''There always seems to be one person who causes friction.''

''I think Iris and Rowena had some sort of falling out just before Rowena ran off.'' Ivalee shifted a banana in the bowl. ''Iris still doesn't like to talk about her.'' She rose abruptly. ''My goodness, where has the time gone? And I haven't even been to the grocery store!''

''Just make me a list, and I'll be glad to go for you,'' Molly offered as her aunt studied the contents of her cabinets. ''Aunt Iris is so attractive,'' she added impulsively. ''I wonder why she never married.''

''Humph! Wasn't because she wasn't asked!'' Ivalee slammed two cabinet doors in succession: Wham! Wham! ''Waited too long for Mr. Right, I reckon. Then she started working for J. B. Gideon—you know, Gideon's Department Store downtown here—and stayed on after Jud bought him out.''

Ivalee Brown leaned against the sink and folded her arms. "You might as well hear it from me: Everybody here thinks Iris and Jud have a thing going."

Molly shrugged. "Do they?"

"Of course not! Iris has done some foolish things, but she's as straitlaced as they come," Ivalee insisted. "Certainly she loves Jud, but not in that way, and I think Jud is genuinely fond of Zebina." She twisted a dish towel in her hands. "Poor little Zebina, in and out of hospitals all the time! She's not strong, you know."

Ivalee draped the damp dish towel over the rack. "Iris has always been one to stick close to home. Our father sent her away to college, but she wouldn't stay after the second year. Daddy begged and threatened, but it didn't do a bit of good! She just came flittering back like a moth to a flame."

Molly, who couldn't imagine Ethan's dignified Aunt Iris flittering anywhere, said she thought that was a waste and a shame.

Ivalee agreed. "My Beckworth said back then that Iris would never marry, never leave Harmony. I guess he knew my sister better than I did," she admitted. "You see, Iris was not quite twelve when we married. I'm almost ten years older than she is."

"You're kidding! Why, I never would have believed it!" Molly vowed with what she hoped was the proper awe. She stood at the living-room window watching an occasional car pass as her aunt made out her grocery list.

"I think we'll christen Myrt's spiced peaches tonight," her aunt mused, jotting down another item. "They're good with just about everything."

"I like Myrtis," Molly said smiling. "Curtis. Is that her maiden name?"

"You don't think she'd deliberately choose it, do you?" Ivalee laughed. "Myrt would be the first to set you straight on that! Yes, Curtis is the name she was born with; parents had a warped sense of humor, I guess, but it sort of suits her, don't you think?" She scribbled something on the back of an envelope. "Don't guess she'll change it now.

"You know," she added, "for a time when they were younger, I thought Myrtis and Jud might marry; they dated for a while, but he ended up with Zebina Murdock from over near Cedartown. Right pretty girl when she was young, bless her heart." Ivalee sighed. "But I believe if she ever had a thought, it would leave a vapor trail across her mind!" She presented Molly with the finished list. "Now, be sure to get those tiny green peas, not those great big marbles that look like horse pills!"

Molly drove to the store wondering if anyone from Harmony had ever enjoyed a long and happy marriage. But then, Myrtis seemed perfectly satisfied with the way she lived. There were a lot of things, Molly reminded herself, that are worse than being single. For the time being, however, she couldn't remember what they were. She missed Ethan; missed his laughter, his roguish, seductive signals when he wanted to make love; the lilting way he said her name. If Ethan were here, he would know what to do about the problem with Joy. But then, if Ethan were here, the problem wouldn't exist.

To her surprise, her daughter greeted her with a smile when she returned from shopping. She was helping her aunt ladle steaming vegetable soup into bowls for lunch, and her cheeks were flushed from the heat.

Molly turned away to put the milk in the refrigerator before Joy could say anything to dim her good spirits, and for a fraction of a second she closed her eyes. Just a little peace at a time, she thought. That's all I ask.

And then Emma Beth came home from school.

They heard her sobbing before the door slammed. "I hate her!" she screamed. "That meddling old witch—I'll get her for this! Just see if I don't." Emma Beth hurled the words behind her as she charged up the steps to her room.

Ivalee, who had just sat down, pushed herself out of the chair. "Oh dear, I'd better go up and see what's the matter."

Molly looked at Joy who sat reading on the other side of the small den. Brows raised, Joy's eyes followed the sound of her aunt's hurried footsteps, then turned to her mother as if she wanted to speak. Abruptly her mouth formed a sad little line as she picked up the book again.

So much for peace and good will, Molly thought. Even in the intimacy of the cheerful room, there remained a barrier between them.

"She won't let me in." Ivalee stood in the doorway looking as if she had just been slapped. "I can't even get her to answer. Do you mind?" Her eyes pleaded with Molly. "Maybe she'll talk to you."

Molly nodded in what she hoped was a reassuring way, but she had no idea what to say as she rapped softly on Emma Beth's door. "It's Molly," she called. "Could I come in for a minute?"

For a while she thought the girl wasn't going to answer. Then the door swung silently open and Emma Beth stood there, her eyes red from crying.

"She told him!" Emma Beth spat out the words. "Miss Curtis told Max those cookies were from me, and he threw them in the trash!"

Molly, who would gladly have thrown Max in the trash at that moment, smoothed the girl's hair with a cool hand.

She had left the cookies on Max's desk in Myrtis's classroom, Emma Beth said, knowing he sat there for algebra the following period. "And she *told* him!" Emma Beth stiffened, clutching a purple panda to her chest. She turned her face aside and whispered, "Everybody laughed! I never want to go back to that crummy school! And I wish Myrtis Curtis would fall in front of a train!"

SEVEN

"IF ONLY HER FATHER were coming home tonight!" Ivalee fretted as her granddaughter rested upstairs. "He'll be
out of town until tomorrow, and I'm going to have the
dickens of a time getting that child to go back to school."

Iris Stonehouse unfolded the afternoon paper with a
brisk snap. "Good thing I never had children, I guess.
Anyway, Mama always said I wasn't strong enough for
childbearing—narrow pelvis, you know."

Ivalee stood as straight and tall as her round little body
would allow. "Well, maybe it's just as well you didn't,
Iris," she began. "My dear Beckworth always said—"

But Molly never heard what "dear" Beckworth always
said because the phone rang and she excused herself to
answer it. And she was glad she did because it was Tyrus
Duncan calling from Harmony's one motel. "I'm back,"
he said. "Learn anything?"

"So soon? I thought you were spending the holidays
with your sister."

"The whole tribe's down with the chicken pox." Ty
paused for dramatic effect. "Not much of a Christmas,
I'm afraid."

It was a lie, of course, an excuse they had concocted between them to explain Ty's presence in town during the
holidays.

"Oh, that's a shame!" Molly said it loud enough so the
sisters could hear, then added under her breath, "Come by
later and we'll find an excuse to go somewhere—shopping
or something."

"What an awful thing to happen at Christmas!" Ivalee put her head on one side when Molly told her about Ty's "poor" sister and all her problems. She seemed so genuinely concerned that Molly felt a slight pang of conscience for taking part in the scheme. "You tell him he's welcome to have supper with us," Ivalee said. "Ham and cheese omelets will stretch to eternity, and I always make too many yeast biscuits."

And so that evening Tyrus Duncan, wearing his Santa Christmas tie with a red-striped shirt, sat eating at the kitchen table with Molly and the aunts and entertained them with anecdotes about his years of teaching high school science in a small city in Tennessee. "Most of these kids don't know a dandelion from a daisy," he said, "so I try to take them on a field trip to a nursery each year." He accepted another biscuit from Ivalee and laughed. "More than one student has confessed he thought we were going to tour a kindergarten!

"But they're never boring," he added, breaking his bread in half. "They're never, never boring!"

Molly exchanged glances with Ivalee, who winked at her. Now and then they heard a low giggle from Emma Beth's room, where the girls were having supper on trays. Once the laughter reached a howling crescendo accompanied by much clapping and jumping about, and so Molly was surprised when Joy came downstairs to announce that Emma Beth wasn't feeling so great, and what was that stuff you take to make you throw up?

"You mean syrup of ipecac?" Ivalee's face turned white.

"She hasn't *taken* something, has she? Is she having stomach pains?"

"Oh, no, ma'am! Nothing like that," Joy assured her. "She's just feeling kinda yucky. You know, nerves and all."

"I think there's still a bottle on the bathroom shelf that I had when she was little; fortunately, we never had to use it. But that's only for emergencies." Ivalee tossed ice in a glass and rummaged in the refrigerator. "I'll take her up a nice glass of ginger ale," she said.

"I'll take it to her," Joy said, watching the bubbles rise to the top. "Thanks!" She didn't even look at Molly, and she had a funny little smile on her face. A smile Molly had seen before, and she didn't like it.

Molly tried to dismiss it from her mind as she and Ty plowed through the crowds in the downtown mall later that night. It was almost impossible to talk over all the noise and bustle until Ty happened to see an empty bench away from the mob and led her aside. "Now," he said, "tell me what you've learned. Any luck with the map?"

Molly shook her head. "I've turned that room upside down. It's just not there, but Ivalee thinks there's a box of Ethan's things in the attic somewhere. I'll try to look up there in the morning before we go for the tree."

"What about this Rowena?" he asked. "Have you found out who left the notes?"

"Some roaming poet named Barlow Jones—sort of a hippie type, they say. Myrtis—that's Rowena's stepsister—says they ran away together." She sighed. "I wish you could remember what you put in that can you buried."

"How good are *you* at ancient history?" Tyrus shrugged. "Other than the plane tickets and the letter, the only other thing I can remember was an arrowhead that was dug up in somebody's yard, and I can't imagine anyone killing for that."

"If it weren't for that scare in the church the other night, I wouldn't be so sure there was a murder," Molly whispered. "There are times when I think I'm letting my imagination, or maybe my grief, get the best of me."

"What about the letters from Neil—the warning notes? You can't ignore them."

Molly jumped as a child shrieked behind her and popcorn spilled all over the brown tile floor. The smell of it made her faintly sick.

"I told you to look where you were going, Randy!" the child's mother reminded him. "Hush that crying now! Santa's looking at you."

"But why now?" Molly persisted. "Whatever is in that can has been there for almost twenty-five years. Why the panic all of a sudden?"

Ty waited until the snuffling boy was led away, then looked at her as if she were one of the students who confused a nursery with a kindergarten. "Because he didn't know it was there." Ty spoke in a low, steady voice. "Molly, when Neil ran into somebody from Harmony at that convention or whatever, he must have gotten into what he thought was a harmless conversation and inadvertently spilled the beans."

"What do you mean?" Molly looked at the shoppers swarming about. As the crowd parted for a second, she thought she saw Reuben Anthony, the red-haired minister, disappear into a store. She played with the zipper on her jacket, wishing she had worn a lighter wrap. There were too many people around her, and she had eaten too many chocolate brownies after supper.

Ty stopped her hand with his. "You know how you search for common ground when you meet someone from a place you've been before: Neil most have said something like, *Oh, I remember! I was in Harmony the Christ-*

mas that girl ran away.... We buried her letter in an old
Prince Albert tin... scared to death we'd be found out.
They probably laughed about it, Neil and the man—or
woman—who was later to cause his death.''

A tired-sounding Santa "ho-ho'd" again from his high-
placed throne as he lifted yet another toddler to his knee.
In a green cluster at one end of the mall, a troop of Girl
Scouts sang, "You'd better watch out, you'd better not
cry..."

Molly shuddered and jumped to her feet. "Let's get out
of here," she said, worming her way through the crowd.
She wanted to feel the cold night air on her face, escape the
crush of shoppers, the hubbub of the mall. And almost
without thinking, Molly reached out for Tyrus Duncan's
hand. The whole time they had been sitting there, she had
felt that someone was watching, perhaps even listening to
every word they said.

EIGHT

MYRTIS CURTIS crossed her arms over the top of the sturdy rail fence as they watched Joy dismount and lead the roan into the stable. "Shortcake's going to miss her when you leave us," she said. "Wish I could get her cousin interested in riding, but Emma Beth won't have anything to do with horses or me." She kicked the ground with a brown booted foot and let out a long heavy sigh. "That young'un! Lord, I wouldn't have hurt the child for the world! Wish she'd just let me get close enough to tell her."

"I know." Molly ran a gloved hand along the rough wood. "But she did go back to school this morning. That must have been hard for her. Why, she was so upset yesterday, I thought she was going to be sick."

Myrtis shook her ragged head. Her hair looked as if it had been cut with pinking shears. "I'm going to have to keep my big mouth shut! But I had no idea she meant for it to be a secret." She reached down to stroke the dog, who pawed her leg for attention, and started back to the house. "And I'll tell you something else," she added. "Little Max will think twice before he messes with our Emma Beth again."

Molly whirled about. "What do you mean?" she asked, falling into step beside her.

"Max was sick today in the cafeteria—violently sick. We had to call his mother to come and get him."

"And you think Emma Beth had something to do with it?" A little bell rang in Molly's head. It wasn't a Christmas bell.

"She was at the table right behind his, and he said his chocolate milk tasted funny. She could have easily switched cartons.

"'Tossing your cookies again, Max?' That's what she said, and she laughed. Emma Beth knew very well that boy was going to be sick because she made him that way, and what's more, she enjoyed it!"

Oh, dear God! Molly thought. I wonder how much of that stuff she gave him? "How is he?" she asked. "Is he going to be all right?"

Myrtis nodded. "Weak as all get out; I called this afternoon, but he'll be okay. And he'd never in a million years admit that Emma Beth had anything to do with it. It wouldn't be cool."

"Hell has no fury like a woman scorned," Molly said. "I'll have a talk with Emma Beth as soon as we get back." She shivered in a sudden gust of wind and glanced back at the stable where her daughter emerged, looking suspiciously smug. "And our young equestrienne as well. Emma Beth didn't plot this thing alone."

"Here, you'll freeze like that. Where's your hat?" Myrtis let the dog onto the porch and hurried inside, where she grabbed an orange toboggan hat with a violent purple pompom and a matching muffler that seemed a mile long. "The colors will keep you warm," she said, wrapping the garish scarf around Molly's shoulders. "Now, do you have a saw? There's a nice grove of cedars just west of that far hill there. Take your pick."

Molly ducked underneath the barbed-wire fence to the pasture, taking pains not to snag her trailing scarf, and held the strands apart for Joy. The faint smell of wood smoke wafted from Myrtis's big stone chimney, and the hot coffee and doughnuts she had shared with her friend earlier settled warm and snug in her stomach. Grass crunched underfoot as they walked, and she saw the green-dotted hillside not too far away.

"'Deck the halls with boughs of holly!'" Joy hummed almost to herself, and Molly laughed, walking a little faster. It was cold; it was Christmas, and she and her daughter were looking for a tree together. "A fat one," Ivalee had said. "One that touches the ceiling. My Beckworth would never allow any other kind!"

Molly remembered the Christmas Joy was four, when she and Ethan had taken her tree hunting on her parents' small farm in North Carolina. When it began to snow, they had all laughed and run around trying to catch the flakes on their tongues. Her brother and sister and their families would be arriving at that same farm soon to spend the holidays sleeping on makeshift pallets and raiding the refrigerator in the middle of the night.

They jumped a brown trickle of creek and circled a clump of white-faced Herefords licking a salt block. Next year, Molly thought. Next year Joy and I will be there, too. "Don't forget we need extra greenery for decorating," she said. "Ivalee likes to make her own wreaths."

"What about some mistletoe?" Joy pointed to the green-topped oak.

"How are we supposed to get it down? Neither of us can climb that high, and we don't have a gun to shoot it."

"Myrtis does. A rifle! There's a gun cabinet in her hall," Joy said. "I saw it."

Molly picked her way past a tangle of blackberry bushes. "We'll see," she said. She doubted if Ethan's aunts would allow them to decorate with the squishy white berries that bonded like glue if mashed into carpeting. Besides, mistletoe was for flirting, for kissing all in fun; she had always hung a sprig at parties. Tied with a red ribbon, it added a festive touch. This would not be that kind of Christmas for her.

At the top of a slight rise they found the perfect tree—a plump, feathery cedar slightly taller than Molly's head. "It's just right!" Joy buried her face in the branches and took a deep breath. "Ummm, smell it! Let's string popcorn tonight when we get home."

Molly laughed. "Remember the last time? More popcorn went into your mouth than on the tree."

"And Dad kept sticking his finger with the needle." Joy disappeared behind the tree and grasped the slender trunk. "You cut; I'll hold it," she said. Her voice had the forced brightness of a game-show host's.

The saw bit into the fragrant red wood, filling the air about them with a deep green smell. "It's all right to cry, Joy," Molly said, pausing to get a better grip on the handle.

"Hurry, will you, Mom? My arms are beginning to itch." Joy shuffled her sneakered feet impatiently and caught the tree as it fell with a crack. They carried it silently between them with Molly hanging on to the heavier end at the rear; the scent of it was overpowering, but the magic spell was gone.

Molly held the trunk on her shoulder as she followed her daughter up the steep creek bank. "That was a dangerous thing you and Emma Beth did, giving that boy ipecac," she said. "How much did he take?"

Joy plodded steadily onward, giving her end of the tree a tug. "What do you mean, *you and Emma Beth*? She's the one who did it! Besides, that Max is a jerk. He deserved it!"

"He could have been a very sick jerk. Syrup of ipecac is a drug, Joy. It could have bad after-effects. You don't mess around with things like that! I want you to promise me you'll never do anything like that again."

"You won't tell Aunt Iris, will you? Emma Beth's kinda scared of Aunt Iris. You know how she is."

"That's between Emma Beth and me," Molly said as they hoisted the heavy tree over the pasture fence and leaned it against a post. "Let's leave this here and go back for the greenery. There's a big plastic bag in the car."

"I'm going to run in and borrow some extra scissors from Myrt," Joy said. "Why don't you go on and let me catch up?"

"I saw a thick pine not too far on the other side of the creek, and it was loaded with pine cones," Molly told her. "I'll meet you there; hurry now. It's getting dark!"

But the tree was farther away than she remembered. Molly was glad for the warmth of her gaudy wraps as the cold wind sliced at her clothing, whipping about the plastic bag she carried under her arm. She stopped to break off cedar branches, stuffing them hurriedly into the sack, and tossed in clusters of sweet-gum balls with the evergreens.

The pine tree she had seen grew halfway up the side of a wooded hill and held its lower branches teasingly out of reach. Molly stood on tiptoe on a mound of stone, and with cold fingers she snapped off twigs of pine, clusters of cones, and dropped them to the ground, then scooped the evergreens into the bag.

Molly scanned the drab landscape for sight of her daughter's blue-coated figure. Her feet were numb from the cold in spite of the snug boots she wore, and the sky had turned a chilling gray. She would be glad to warm herself by Myrt's comforting fire before starting back to Harmony, but she was also eager to learn if Tyrus Duncan had gathered any further information about the elusive Rowena Sterling.

"People here don't know me yet," he had pointed out the night before. "Give me a chance to ask around, find out who her friends were."

"I know who her friends were," Molly said. "Iris, Myrt, Judson Horne, and Reuben Anthony, to name a few."

"Those were the ones she was seen with," he said. "There had to be others like Barlow Jones. Something tells me our Rowena wasn't a one-secret kind of woman."

"Rowena worked at the drugstore," Molly reminded him. "Why not ask there? Maybe some of the same people are still around."

She smiled now as she started down the hill, dragging the bag of greenery behind her. Maybe Ty would come by tonight in time to help decorate the tree. If Aunt Iris would play the piano, they could even sing carols.

Suddenly she was on her hands and knees with one throbbing foot in a stump hole, her face buried in pine straw, and her rear end in the air. That was when someone chose to take a potshot at her.

"Hey, watch out! Stop shooting!" Molly pressed close to the ground, spilling evergreens all around her. The sharp, fresh scent of pine engulfed her as someone fired again. This time the zing of the bullet seemed even closer.

Pushing up on one hand, Molly waved her orange muffler in the air. "Don't fire! I'm over here!" she screamed. Whoever it was would have to be both blind and deaf not to see or hear her. Surely no one had mistaken her for a deer! Maybe Joy had talked Myrtis into shooting down some mistletoe, she thought; but the tree was on the other side of the pasture.

After waiting for what seemed like a safe length of time, Molly crawled to her knees and shouted, "Myrtis? It's Molly! Where are you?"

An answer came sooner than she expected as a shell hit the ground somewhere behind her. For the first time Molly realized her danger. Someone was deliberately shooting at her!

Tossing aside her vivid wraps, Molly rolled down a slight hill into the sparse protection of a thin strand of pines and sat with her back against a tree. Surely whoever was stalking her could hear her loud, frantic breathing. I'm going to freeze to death crouched against this damned tree, she thought. They won't even have to shoot me. Still she waited. Listened. From somewhere on the other side of the hill behind her came the distant drone of heavy equipment, probably earth-moving machinery clearing land for the new shopping center. A dog barked. The Colonel, she thought, as it seemed to come from Myrt's.

And where was Myrtis? Did she allow just any maniac to run around on her property shooting at will? Molly rubbed her ankle; she had forgotten about the injury in her panic to survive. If she could just stay under the cover of trees, maybe she could work herself back to the house. But she would have to cross a wide span between the hill where she was hiding and the bramble-covered creek bank. Foliage was gone now from oak, redbud, and dogwood; only naked limbs remained.

Molly inhaled deeply and stood. Bending over, she zigzagged from one tree to the next until she reached the edge of the little thicket. Thank God Joy had stayed behind! she thought. She must have decided to visit a while with Myrt by the fire—a wise choice! Molly hugged herself for warmth. At least her daughter was out of harm's way. She looked out at the bare, rolling pasture, a soft blend of gray, brown and green, and wished she could become a part of it, like speckles of mist on a watercolor painting. Nothing moved. And then a twig snapped in the darkness. It was only a tiny noise, but it sounded like a firing squad in the smothering twilight.

NINE

INSTINCTIVELY, MOLLY BACKED into the shadows as the needles from an overhanging pine bough tickled her cheek. This is a bad dream, she thought, groping blindly for a weapon, anything to defend herself. Her fingers closed around a broken limb at her feet; it fell apart when she picked it up. The screen of branches around her rustled and parted.

"Mom?" Joy stood in the opening, her face in shadow. "What's wrong? Why are you standing here? I thought you wanted some—"

"Sh!" Molly snatched her daughter to her. "Be quiet! Somebody's out there—somebody with a gun!"

"Huh?" Joy tugged at her hand. "You're kidding, aren't you? Come on, Mom. It's getting dark."

"You didn't see anyone out there?" Molly took a tentative step forward. "Some maniac's been shooting at me. Didn't you hear it? Where have you been?"

"Cutting evergreens. I found some real pretty pine trees behind the stable—all different kinds. The car's piled high with greenery. Let's go."

Molly felt for her daughter's hand. "You didn't hear me call? Or the shots? How could you not hear something that loud?"

"I guess I did hear a noise; I thought somebody was shooting off firecrackers. You know, celebrating Christmas early." Joy shrugged. "And then Colonel Sanders was barking, so it was hard to hear much of anything. Myrt had him shut up on the back porch so he wouldn't follow us." Laughing, she knelt and spread her arms. "See, here he comes now!"

A light went on in Myrt's kitchen as the big dog ran across the pasture to meet them and skidded into Joy's embrace. "Hurry!" Molly pulled her daughter to her feet. "Let's get out of the open."

"You're serious, aren't you?" Breathless from running, Joy crawled between the strands of barbed wire. "Was somebody really shooting out there? Why would they be shooting at you?"

"That's what I want to find out." Molly paused by the back steps as she heard the sound of a car approaching and yellow headlights swept the dark yard. "Here comes somebody. Where's Myrtis?"

"Right here." Myrtis stepped outside and held the door open wide. "I was about to send a search party for you. You didn't get lost out there, did you?" She shivered. "Come on in and get warm. This must be Jud bringing my feed from town; he picks it up from the feed store and brings it over in his truck. Sure saves me a lot of trouble." She prodded Joy on the shoulder. "Run down to the stable for me, would you? Ask him to come in for a drink. You're not in a hurry, are you?" Myrtis stared at Molly in the bright light of the kitchen. "Good lord, woman! You look like you've just walked barefooted through the barnyard after dark! What in the world happened to you?"

Between sips of a very strong drink, Molly told her. "I'm afraid I shed your hat and scarf back there," she said. "They're somewhere out in the pasture along with a few spent bullets. When I learned I was meant to be the target, I wanted to be as inconspicuous as possible."

Myrtis sat with her red-stockinged feet on the Colonel's brown back. "It could have been somebody shooting for mistletoe; it's all in those trees over there. And once in a while I get a hunter who can't or won't read the '*no trespassing*' signs.'' She leaned forward. ''I'm glad you're all right. You must have been scared to death!'' Myrt shook her head. ''I can't imagine why they didn't see you.''

Molly set her drink on the table. ''I screamed. I shouted. I waved my muffler in the air. I did everything but dance the hula! Whoever was shooting knew I was there, Myrt. It was no accident.''

The woman's square, friendly face looked grim. ''It must've happened while I was over at Jessie Oglesby's,'' she said, nodding in the direction she had gone. ''Jessie's my closest neighbor—lives about a half-mile down the road. She asked me to feed her cats while she's visiting her daughter in Birmingham.'' Thoughtfully, Myrtis leaned over and ruffled the sleeping dog's fur. ''I left the Colonel here at home—he doesn't socialize well with Jessie's cats—and took the back path over there. I try to walk as much as I can,'' she added with a grin. ''Keeps my come-hither body in shape.''

''You didn't hear the shots?'' Molly wasn't in the mood for jokes.

''Well, no, but I wasn't listening for them, either, and I had that old hat pulled way down over my ears.'' Myrtis slapped her knees with both hands—a signal that meant she was ready to change the subject. ''And then I had to go inside to get the cat food.''

Molly frowned. ''You don't believe me, do you?''

''Believe what?'' Judson Horne came in rubbing his reddened hands and backed up to the fire. ''You did offer me a drink, didn't you?'' he reminded Myrtis.

While their hostess was in the kitchen, Molly repeated the story.

Judson frowned, rocking back and forth on his toes. ''Joy mentioned something about that down at the stable," he said as her daughter sat on the rug and took the Colonel's big head in her lap. Jud shook his head. "I just don't understand it, but I'll drop by in the morning and see if I can find those shells. I'm afraid this new shopping center will bring in all kinds of unwanted visitors."

Myrt smiled as she brought in his drink. "Jud's jealous because I wouldn't sell him the land so *he* could develop a shopping center," she said.

But Judson Horne only laughed. "Just you wait," he told her. "Wait until your orchard's full of beer cans and somebody over there opens a used-car lot, complete with searchlights and loudspeakers!"

Myrt rested a hand on Molly's shoulder. "Don't get me wrong," she said. "I do believe it happened; I just don't understand why."

No, I guess you don't, Molly thought. And I don't understand why somebody sent my husband off the side of a mountain, either. Suddenly she felt alone and afraid. These people were supposed to be old family friends, yet she felt she couldn't trust either of them with her suspicions. Not yet.

The reflection of orange flames in the dark window told her that night had indeed come. "My goodness, we have to go, Joy! Aunt Ivalee will have the state patrol out looking for us, and I still have to get that big tree in the car."

"Let me help. If I stick around long enough, maybe Myrt will offer me a piece of that fruitcake I know you brought her!" Jud followed them to the car, where he hoisted the bushy cedar into the trunk and tied down the lid with a length of twine. "Ask your aunts what they think of a caroling party after the pageant rehearsal Friday. Everybody can bring their specialty. We'll start at your place and eat our way to my end of town."

Molly laughed. "I thought the purpose was to sing."

"That, too," Jud said, opening her door on the driver's side. "And try not to worry about this other. I'll check out those casings as soon as it's light. Maybe we can find out who's responsible."

"Let's not say anything to the aunts about this," Molly warned Joy as they drove home. "It will just upset them, and I don't want to spoil their Christmas." She took a deep breath, inhaling the fragrance of the cedar and pine Joy had piled into the back.

"Are you going to tell them about Emma Beth?" Joy asked as they bumped onto the dark driveway.

"I'll have to say something to Asa. He's her father; he needs to know." Molly switched off the engine and sat for a moment in silence. "But I'll wait until Emma Beth's asleep. And Joy," she added softly, "I'd just as soon you didn't mention anything to her about it. Okay?"

"Okay." Joy jumped out of the car, slamming the door behind her, and ran across the front porch. "We're home!" she called brightly, sticking her head in the door. "And wait until you see the tree!"

Asa set up the cedar in the living room, where it filled most of the wide front window, and the aunts served a light supper on the coffee table so they could trim the tree while they ate.

"Mr. Horne says we're having a caroling party after pageant rehearsal," Molly reminded them as Asa plugged in the lights. "Everybody's supposed to bring something to eat."

Ivalee smiled. "That Jud! He loves to party better than anyone I know."

"I guess I'll stir up some of those little fruitcake cups," Iris said. "Everybody seems to like them."

Asa laughed. "What they like is the booze you put in them!" He ran upstairs to escape his aunt's reply and came down a few minutes later with a worried frown. "Has anybody seen the flat white box I left on my closet shelf? I'm sure I put it there, and I can't find it anywhere."

Iris shook her head. "I don't believe so. How big a box?"

"Small. About so." Asa measured with his hands. "It was there when I left here Monday." He turned to his daughter. "Emma Beth, you haven't been in my things again, have you?"

"Why do I always get blamed for everything? Can't I ever do anything right?" Emma Beth dropped the scissors she was using to curl paper ribbon and stamped her foot, knocking over a bottle of Coke in her hurry to get away.

Her father looked at the puddle seeping into the rug. "You just get yourself over here, young lady, and clean up this mess!" he shouted after her.

"I just had that carpet cleaned," Iris muttered on her way to the kitchen. "Money down the drain!"

But Ivalee shoved her aside and was back in an instant mopping the spot with a towel. "The child's had a difficult week, son. You really shouldn't have accused her of getting into your things."

Asa sank into the chair with a groan. "Oh, did I accuse her? Funny, I don't remember that!" He covered his face with his hands as if he wished they would all disappear.

Ivalee blotted the remains of the stain. "Never mind. I'll go and talk with her, try to calm her down."

Asa sighed. "No, Mother. I'll go. I'm afraid my little chat with Emma Beth is long overdue."

Molly glanced at Joy, who silently left the room. She heard her soft tread on the stairs. "Before you talk with Emma Beth," Molly said to Asa, "there's something else you should know."

TEN

ASA PACED from one end of the long living room to the other, pausing only to sidestep the damp spot on the rug. "I don't know what I'm going to do with her," he said, flinging his arms about. "What brought that on in the first place, this crush on the kid in her class?"

Molly collected empty ornament boxes and stacked them to one side, glad to have something to do with her hands. She certainly didn't know what to do with Asa. His ineptness as a parent embarrassed her because it was a little too close to home.

"One of her girlfriends told her Max liked her," Molly explained, piling used paper plates onto a tray.

Asa stared at his shoes. "Well…that's what Emma Beth said—what she chose to believe. Unfortunately, it might not be true. My daughter can stretch the truth like a rubber band!"

He picked up a plump sofa cushion and plopped it against his leg. "I know she took that box from my closet," he said. "There's no telling what she did with it. I'll probably never see it again."

"What was in it?" Molly asked.

"A pearl pendant; nice one, too. Looks like a bunch of grapes."

"For Corrine?"

Asa smiled and shook his head. "No, for Emma Beth—but she didn't know that, of course."

"I expect she just wants attention," Molly said. "She loves you, you know."

He nodded. "I know. I can't be here as much as I like; traveling's part of my job, and then Mother overcompensates." He laughed. "To hear her tell it, Emma Beth does no wrong, makes no mistakes. Hell, everybody makes mistakes—even me! My worst one was marrying Em's mother. She left us, you know, without so much as a backward look. Em has a hard time with that."

It wasn't so different, Molly thought, from the trouble Joy was having with Ethan's death. "It's hard going on your own," she admitted. "Sometimes it's scary being a parent."

"And lonely." Before Molly knew it, Asa had placed himself behind her and was leaning over the back of the sofa with his face close to hers. His hand trailed lightly across her shoulder to the nape of her neck. All she had to do was turn her head a fraction of an inch, and his lips would be there—waiting. It was not an unpleasant awareness.

"Mom!" Joy stood at the foot of the stairs. "Emma Beth won't stop crying, and she has the hiccups."

Molly sat abruptly forward while Asa ran upstairs. She heard him calling softly to Emma Beth from the hall as Joy clung to the acorn-carved newel post and stared at her. How much had she seen? And how much more would she have seen if she hadn't made herself known?

She jumped when the phone rang. Since Joy made no move to answer it, Molly hurried past her into the hall, hoping it would be one of her daughter's friends—even the arch-nuisance Dwayne. Anything to relieve this curious silence.

But it was Tyrus Duncan calling from a restaurant outside of town. "I've tracked down a friend of Rowena's who used to work in the drugstore," he told her. "And she thinks Rowena might have been seeing somebody besides the Jones guy—someone from right here in town.''

"You don't know who it was?"

"No, and neither did Shirley Jo Hufstetler." Ty yawned. "Had to drive almost all the way to Marietta to find her." He paused. "Don't guess you've uncovered that map?"

Molly watched her daughter's fuzzy-clad feet plod slowly up the stairs and disappear over her head. "No, but I had an exciting day nevertheless," she said, and told him about the Christmas tree sniper.

"Well, that should dispel any lingering doubts," he said crisply. "Someone thinks you're too dangerous to have around. Molly, I think you should go to the police."

"Not yet! We don't know any more than we did. Besides," she added, "you were the third of the three who buried whatever this person is after. You're in more danger than I am."

"Look, if somebody wanted to get rid of me, I'd already be out of the way," he reminded her. "I don't think he knows who or where I am—unless you've let it slip."

"Of course not!" Molly was tempted to hang up on him. She felt suddenly tired and weepy and she wanted to be held and comforted by someone who loved her, someone she could trust.

"Are you all right?" He sounded a bit contrite.

"No, I'm not all right! How would you feel if somebody shot at you?"

"I can be there in half an hour."

"No, really. I just need some sleep." Molly looked at the grandfather clock that stood in the hallway. It was after eleven. "But come by in the morning, and we'll look for that box of Ethan's things."

A light was on in Emma Beth's room when Molly passed her partially open door. She heard Asa's voice in a gentle questioning tone, and wondered if he had learned anything more about the missing jewelry. Her own daughter was inert under a mound of covers with her face turned to the wall. She kissed a mat of brown hair and said good night, then went into the bathroom, turned on the shower full force, sat down on the john, and cried.

She felt as if she were walking barefoot on a fence with broken glass on either side. Had the person shooting at her today really been trying to hit her, or merely attempting to scare her away? Had that same person waited in the darkness of the empty church? She would like to take the two aunts into her confidence, but Ivalee would do anything to protect Asa and Emma Beth, and there was a reserve about Iris that made her seem a bit unsympathetic.

Molly threw cold water onto her red face and toweled it briskly. Several times she had come close to saying something to Myrtis when they were discussing Rowena. It was easy to talk with Myrtis; perhaps too easy, and Molly was glad she hadn't given her secrets away. After all, the woman was Rowena's stepsister, and Ethan's death was, in all likelihood, a result of that mysterious message to Rowena Sterling. Also, the orange hat and muffler that Myrtis had insisted she wear had made her conspicuous as a target.

Molly hurried to put on warm flannel pajamas. Iris had already turned down the furnace for the night, and the big house was beginning to lose its heat. Myrtis Curtis could easily have taken those shots at her in the pasture, she thought, shivering between cold sheets. Or perhaps the gregarious Judson Horne had made a brief detour before delivering Shortcake's feed.

A floorboard squeaked in the hall, and Molly stiffened. She listened as footsteps passed her door and continued down the all. Tired footsteps. Poor Asa had had a long night. How early had he returned from his travels? Molly wondered.

Just before she went to sleep, it occurred to her that the phantom sniper might even be Tyrus Duncan. After all, what did she know of him other than what he had told her? For all Molly knew, he could have been in the vicinity on both occasions.

She tried not to think of that the next morning as she welcomed him into the warm, pine-scented kitchen where Ivalee and Joy wired boughs of evergreens to make a swag for the stair rail.

"Ty's going to help me look for those things of Ethan's," she explained, pouring them both mugs of coffee. "Aunt Iris said she thought there was a box of them in that old dresser at the far end of the attic." She looked at Joy, who was clumsily twisting florists' wire around a fistful of pine. "Wanna come up with us?"

Joy examined her rosin-smeared hands. "Guess not; too sticky. But if you find any stuff of Dad's, I want it." This was said with a significant look at Ty.

Ivalee smiled over Joy's head. "Be sure and wear something warm. It's freezing up there!"

"Brr!" Ty slapped his hands together as Molly clicked on the attic light. "What brought on Joy's frosty attitude? It's chilly enough as it is."

"To put it bluntly, she resents you because you're alive and her father isn't," Molly explained. "Nothing personal." She wasn't going to tell him what almost happened with Asa the night before.

Ty smiled. "Should I apologize?"

"Nah! We'll let it go this time." Molly shoved aside a box of books and squeezed between a crib (Asa's? Emma Beth's?) and a massive oak desk that looked as if it had taken root from the floor. Tyrus ran his fingers across the strings of a horribly out-of-tune guitar until Molly clamped her hands over her ears and begged him to stop.

"Here's the dresser! Over here in the corner!" she shouted. Dusty, tattered volumes of encyclopedia were stacked on top of the chest. She pulled at a drawer. It was filled with old grammar school workbooks.

"Something tells me this is going to be a hopeless project," Ty said, trying to work the large bottom drawer loose. Inside they found a shoebox filled with letters, drawings, and an occasional school paper. Molly carried the box beneath the window where the morning sun offered a fainthearted light. "You take half and I'll take half," she said, sitting on the bare attic floor. "I think we'd better go through this before we take it downstairs."

Molly was grateful for the tissues in her pocket as she sorted through part of her husband's childhood: letters he had written to his grandparents; letters his mother had written to him during the times he visited in Harmony; a composition on fishing (sent by Ethan's father) that had earned him an A in the sixth grade; and two boyish sketches of sailing ships. Molly looked forward to reading the letters more thoroughly, but right now she was looking for a map. She sighed and examined her stack again. No map.

Ty shook his head and shrugged. "Nothing! Want to swap?

"Wait a minute!" he said as they traded papers. "Think. If you're a kid visiting relatives and you want to draw a map, what do you use for paper?"

Molly frowned. "Ask for some, I suppose."

"A *secret* map."

"Then I guess you'd use what's on hand in your room—the back of a letter or something."

Ty nodded. "Right! A letter from home."

The map was drawn in pencil on the back of a letter from Ethan's mother that was written during his Christmas visit to his grandparents. In typical childish fashion, Ethan had used paces and arrows to show the location of his "treasure": five paces left, then two paces right from corner of doghouse; six paces from green bench; three paces from trunk of magnolia under lowest limb.

Molly read it aloud twice, then grinned. "Why not just skip all that about the doghouse and the bench and say it's under the magnolia?"

Ty shook his head, smiling. "I can see you've never had any pirate experience."

Molly tucked the letter into her sweater pocket as they went downstairs. She put the box of Ethan's letters on the hall table and stood for a minute watching Joy and her aunt trail the swag like a long green snake between them. Now and then a strand would come apart from the rest, and the two of them stopped to reattach it, giggling like conspirators. Following Ty's lead, she tiptoed through the kitchen and into the Stonehouse back yard.

There wasn't a magnolia tree in sight.

ELEVEN

"I THOUGHT YOU SAID it was hidden here in the back yard," Molly said as Ty stood on the flagstone walk beside her. "Where's the magnolia? Where's the doghouse? I don't see any of those things."

Ty strolled past the sagging gazebo to the end of the garage, studying the ground as he walked. "I don't understand this—" he began, but was interrupted by two short blasts of a car horn as Myrtis pulled into the driveway.

"Lost a contact?" she shouted, rolling down her window. Ty smiled, pretending he didn't hear.

"Gotta rush! I'm here on my free period," Myrt said as Molly hurried to the car. "Just wanted you to know I couldn't sleep worth a hoot last night for worrying about what happened out in the pasture; went out there with Jud early this morning and combed every inch of that hillside." She shook her head. "Nothing. Except that godawful hat and scarf. They were just where you said you'd left them." Myrtis made a face. "One of my students gave them to me—can't get rid of the darned things!"

Molly braced herself against the car. "I didn't imagine those shots," she said.

"No, no. Of course not," Myrtis answered. "Probably came from that hill behind me where they're clearing land for the mall. Pack of fools get up there shooting at beer cans, never thinking somebody's on the other side of the hill." She reached down beside her and handed Molly a newspaper-wrapped bundle. "Mistletoe," she said. "For Joy. She told me she wanted some, and the Future Farmers club was selling it. Just don't tell Emma Beth where you got it," she added in a whisper.

"Thanks. We can use it for the party tomorrow. Joy and Ivalee are decking the halls right now." Molly waved to Tyrus, remembering the two had never met, and introduced him to Myrtis. "Tyrus is an old friend of Ethan's," she explained. "He was planning on spending the holidays with his sister in Atlanta until her kids came down with the chicken pox."

Ty looked duly disappointed. "I haven't had them," he said, managing somehow to seem disadvantaged because of it.

"Will you be with us for Christmas?" Myrtis glanced at the crowded Stonehouse residence as if she were wondering where in the world they would put him. She smiled. "You'll be able to come to our caroling party tomorrow!"

"Ty's staying at the Inn and Out," Molly said, using Asa's term for the Harmony House Motel. "And yes, he'll be staying for the party—or at least, I hope he will." She glanced at Ty expectantly, remembering that she hadn't thought to invite him.

"When you hear me sing, you'll wish you hadn't been so hospitable," Ty warned them.

"No matter. After we've all had a few eggnogs, nobody will care." Myrt began to ease backward out of the driveway, then stopped the car abruptly and stuck her head out of the window. "And the motel is no place for anybody at Christmas. You're welcome to stay with me—or with Jud, if you're afraid of gossip." She laughed and waved, leaving them standing there in the yard. "Get back to you later!"

AND SHE DID. By midafternoon Tyrus and his belongings had been transferred to a comfortable room in Judson Horne's refurbished Victorian house a few blocks from the center of town. Molly drove past there with Emma Beth on her way to the A&P for more fruitcake ingredients and was a little resentful of Ty's good fortune. Painted a decorous Williamsburg blue, the spacious old home stood on a slight rise on about two acres of land looking like a picture on a Christmas card. A fresh balsam wreath hung in every window; the wrought-iron hand railings that led to the porch were entwined with greenery. Even the iron deer in the yard wore a festive circle of ribbon-laced cedar. The house also had a turret, Molly noticed, and she wondered if that was where Ty would sleep. She had always wanted a house with a turret.

"Grandma says this belonged to the Saxon family when she was growing up," Emma Beth pointed out. "They musta had lots of money." She gazed wistfully out the window as they stopped for a traffic light. "She said they owned the cotton mill here, and most of Harmony, too."

"I wonder what happened to them," Molly said.

Emma Beth shrugged. "Oh, they moved away a long time ago, and the people who bought the place didn't take care of it. It looked awful until Mr. Jud got it and fixed it up. He said he always wanted to live there."

Molly smiled. No wonder Judson Horne liked to give parties in such a house. She found herself looking forward to caroling and to seeing the fascinating turret room from the inside. But an annoying little pang of guilt reminded her that partying was not the reason she had come to spend Christmas in Harmony. It was merely a means to an end.

"It seems a shame Jud and his wife had no children," Molly remarked to the family after supper that night as the

tiny fruitcakes cooled on the counter. Earlier, Iris and
Emma Beth, cohorts for an evening at least, had run everyone else out of the kitchen while they chopped and
snipped and dredged the candied fruit and nuts before
drowning them in whiskey. Molly thought it smelled deli-
cious, and she usually didn't care for fruitcake at all.

"Zebina has always been frail; I doubt if she could have
children." Iris shifted an ornament on the Christmas tree
and stood back to see if it made a difference.

"That Zebina! So sweet, you know," Ivalee said.
"When she came here after they first married, she just
smiled all the time about nothing and played that autoharp. Got right up in the pulpit at church now and sang
those simpering little Jesus songs. Remember, Iris? Mama
like to have had a fit!" She looked at Molly and grinned.
"Sometimes I wonder if Zebina Horne even knows where
babies come from!"

"Jud's been mighty good to his nieces and nephews,
though," Iris added. She sat peeling a tangerine on a
newspaper in her lap, and the tangy smell of it filled the
living room. "Educated two—no, three of them now, and
Floyd's gone on to medical school. That's Jodean's son,"
she said to Molly, as if it made a difference.

Asa grinned at her as he got up to add a log to the fire.
"Jud has several sisters," he explained. "Jodean's the
oldest. That's her baby, Larry, who plays Joseph in the
pageant this year."

Iris nodded. "Beautiful voice! He'll be studying music
at Shorter College after he graduates next spring."

"You'll meet them all at the party tomorrow," Asa reminded her. "Most of Jud's relatives like to sing, and all
of them like to eat!"

Molly, who had picked up the nutcracker and a handful
of English walnuts, put them back in the bowl. "With all

this talk of food, something tells me I'd better save room for tomorrow night."

"Oops! Sorry I said that!" Asa snapped his fingers. "I was going to ask you out for a drink later on."

"Why go for a drink?" his mother said with a teasing glance at Iris. "Just stand in the kitchen and inhale the fumes."

Molly laughed, glad of an excuse to ignore Asa's invitation. She had been avoiding his signals for most of the evening and was running out of places to hide. Feigning sleepiness, she left the two girls watching television in the den and went upstairs to her room.

Again she looked at Ethan's crude map. She wished she had had more of an opportunity to discuss it with Ty. Jud had dropped by early that afternoon to hustle him away for the historic tour of Harmony, which, according to Emma Beth, included the Confederate cemetery, the tiny Episcopal church, the old Henderson place—once a plantation—and the depot, which now served chicken salad and cheese straws to anybody who wasn't sick and tired of them. Everything on Judson's tour was at least one hundred years old, except for the chicken salad, and Emma Beth wasn't sure about that.

Molly spread the map on her bed and tried to put it in perspective: the doghouse, the green bench—those were things that time could have erased. But a magnolia tree was usually there to stay—for a long time, at least, and she had not had a chance to question the aunts without being obvious. Ty had seemed certain they had buried their "capsule" in the Stonehouse yard, but it had been almost twenty-five years and they were only children then. Surely there was a chance he was mistaken.

She jumped as someone knocked at her half-open door and hurried to hide the map under her pillow.

Asa stood in the hallway. How long had he been standing there? "Sure you won't take me up on that drink?" he asked.

Molly started to decline, then thought better of it. "It's a little late to go out, but I'd love to sneak down to the kitchen for a cup of cocoa." And maybe a couple of those little cakes, she thought. The rich aroma still filled the house.

But Iris had hidden her fruity confections safely from midnight snackers, so Molly had to be content with what was left of Emma Beth's cookies.

Asa crumbled cookies into a mug of hot chocolate, then plopped marshmallows on top of that. Molly wondered how he could stay so thin, then realized the man could barely manage to sit still five minutes. His lean body obviously ran on nervous energy. She was surprised to learn that Asa had had ambitions of being a college professor and had planned to pursue a graduate degree in English when his not-yet wife became pregnant with Emma Beth.

"Of course I had to give that up and start earning steady money," he said, pulling a cigarette from the pack. "Subconsciously, maybe I resented Emma Beth—resented her mother, too." He puffed, frowning intently. "God, I hope not!"

"Oh, come on, Asa! The woman didn't get pregnant by herself," Molly said. "And if you really wanted that graduate degree, you could have gotten it. You still can."

"Well!" Asa drew back, pretending injury. "I can see I'll get no sympathy here."

Molly smiled. "I'm afraid you hit me at a bad time."

"I know. I'm sorry." He jabbed at her with the handle of his spoon. "But you have to get on with living, Molly. Ethan would want that. You know how he loved a good time!"

"He loved coming here, too." Molly jumped in with both feet. "Ethan used to talk about a big magnolia tree somewhere around here. Is that next door? I didn't see it in the yard."

Asa laughed. "The reason you didn't see it is because Grandpa cut it down! I'll swear, if they hadn't been married so long and weren't so set in their ways, I think Grandma would have divorced him for that. I've never seen her so furious!"

"Why would he do that?"

"Said it had blight and was dying," Asa explained, "and maybe it was, but Grandpa hated that tree. I think he just got sick and tired of cleaning up all those leaves." Smoke curled about his face as he spoke. "Frankly, I believe he did it for spite because Grandma had old Shep put to sleep. Shep was Grandpa's dog, and the poor thing was so old and sick, he could barely walk. Grandma finally did what needed to be done."

"When was this?" Molly asked.

Asa smiled. "It was the summer I turned thirteen, the summer they built the gazebo. Grandma had always wanted one, so Grandpa had it built where the tree used to be. Guess he thought that would pacify her."

"And did it?" Molly asked.

He tapped ashes into a saucer. "Well, at least she started speaking to him again."

MOLLY STARED AT the glimmer of streetlight under her windowshade long after she had gone to bed. If you peeked through the latticework beneath the gazebo, you could see the stump of the ill-fated magnolia, Asa had said. And the lowest limb, the one she told him Ethan had liked to climb, grew facing the back of the house.

Molly turned her pillow for the third time. If Tyrus Duncan had lived in Harmony as he claimed, why hadn't he remembered that?

TWELVE

"BECAUSE," he reminded her, "we didn't stay in Harmony that long. Molly, do you realize how many places I've lived? After a while they become blurred together." Ty stood under the pale yellow lamp outside Harmony's First Methodist Church. Pageant rehearsal was over, and the cast members chatted and laughed as they emerged from the building dressed warmly against the chill.

"Sorry." Molly touched his arm. She was tired of feeling alone, and was frightened, too, after the mysterious events of the week. "But how are we ever going to dig up—"

"Dig up what?" Asa stood beside her.

"Dig up enough food to feed all this crowd!" Molly said with a frantic look at Ty.

"Don't worry—Mother's been cooking ahead for weeks, like everyone else. Just wait and see." Asa sniffed and looked about. "I smell snow. Can you believe it? I think it's going to snow!"

"Oh, I hope so! Wouldn't that be fun?" Emma Beth reached for her father's hand, apparently without even thinking, and he tucked it under his arm. "The angels sounded great tonight!" she called to Joy.

"Thanks, but Mom about blinded us with all that mist!" Joy rolled her eyes. "For gosh sakes, go easy on the dry ice, will ya?"

Molly, who thought she had done rather well, was relieved when the aunts bustled out to hurry them home. She watched Judson Horne having an earnest conversation with Louann Dobson's mother as they paused on the sanctuary steps while Louann trailed unhappily behind them.

"Next year the innkeeper's daughter," Jud was saying. "A part I've been meaning to emphasize—perfect for it!" He seemed relieved to see his wooden-faced housekeeper plodding up the walk to meet him. "Ah! Here's our Mrs. Larsen! You've brought Zebina? Good! Mustn't keep her waiting." Jud beamed at Louann and her mother, who seemed to have mellowed some. "We'll see you at the party, I hope?"

"Yeah! We're starting at our house," Emma Beth said. "Come on, Louann, you can ride with us."

The girl smiled and followed them to the parking lot, obviously glad to be away from her mother, if even for a little while.

"Here. Don't forget these." Mildred Dobson shoved a foil-wrapped container in her daughter's lap as Louann squeezed into the back seat with Joy and Emma Beth. "I didn't mess up my clean kitchen baking all day for nothing!" And she slammed the door and marched away.

Molly tried not to respond to Ty's playful nudge as she drove out of the parking lot. She knew he would be willing her to laugh and make a fool of herself. Well, she wasn't going to do it!

"You're supposed to act like a child at Christmas," he whispered to no response. But certainly everyone else seemed to be doing it, Molly noticed as they piled out of the car and into the aunts' crowded hall, where the traditional sprig of mistletoe hung invitingly over their heads. A boisterous group of men clustered there, eagerly taking advantage of it. With a lifted eyebrow, Ty glanced from the mistletoe to her, but Molly smiled and shook her head.

If she ever kissed Tyrus Duncan, it wouldn't be in front of all these people.

"Where in the world did all this food come from?" Molly asked Iris, who was ladling cups of cranberry punch.

"Ivalee made most of it," her aunt said. "But some of the carolers aren't on the route, so they bring their special dishes here or to Jud's." She pulled Molly aside, whispering, "That's Ouida Kirkpatrick's fruitcake over there. She puts that nasty citron in it, and no spirits at all." She sniffed. "Now mine's on the sideboard on Mama's blue Limoges plate. She always served it on that."

Molly nodded and headed for the sideboard. If she absolutely had to eat fruitcake, she preferred Iris's recipe.

"Here, try some of Iris's little fruitcakes!" Myrtis, standing by the sideboard, slipped two onto Molly's plate and peeled the wrapping from another. "Hmm! I just can't seem to stop."

"Aha! Caught in the act!" Jud poked a playful finger at Myrt as he filled a small plate for Zebina, who sat like a fragile antique doll on the living-room sofa.

Myrtis smiled at him with her mouth only. "Jud, I need to talk with you," she said in a husky whisper, glancing about to see if anyone had heard.

Molly moved away and turned her back, pretending to converse with Ty, but both of them listened shamelessly.

Judson Horne laughed. "About what you want for Christmas? Well, have you behaved yourself this year?"

"Oh, stop it! I'm serious." Myrtis sounded tired and a little frightened. Her words were barely audible. "Jud, I've just had the most godawful notion—"

"Mom! You've got to taste these little chicken wings!" Joy stood before her with barbecue sauce on her chin. She grabbed her cousin's arm. "Try one, Emma Beth; they're yummy."

"Don't tempt me." Emma Beth crunched on raw vegetables from a parsley tree. She looked absolutely miserable. "This is awful!" she wailed. "What's the fun of a party if you can't eat?"

"Try a little exercise." Joy slipped an arm around her. "Come on; they're getting ready to leave in a minute. We'll *run* from house to house."

"Did you find out what 'godawful' notion Myrtis had?" Molly asked Ty as they lagged behind the others. "She doesn't seem herself tonight. Have you noticed?"

"You forget, I've only met the lady once," he said. "But she does seem kind of subdued." They lingered on the fringes of the group as the carolers gathered on the lawn of a small brick house with a lighted tree in the window.

Myrtis stood on the bottom step in her glaring orange hat and scarf and bulky brown jacket. "Sing out now," she directed them. "Look happy!"

"Oh, come on, Myrt, it's a party!" someone called out.

"Yeah, loosen up! Somebody give Myrt a drink!" The red-faced man who suggested this sounded as if he had already downed a few, and Myrtis laughed along with the others, but Molly thought she seemed ill at ease.

Behind her she heard Emma Beth mutter, "Wish she'd just go home and leave us alone!"

The porch light came on as the carolers began with "Here We Come A-Wassailing," and a smiling gray-haired woman came outside in a sweater and passed around plates of divinity.

Molly looked about her. Who in this merry group was hiding a secret? A secret so terrible they would kill to keep it! She felt Tyrus nudging her. "Look over there," he whispered. Sonny Earl Dinsmore stood to one side sing-

ing, his worn red cloak wrapped about him. A rope of
plastic holly was twisted around the crown of a visored
garrison cap; she supposed the hat had belonged to his father. He seemed to be familiar with the words to the carols, Molly noticed, but his voice was oddly out of tune.

Judson Horne walked over and put an arm around him.
"Are you sure you're warm enough, my old friend?" he
asked. Sonny Earl nodded as he continued to sing, even
after the song was over. Myrt shared her divinity with him
and whispered something in his ear, to which he smiled in
response.

A few streets away the older singers were rewarded with
warm mulled wine and the younger ones with hot apple
cider, and Molly noticed that Asa's friend Corrine Harris
had joined him. He introduced the two women casually
with one arm around each, and Molly smiled when Asa
made a point of addressing her as his cousin.

Corrine sang in a high monotone, but she seemed to be
enjoying herself, and the bright face that peered from beneath the soft blue wrap was pretty enough that Molly
could see why Asa wasn't interested in her spaghetti (or her
voice) alone. Emma Beth, she saw, made an issue of ignoring them.

They turned down a winding side street lit by fanciful
sandbag lanterns and kicked up brown leaves as they
walked. Molly studied the tall man behind her, who sang
tenor slightly off-key; a round-faced matron who reeked
of Tabu. Could one of them be her enemy? She moved
with the current of carolers, who seemed to be drifting
down a cold, dark river strung with tiny colored lights. It
gave her an uneasy feeling to be welcomed at every door
where people called one another by name and seemed
genuinely glad of their coming. The Tudor house closed in
by hedges resembled Snow White's cottage. Was the witch

nearby? Gradually the singers became louder, a little row-
dier, in spite of Myrt's half-hearted protests, and Molly
found herself laughing along with them. This night she
seemed to have tenth-grade emotions in an adult body.

But she wasn't in high school. She was a grown woman
with a half-grown daughter whose father had been killed
because of something that had happened in Harmony.

An hour later, throat hoarse from singing, Molly shivered as she merged with the crowd to serenade the Baptist
minister's family at their gray stone parsonage across from
the church. Her icy feet felt as though they might shatter,
and her fingers had no feeling at all. When Tyrus wrapped
a warm woolen arm about her, she did not protest in spite
of Joy's sullen glance.

"Let's sneak back to that place where they served the
hot wine," Ty whispered, holding her warm against him.
"Or better still, hitch a ride with Jud and what's-her-
name." He sighed. "Now that's caroling in style!"

In spite of her discomfort, Molly wouldn't want to ride
from house to house with the ailing Zebina Horne, even to
keep warm. The woman seemed to exude sorrow.

"She usually doesn't bother to come at all," Iris said.
"Guess she was afraid she was missing out on something."

"Just thank the lord she didn't bring that autoharp!"
Ivalee said under her breath.

Then why had she come? Molly found herself watching
the pale, pinched face. Swathed in a gray plaid robe, Zebina sang mechanically, her dark eyes taking in the revelry about her, but she smiled when they came to rest on
her husband. Jud leaned down to whisper to her, then
hustled his wife into the car.

"Guess they're leaving early to see to things at their
place," Ivalee said, watching them. "I suppose that fat

housekeeper with the tacky yellow hair has everything ready for us by now." She gave Molly's shoulder a hearty whap. "Brace up! We've only a few blocks to go!"

"Wait a minute, Jud!" Iris called, taking Sonny Earl's hands between her own. "Sonny's freezing out here. We've got to get him home. I wouldn't be surprised if we all got pneumonia!" Molly noticed that someone had thrown a heavy man's topcoat over the thin cloak.

"Yes, home," Sonny Earl echoed. "I'm tired."

Jud held the open door of his car. "Your carriage awaits," he said, returning the topcoat to Reuben Anthony as Sonny climbed inside.

Ty looked at Molly and smiled. "They take care of each other, don't they?"

But at what price? she wondered.

Gratefully, Molly allowed Tyrus to lead her as they ambled into the street singing "We Wish You a Merry Christmas." By the light of the corner streetlamp, she noticed the vivid red plaid of his jacket in loud disagreement with the crimson of his hat and wondered who picked out his clothes.

Ty had never married, he had told her earlier, although he'd seen someone on a fairly regular basis for almost five years. "I just couldn't make a commitment," he admitted. "Somehow I knew it wouldn't be right. She finally married someone else."

"Were you sorry?" Molly asked, and Ty had grinned. "Hell, no! I was relieved!"

Why had she felt so comforted by his admission?

Suddenly something soft and cold touched her face, and in the light of a doorway she saw the first flakes of snow drifting down.

They walked in quiet little clusters the remaining distance to Judson Horne's, talking and laughing softly among themselves, but Ty hung back from the rest and tucked Molly's gloved hand in his own. "I wish it could stay this way," he said when he finally spoke. His fingers gripped hers, held her back. "Listen to the snow. There's something peaceful about it." He covered her eyes with his hand. "Close your eyes and be still. You can hear it."

Molly stood on the cold, quiet street with a strange man's hand over her face and listened to the hushed whisper of falling snow. Suddenly she felt warm.

"When I was a boy," Ty told her, "we lived near some woods. I would go there when it snowed and just lie down in it. I liked to close my eyes and feel it touch me; listen to the stillness of it. Somehow it made everything seem right."

"Do you think everything will be right now?" Molly asked as they walked along.

"No," he said. "I don't. In fact, I have a bad feeling about tonight."

Molly hurried to keep up with him as they followed the others through wrought-iron gates and up the winding path to the Hornes' festive home. And this time Ty paused to kiss her lightly on the lips as they stood beneath the mistletoe in the hall.

The party grew merrier as they gathered around the warming blaze of the fireplace in the dining room sipping frothy eggnog from silver cups. Molly tasted the rich blend, licked nutmeg from her lips, and found it just right. Someone started to play Rodgers and Hammerstein's "My Favorite Things" on the grand piano in the corner, and several people began to sing.

For a few minutes Molly wanted to become a part of them: forget Ethan, forget why she was here, and lose herself in the joy of the moment. But she couldn't. Something was wrong and she felt it. Molly looked about her at the guests, wishing she could warn them. But warn them of what? Yet like Tyrus Duncan she had a dull, cold feeling, almost a "knowing" that something terrible was going to happen in this house.

THIRTEEN

"I CAN'T DANCE," Ty said as Molly hobbled to a chair on the sidelines. "Sorry, two left feet. Guess I should have warned you."

Molly rubbed her bruised ankle and laughed. "Next time we'll try it barefoot!" Most of the partygoers had collected in the Hornes' large basement recreation room, where a jukebox blared a Beach Boys song. She smiled to see Asa swinging his Aunt Iris to "Help Me, Rhonda."

Jud said something to Zebina, who watched the dancers from a wicker settee, then went over to ask Myrtis to dance, but she only smiled and shook her head. Molly wished he would ask her. Her feet—or what was left of them—were about to shag off somewhere on their own.

Louann Dobson, she noticed, had maneuvered Jud's good-looking nephew Larry into a private corner, and Joy was flirting in earnest with an older man who looked to be at least fifteen.

Molly tried not to seem too eager when another song began and Asa led her to the dance floor. He was a smooth dancer, and they moved together as if they had been partners for years. Later, dancing with Jud, she noticed Asa gliding about with Corrine Harris tucked under his chin like a priceless violin. Corrine had a sleepy little smile on her face and danced with her eyes closed. She looked a bit put out, Molly thought, when the song ended and Asa abandoned her on the sidelines to dance with Emma Beth.

Later, as they moved into the dining room, Molly was glad she had only nibbled at the plate of refreshments someone had served her earlier. The room was filled with good breakfast smells. How could she possibly be hungry?

"I've decided I want to live in this town," Ty said as he filled his plate. "I'll just drift from house to house, meal to meal, and eat myself into oblivion."

Molly helped herself to the cheese grits—only a tiny serving, but they looked so good. And the sausages were a crusty brown.

"Molly." Ivalee, dressed for the outside, came up behind her. "The girls are ready to leave. Emma Beth's tired and Joy doesn't want to stay without her, so I'm going to walk on home with them."

"But you'll miss breakfast," Molly protested. "I'll go with them, Aunt Ivalee."

But her aunt was firm. "Frankly, I'm exhausted. It's been a long day, and I'm ready for bed." She smiled. "Stay as long as you like, and don't worry; we'll be fine."

"It's stopped snowing now," Iris assured Molly as they carried their plates downstairs. "And the walk will do Emma Beth good. Besides," she added, "you don't want to miss the charades."

"We always end up with charades," Jud told her, balancing a plate in each hand. "It's the best part of the party!" He placed a plate in front of Zebina. "Now, I want you to eat every bite! Promise?"

His wife managed a fleeting smile. "I'll try, dear, but I'm afraid I'm not very hungry. I've eaten more than I should already. Dr. Rosenberg will be cross with me."

Jud laughed and patted her hand. "Well, what Dr. Rosenberg doesn't know won't hurt him," he told her. "Look, Undine has made those biscuits you like so much."

"Does your Mrs. Larsen do all the cooking?" Molly asked. "Everything has been wonderful. I'd like to tell her so before I go."

Jud nodded, beaming. "Oh, yes . . . well, except for the eggnog, which is my own recipe, and Zebina's special fruitcake. I'm afraid Undine's retired for the night, but I'll certainly relay the compliments. She's quite a cook, isn't she? We're lucky to have found her."

But Molly noticed that Zebina barely picked at her food, and when her husband announced it was time to choose sides for charades, she excused herself, saying she would much rather watch.

"Where's Myrtis?" Asa asked. "I want her for my team. She knows every song that's ever been written."

"She left a little while ago," Jud said. "Said she wasn't feeling well. It's been a hectic week for her, I'm afraid."

Ty frowned. "Will she be all right to drive home?"

"I think so. Her car was just out front, and it isn't that far." Jud appeared sure of himself, but his voice left room for doubt. Myrt had seemed unusually pale and quiet, and Molly had noticed that her face was beaded with perspiration as she watched the dancers earlier.

Most of the people who stayed to play charades were members of the older crowd—the "diehards," Iris called them. Molly found herself looking from face to face. Which one? she wondered.

She noticed that Jud left the room briefly as she wrote down the titles for Asa's team, and that he was white-faced and fidgety when he returned. Molly wondered if he and Myrtis had picked up the same virus. But she forgot him momentarily as Asa took the floor and began acting out the title of his charade.

"Not fair!" Tyrus yelled. "There should be a word limit."

"Sixteen words!" Iris Stonehouse frowned down her long, slender nose. "Whoever heard of a song title with sixteen words?"

But Asa had, and he proceeded to share it silently with them.

"Of course! I remember now!" One of the quieter choir members jumped to his feet in a flash of inspiration: "'I Built a Bar in the Back of My Car, and I'm Driving Myself To Drink!'" He counted the words on his fingers.

Ty seemed stunned. "How on earth did you know?"

The man slapped his knee and laughed. "Because he did the same one last year."

"I think something's the matter with Jud," Molly whispered to Asa as their host reentered the room for the second time looking decidedly uncomfortable. "Maybe we'd better go."

But Asa only shook his head and held a finger to his lips. Zebina had apparently changed her mind and was standing, acting out a title for Jud's team.

"What is it?" someone asked as she bent over, clutching her stomach. "Book? Movie? Song?"

Zebina groaned.

"'Birth of a Nation!'" Asa shouted.

Zebina looked wildly about as if she didn't know where she was, and when she tried to speak she sounded as if she had a mouthful of mush. Molly thought her complexion seemed even paler than usual.

"Hey! You're not supposed to talk!" a member of the opposing team reminded her.

"'The Agony and the Ecstasy'?" someone guessed.

The players were so caught up in the game that only Molly seemed to notice when Zebina Horne pitched forward, still grabbing her stomach. She watched, horrified, before she willed herself to move. And still for a moment she thought that Jud's usually quiet wife had merely become carried away with excitement.

But Zebina Horne didn't get up.

"Somebody call a doctor!" Molly put a hand on the woman's forehead. It was cool and clammy, and the pulse at her neck was slow. Again Zebina grabbed violently at her middle and moaned.

"Oh, God! What's wrong?" Judson sank to his knees at his wife's side, looking almost as ill as she. "It's her heart again—I know it!" He stroked her thin graying hair. "You're going to be fine, sweetheart. The ambulance is on the way."

Undine Larsen, who had undoubtedly heard the commotion, stumbled downstairs, breathless and red-cheeked in a pink flowered robe. "What's wrong? Is someone sick?" Her pale blue eyes flickered from face to face and came to rest on Jud cradling his wife on the floor. "Oh no! Not Zebina!" she cried. "Not Zebina!"

"Do you think it could be a stroke?" Molly asked Tyrus as they waited upstairs for the ambulance to arrive.

He stood at the window listening. "Maybe—or her heart." Ty gave the curtain an impatient twitch. "It looks bad. Wish they'd hurry."

Molly sat on the bottom step next to a bright red poinsettia; there was one at the end of every stair. Only a few hours ago the large entrance hall with its rose-flowered wallpaper and shining parquet floors had been filled with laughing people. Now it was silent. Asa had left with Corrine, who had had too much to drink and didn't look much better off than Zebina. Iris planned to follow the ambulance to the hospital in Judson's car.

Molly switched off the lights on the big cedar tree in the bay window. The decorations seemed improper, out of place, and she didn't want to look at them anymore. All she wanted to do was get out of this house. She glanced up to find Tyrus watching her with a kind of tired and gentle look about him. Poor Ty! He would have to spend the night in this house with the stolid Mrs. Larsen and Jud's assorted relatives. She didn't envy him.

The telephone rang as the ambulance swung into the driveway. It was Ivalee, and Molly sensed right away that she was trying not to cry. "I think you and Asa had better come home right away," she said. "We've had an intruder here and the girls are upset. I can't get them to settle down."

Molly and Ty left without saying a word to anyone. Jud followed his wife's stretcher to the ambulance, and Iris followed Jud. Neither of them needed something else to worry about just then. Besides, Aunt Ivalee had said the girls were upset. If they had been harmed, they would be at the hospital—wouldn't they? She saw her daughter's face in front of her all the way to Muscadine Hill.

Asa was there before her. "They're all right," he said as she and Tyrus ran across the yard and up the front steps. "The police have been here, but nothing was taken, and there are no signs of a forced entry."

Molly looked about the living room. Even the presents under the tree seemed to be undisturbed. The two girls sat on the sofa with Ivalee between them. Emma Beth was red-eyed and sniffling; Joy sat stiffly under a blanket. She tossed it aside when she saw her mother and ran into Molly's arms.

Molly sank into the large armchair with Joy on her lap, feeling suddenly weak and shaky. "When did all this happen?"

"We didn't notice anything unusual when we got home," Ivalee said, "but I believe somebody was already here. Hiding. I think we surprised them."

"She was in our room, Mom." Joy's greenish eyes were round and solemn. "She was in there the whole time."

"The girls went right to the den and turned on the television," Ivalee said, "and I picked up a few things in the dining room. Later, when Joy and Emma Beth started up to bed, she must have heard them coming and panicked—"

"Somebody turned off the hall light," Joy said. "Somebody wrapped in a dark coat ran past us on the stairs." She held tightly to Molly's hand. "She almost knocked me down."

Tyrus frowned. "She?"

"I think it was a woman," Joy said.

"I know it was a woman," Emma Beth announced. "It was Myrtis Curtis, and she was wearing that awful orange hat. I saw it!"

FOURTEEN

THE MAP WAS GONE. Molly knew it would be when she dashed upstairs and dug frantically in her top dresser drawer. She had tucked Ethan's yellowing diagram beneath a favorite green sweater. Now she shook the heavy sweater, felt its empty sleeves, and took everything out of the drawer one at a time. But none of it was going to bring back the map, she thought, because whoever had been in her room had taken it.

"It could have been Myrtis," Ty reasoned before he left for the hospital to check on Zebina. "She left early, remember? She had plenty of time."

But why would Myrtis want to know where three kids had buried an old love note? Molly wondered. Why would anyone—unless it contained something they didn't want revealed?

She wasn't surprised when the sound of someone digging woke her a few hours later. It was a muffled noise, a muted scraping of sharp metal on the frozen earth. Molly sat up in bed. She felt heavy, dull—as if she were wearing a suit of armor. Joy's cot was empty and she remembered that her daughter was sleeping with Emma Beth that night.

Shivering, Molly wrapped herself in the faded blue flannel robe she had worn for years. Ethan had made fun of it, but it was the warmest thing she had and she couldn't bring herself to part with it. From the bathroom window she could see a dark figure crouched near the gazebo. A sharp wind had blown away most of the snow, but white patches still lay over the black earth. As Molly watched, a dim yellow light flickered briefly as if the treasure seeker wanted to be sure he was digging in the right place.

Molly touched the cold window glass. Whoever it was, she had to stop him! But how? Suppose there was more than one? She thought of Asa. His door was closed, but that might mean anything, and she was sure he knew about the map. Also, he was there when she reached home that night. How long had he really been back?

With cold, bare feet Molly hurried downstairs to the kitchen and switched on the outside light. What if whoever was out there came charging inside? What if he had a gun?

But when she looked out the window the nocturnal visitor had vanished. The gazebo stood, a fragile old ghost of a building, looking worse for the wear and in need of paint.

"What on earth are you doing down here at this hour of the night?"

Molly stifled a cry as she turned and saw Asa standing behind her. He wore a dark coat over his pajamas and his damp sneakers left tracks on the kitchen floor. His hand was cold on her wrist. She pulled away. "I might ask the same of you! I thought I heard someone outside, out by the gazebo." Molly quickly managed to put the kitchen table between them. "You almost scared me to death!"

"Sorry. I couldn't sleep; got to thinking about Zebina, about what happened tonight. I went out on the porch and smoked a cigarette." He looked at his feet and frowned. "Afraid I've tracked in snow."

"You didn't hear anything out there?" Molly pulled her robe together. He did smell like tobacco, but then he always smelled like tobacco.

"No. Should I have?" Asa smiled. "Maybe we've both been eating too much rich food; and it's freezing cold down here. We'd better get some sleep."

He made it sound as if she had been dreaming, Molly thought, but she was too sleepy to argue.

"Look at this!" Ty said the next morning, calling Molly's attention to a shallow hole in the back yard. "They've been digging in the wrong place. The magnolia limb would have been about in the middle of where the gazebo is now, so the box should be just inside the foundation." He touched the rotten latticework with the toe of his shoe and a piece fell away. "About here."

"Whoever was out here last night had big feet," Molly pointed out, trying to avoid tramping over the fresh tracks where water from the melting snow had softened the ground. "And look—the soles have a peculiar pinwheel design."

Tyrus frowned. "They look like they were made by heavy boots," he said. "Probably men's boots." He looked around him. "If you can find me something to dig with, now is as good a time as any."

Molly agreed. Ivalee had gone to the hospital, Asa had taken the two girls ice skating in Atlanta, and Iris, who had come home at dawn, was sleeping upstairs. Molly thought it would take more than a little shoveling to wake her.

"Zebina's very weak," Iris had reported. "Her blood pressure went sky high, and she doesn't seem to know anyone. Poor Jud! What an awful thing to happen here at Christmas! I had to make the man go home and get some sleep. He was sick and exhausted."

Molly wondered if Judson Horne had gone directly home, and then was ashamed for even considering such a thing.

Since the floor of the gazebo wouldn't allow the leverage to work with a long-handled shovel, Ty had to make do with a small garden trowel. But the dirt underneath was fine and moist, and even from his awkward kneeling position, he soon had scooped out a hollow several inches deep. He lay on his stomach with a smear of dirt on his cheek. "I think I'd better prepare you, Molly: the soil should be packed harder than this. It's too easy to dig here. Somebody's been here before us, I'm afraid."

"Maybe this isn't the right place." Molly groaned. "I wish we'd looked at that map better!"

"Can you see anything?" Ty asked as Molly squinted inside.

"Not yet." She sat on the summerhouse steps and watched the mound of red dirt grow larger. "Ty, we have to find that box today—before whoever was here last night comes back!"

Ty reared back on his knees and stretched. "Who else knew you had that map? Think."

"Asa knew, I'm sure, and probably Myrtis, too. Remember? She drove up in the yard the other day when we were trying to figure it out." Molly pulled off her hat and ran a hand through her hair. The midmorning sun had melted what little snow was left, and Ty had already peeled off his heavy jacket and tossed it aside. "Of course," she continued, "if they knew, they could have told someone else."

"What worries me is, what are we going to do when we find it? Will we know when we see it exactly what this person is after?" Ty wiped his forehead with a grimy arm. "What may seem innocent to us could be deadly to someone else."

Molly suddenly felt cold again. Two people were dead, maybe more. She hadn't fooled anyone about her reasons for being in Harmony, and now someone was trying to stop her. She watched silently as Tyrus scraped the dirt away, slowly enlarging his excavation. It had been almost a quarter of a century since the three children had buried a secret "treasure," drawn a crude map of its location, and forgotten the whole thing. Until now. It would be a surprise if it was still there, and an even greater shock if they learned anything from it.

She was jolted by the *thunk* of the trowel striking something hard. Ty pressed himself to the ground to explore the area, groping with an outstretched arm.

"I can't see a damned thing," he told her, "but I feel something—something hard; maybe a rock. No...it has corners." With a groan Ty brought forth a dirt-encrusted package wrapped in layers of plastic that clung to the sides of the box. "This hasn't been under here for any twenty-three years," he said, unwrapping the package. "It's a trash bag—one of those heavy-duty ones." But the small metal box inside had obviously withstood years of weather. It had once held peppermints; a portion of its label was still readable, but little remained of the original design. Inside was an even smaller tobacco tin.

Ty held the box between his knees and strained to pry off the lid, his fingers clumsy in mud-caked gloves. "It's rusted on," he said, shaking his head. "A hammer should do it, or a screwdriver."

"Let's go inside." Molly found herself tugging at his arm, trying to pull him to his feet. "I don't like being out here. Anyone could be watching." She glanced nervously at the house next door.

Ty snatched up his jacket and tucked the box under his arm. "How do you know we'll be any safer inside? Besides we might wake your Aunt Iris."

Feeling extremely vulnerable, Molly followed him to the garage where he replaced the trowel and quickly removed the lid of the tin with two heavy blows of a hammer. The contents of the box were enclosed in yet another plastic lined envelope.

"Thorough little pirates, weren't you?" Molly remarked as Tyrus carefully slit open the bag. She could imagine Ethan at twelve, eyes gleaming with excitement, as he placed the articles in the box on that long-ago winter day. She smiled as the first objects slid out: a small metal whistle on a plastic lanyard, like the kind made at summer camp; a white arrowhead still streaked with red clay; a shark's tooth from a vacation at the beach; and a large yellow marble Ty called a "cat's eye."

"There has to be more than this!" Frowning, Tyrus shook the contents of the envelope onto the dirty cement floor. A baseball card featuring Mickey Mantle, a folded page from an old newspaper, and a ball-point pen from the Bank of Harmony tumbled to the ground. And in the middle of the clutter lay a small metal key.

"This has to be it!" Tyrus snatched it up with one scoop of his fist. "Do you have any idea what it's for?"

"You were one of the three junk collectors," Molly reminded him. "How should I know?" She held out her hand and waited until he placed it in her palm. "Looks like it might fit in a chest of drawers or a desk or something. Maybe one of the aunts will know." Her eyes met his in the silence of the dark garage. "We have to ask, Ty. I have a feeling time is running out."

"I'M GLAD YOU ASKED me instead of Iris," Ivalee admitted a short while later as she studied the key in the quiet kitchen. "I think it belongs to that old desk I gave away— that ugly old pine thing that used to be in the upstairs hall." She smiled. "We were all supposed to do our schoolwork on it, but we never did. It stayed in the attic for years. Ethan seemed interested in it when he was here last. Told him he could have it, but then . . ." She looked away before reluctantly meeting Molly's eyes. "I'm sorry. I had no idea you wanted it. Maybe I can—"

"No. No, that's all right. But why did you give it away?" Molly tried to keep her voice from rising.

"Sh! Iris doesn't know yet." Ivalee held a finger to her lips. "Old thing was just collecting dust, and we have too much junk as it is. Our church sponsors a Boy Scout troop and they had a big yard sale for their Christmas service project. So when Reuben—you know, Reuben Anthony, our minister—he helps with the troop. Well, when Reuben asked for donations, I just told him to help himself."

"Was there anything in there?" Ty asked. "It must have been empty when he took it."

"All except for that drawer," Ivalee said. "Darned thing was either stuck or locked, and of course I couldn't find the key. I just told Reuben to jimmy it open and throw away what was inside, unless it was something we might want to keep." She frowned. "I remember Ethan went up and looked at it while he was here, but I just assumed he decided it wasn't worth the effort. It needs an awful lot of work." Ivalee poked her head in the refrigerator. "How does an omelet sound to you?"

But Molly wasn't hungry. "And did he?" she asked.

"Did who what?"

"Did Reuben throw away what was inside?"

Ivalee shook her head. "You know, I suppose he did. He never said anything about it. Where did you find that old key, anyway?"

"It was in that stack of Ethan's things," Molly said, avoiding Ty's eyes. "Those papers I found in that attic."

She watched her aunt take cheese from the refrigerator. "When did they have their sale?" she asked.

"Oh, several weeks ago, I think. You might call Reuben at home. He left the hospital when I did . . . Poor Zebina's about the same . . . just lies there! Anyway, I imagine he's gone home for a sandwich. That's all the man knows how to fix."

It seemed that Molly had caught the minister with his mouth full when she telephoned. "Oh yes, I still have that little desk," he said finally. "In fact, I liked it so much I bought it myself. I was going to refinish it for my niece for Christmas, but somehow or other I just haven't found the time." He chuckled. "Maybe I'll get to it before she graduates from high school!"

"He's going to be at home for about an hour or so," Molly whispered to Ty in the privacy of the downstairs hall. If there was anything important about Rowena's disappearance, it was going to be in that desk drawer.

Tyrus nodded. He was reading the folded section of newspaper that had been in the buried box. "Look at this: the front page of *The Harmony Herald* from the week Rowena disappeared."

Molly looked over his shoulder. "'Santa Arrives in Christmas Parade,'" she read aloud. "'Local Schools Begin Holidays; Tree Lighting Scheduled for Town Square.' Looks like big doings. Guess you three thought it was important enough to save for posterity."

But Ty had turned the paper over and was studying the back. Among the seasonal garden-club socials and an item on the monthly meeting of the DAR was an article on a Christmas party for the college-age set hosted by Miss Iris Stonehouse, and those attending were listed by couples. Tyrus planted his finger in the middle of the page. "Myr-

is came with Judson Horne and Iris had invited some-
ody named Ralph Barr for herself; but look who was
Rowena's date!'' His finger trembled on the paper. ''Your
good minister, Reuben Anthony!''

FIFTEEN

REUBEN ANTHONY came to the door munching a huge kosher pickle and smelling delightfully of garlic. "I'd offer you lunch," he said, extending his hand, "but I'm sure you could do a lot better at Ivalee's." He was a big, jovial man who would look more at home behind a plow than a pulpit, and Molly couldn't imagine him harboring dark and terrible secrets. However, as Ty had pointed out on the way over, you couldn't judge by appearances.

"I'll be glad to have that key; hated to break the lock." Reuben flicked on the light at the top of the basement stairs. "The desk's down there against that far wall," he told them. "Just take your time; I'll see if I can cram all this stuff back in the refrigerator." Molly looked at his cluttered kitchen and wished him luck.

She hesitated at the bottom of the stairs and glanced over her shoulder at the lighted kitchen above them. The basement was damp and musty, and she wouldn't want to spend much time there. For all she knew they might not have the right key, or someone might have been there before them to empty the drawer of its contents. Had Ethan already taken what was there?

But the old key turned smoothly in the lock, and the desk drawer slid open without so much as a creak. In a long white envelope at the back of the dusty drawer were two airline tickets and a typewritten note. The tickets were made out to Rosie and Charlie Alnutt.

"Who's that?" Ty asked. "How do you suppose they came up with those names?"

Molly frowned. "I don't know, but they sound familiar." She resisted the impulse to peer up the stairs behind them. She could hear water running in the sink and Reuben's heavy footsteps as he moved about the kitchen.

"He doesn't even know it's here," Ty whispered, guessing her thoughts. He unfolded the mildewed note and laid it on the desk beneath a dirt-smeared window. The letter, written on plain blue stationery, consisted of two brief sentences:

My Rowena,
Fly away with me! Meet me tonight at the usual place and time.
Your "Christmas Mouse"

Molly rolled her eyes upward. "His nickname?"

Ty shook his head. "Can you imagine him ever being small?" At the sound of Reuben's approaching footsteps, he quickly put the items back in the envelope and stuffed it inside his coat.

"Some old letters of Aunt Ivalee's," Molly explained to Reuben as they tramped back up the stairs. She hoped the darkness concealed her face. "I imagine she'd like to have them back."

The minister nodded, smiling, and walked with them to the door. She could tell he was eager for them to be gone.

"I hadn't realized you had grown up here," Molly said to Reuben Anthony as they paused in the hallway. "Aunt Ivalee said you and Aunt Iris were in the same class." She smiled brightly. Lying was becoming almost easy.

"I'm flattered, but Iris was actually in the class behind mine," Reuben Anthony said. "It's unusual for a Methodist minister to come back to his own home town, but I only lived here for a few years during high school and college." He smiled. "My father was a minister, too, so we moved around quite a bit."

"Harmony must have been a nice town to grow up in," Molly said, pretending to become interested in the small nativity scene on the table. "I guess you had a lot of parties—things like that?"

He laughed. "We had our share."

"Do you remember anyone in your crowd using the nickname 'Mouse'?" Ty asked. "Ethan's aunts were arguing about that the other day, and Ivalee said she was almost sure it was someone in your group."

Molly smiled; Tyrus was getting to be as skilled at lying as she was. But Reuben didn't change his expression. "Don't believe I've ever heard that one," he said with a large hand on the doorknob. "You must think I'm awfully rude rushing you out like this," he added, "but I have an appointment in a few minutes. I wish we could talk longer."

Molly put her hand on his. "I'm sorry. I'm the one who's being rude." She took a deep breath and plunged ahead. "Reuben, do you know who Rowena Sterling was seeing before she disappeared?" There. She had said it! Ty's fingers were firm on her arm. The buttons of his coat pressed into her back, and she felt oddly comforted.

"I assumed she went away with that Jones fellow—the one who wrote poetry." The minister's face was flushed, but his eyes were steady.

"Someone else, I mean." Molly felt like a human wedge. She wanted to walk out the door, but the opening was still too narrow.

Reuben managed a laugh, but his eyes were not amused. "Well, I saw her a few times myself—strictly on a platonic basis. Rowena was pretty; she was fun. She had a lot of dates." He looked from Molly to Ty. "Why do you ask? That was years ago."

"I wish I could tell you," Molly answered. "Maybe I can soon." She slipped outside, pulling Tyrus behind her. When she looked back, Reuben Anthony was still standing in the doorway frowning into the sun. "Now I'm hungry," she admitted. "Fear does something to my appetite."

Two chili dogs later, they turned off Shake Rag Road onto the long graveled drive leading to Myrtis's place. "She wasn't feeling well last night at the party," Molly said. "I'm worried about her. And she might be able to tell us who was called 'Mouse.'" She looked at Ty, who was trying to drain the last of his chocolate shake. "Do you still think it couldn't have been Reuben?"

"I don't think Reuben's our man," Ty said. "But I believe he knows who was."

"Surely you don't think he's protecting a murderer!"

"Maybe he doesn't think there's been a murder," Ty reminded her.

Molly was silent as they drove into Myrt's yard. *Rosie and Charlie Alnutt.* Where had she heard those names? Something to do with gin... and tea...

The Curtis farm was quiet and still. No smoke rose from the great stone chimney. At the sound of the car, Colonel Sanders careened from behind the house barking to show who was boss. Then he wagged his tail at the sound of Molly's voice and jumped up on her with muddy feet.

Molly shoved him away with both hands. "Get down, Colonel! I know you're glad to see me." She frowned. Myrt's car was in the shed, but she didn't see a light in the house. She tried to peek inside while Ty knocked at the kitchen door. The only festive decoration was a quilted calico wreath that hung on the gray porch wall.

"Maybe she's gone next door to feed the cats," Molly said. Then she remembered that Myrtis would have left the dog on the porch to keep him from following.

"I'll try the front," Ty said finally. "She might be on the other side of the house." But he didn't sound convincing.

Molly looked in the big kitchen window. A fat Santa candle stood in the center of a pine trestle table along with one coffee mug and a paperback book open face down. He looked lonely. Then Molly thought she saw something move: something large and brown. A tall figure slowly emerged from the doorway leading into the hall. It looked a little like a bear learning to walk on its hind legs. A very sick bear. Myrtis!

It seemed to take Myrt forever to undo the latch, and by that time Ty had raced back around the house in answer to Molly's frantic call. With one of them on either side of her, they made it to the living-room sofa. "Well, I've had one hell of a night," Myrtis said in a weak, rasping voice. Her face was ashen and gaunt, and there were dark circles under her eyes. She wore white cotton socks and a bathrobe that looked as if it had been made from an old army blanket.

She had left Jud's party early, Myrtis told them, because she hadn't been feeling well, and shortly after arriving home had suffered from severe stomach cramps, vomiting, and diarrhea. "I've never in my life been so sick I actually wanted to die; and then I thought maybe I *had* died and had ended up where a lot of folks always said I would." Myrt allowed Molly to tuck a pillow behind her and accepted a glass of ginger ale, sipping it a little at a time. "Thank God I don't even remember half of it," she said. "That's one night I'd just as soon forget!"

"I wondered where you were last night," Molly said. "We didn't see you leave."

"Huh! Didn't have time for polite good-byes. Didn't even have time to hunt up my wraps," Myrt said. "I just grabbed an old sweater of Jud's and went home!"

"Do you think it might have been something you ate?" Molly asked.

"Wouldn't everyone else be sick, too?" Myrt set the glass on the coffee table. "No, I guess I just picked up a virus—or it picked up me. Whatever it was, I hope to God I never have it again!"

Ty had lit a fire in the fireplace. Now he drew the screen across it and leaned on the mantel. "They rushed Zebina Horne to the hospital last night," he said. "From the last report, she wasn't doing all that well."

"Oh lord! Poor Zebina." Myrtis closed her eyes. "Well, she's always been frail, and she has a weak heart. This isn't the first time she's had a close call."

"Iris said Jud was sick, too," Molly told her. "I wonder how he is."

Ty picked up the telephone. "I didn't see him when I left the house this morning. It was early, and I just assumed he was either asleep or at the hospital with Zebina." Quickly he dialed the number Myrtis gave him and spoke briefly to someone on the other end. "That was the housekeeper, Mrs. Larsen," he told them, replacing the receiver. "She says Jud was sick all morning, but the doctor thinks he's going to be all right."

Molly refilled Myrt's glass and brought a blanket to throw around her. Sitting beside her on the sofa, she glanced at her friend's ungovernable hair and considered a hairbrush, then thought better of it. What difference would it make?

"Just to be sure, I think you'd better let a doctor look you over," Molly suggested. "Maybe it is a virus, but if the three of you ate something that made you sick, we need to find out about it."

"Please don't talk about eating," Myrtis begged, turning her head away. "Besides, I don't like doctors. They give me the creeps."

"Oh, come on, Myrt!" Ty laughed. "They don't use leeches anymore."

Leeches. Gin and tea. Molly smiled. *"The African Queen!"* she said aloud.

But Myrt didn't hear her. "Well, it's what I deserve for making a pig of myself. I swear I'll never touch fruitcake again!"

"What was that all about?" Ty asked as they drove back to town. "Were you still playing charades?"

"Rosie and Charlie Alnutt were the characters from *The African Queen*, remember? Those were the names on the plane tickets! Be we never did ask Myrt about the 'Christmas Mouse,'" she said as they drew close to town. "Do you think she'll be all right?" They had fed the animals before leaving and had made Myrt as comfortable as possible.

"The doctor said he'd drop by later on," Ty reminded her. He grinned. "I didn't know they still did that."

"I think he's one of Myrt's former students," Molly said. "She said he'd probably charge her double just for spite!" Molly suddenly sat up straighter and shuddered as if someone had dumped snow down her back.

"What's wrong?" Ty had stopped in the Stonehouse driveway before continuing to the hospital to ask about Zebina.

"Nothing." Molly quickly stepped out of the car. She had just had a horrible thought, and she wasn't ready to share it.

As she closed the car door behind her, Ivalcc called from the porch. "Wait! Tell Tyrus not to leave yet! Someone wants him on the phone."

"Must be my sister." Ty hurried inside. "Hope nothing's wrong—other than the chicken pox, I mean," he added after a look from Molly. She heard him answer on the telephone in the downstairs hall while Ivalee rushed to the kitchen to rescue her pumpkin bread.

I will not eat another fattening thing today, Molly told herself, but the spicy aroma pursued her with its rich, warm summons. She fled through the kitchen to the den. Apparently Asa had not returned with the girls, and the big house was quiet. Molly collapsed into an armchair and picked up a magazine. She could hear Tyrus talking softly in the hall.

"Of course I haven't told her," he said in a confidential tone. "No one knows. No one's going to know, I promise." There was a pause, then Molly heard him telling someone about the envelope they had found. The conversation was indistinct, but she definitely heard the words *mouse* and *desk*. Quietly she crept to the door, straining for every word. "Not where we thought . . . led me right to it . . . let you know when I learn anything more." His voice grew louder. "Give the children my love," Ty added before hanging up the receiver. He almost collided in the hallway with Aunt Ivalee and a pot of Russian tea.

"I thought you'd like a little taste of pumpkin bread," she said, putting the tray on the end table. "I made a loaf for the mailman and one for that nice young clerk at the bank, but I always bake an extra for us."

Tyrus gave Ivalee a kiss and broke off a bite of the bread. He was getting to be like one of the family, Molly thought. "Umm, you're a wonder," he sighed, licking his fingers. He smiled widely at Molly who ignored him.

Ivalee sipped her tea. "By the way," she said, "did you find anything in the desk?"

Tyrus stood to go. "Just a few old papers. We didn't think you'd want them." He paused in the doorway and asked, as if it were a spur-of-the-moment question, "Mrs. Brown, do you remember anyone going by the nickname 'Mouse,' or even 'Christmas Mouse'? Someone in Iris's group of friends?"

"Christmas Mouse!" Ivalee laughed. "What a funny name! Sounds like a children's story." She took another sip and set her cup aside. "No, I don't remember that. Why don't you ask Iris? She just ran to the store for eggs. She'll be back in a minute."

But when Iris Stonehouse charged in the kitchen a few minutes later, slamming the back door with a bang, she was in no mood to be questioned. "You'll never guess what I heard at the store!" she exclaimed, setting down the grocery sack with an alarming crunch. Her green eyes were wide and gleaming. "They've dug up a body—a skeleton—out where they're building that new mall, and it was right out there behind Myrt's place!"

SIXTEEN

MYRTIS APPEARED QUIET and pale at church the next morning, but the organ blasted out "Joy to the World" with its usual intensity. Molly felt relieved that at least one component in Harmony's scheme of things was as it should be.

The little town was all aflutter over the recently discovered skeleton, and the congregational chatter before the service had been of nothing else. "It's like throwin' one corn pone to a pack of hungry dogs," Ivalee had observed as they stood in front of the sanctuary. "They all want a little piece of it."

"They say it scared the workman who found it so bad, they could hear him yelling clear over in Floyd County," said one of a group of men.

Another laughed. "Yeah, I heard he was runnin' so hard, his shadow was two miles behind him!"

Molly was sure everyone had speculated as to whose skeleton it might be, but they weren't discussing the identity—or lack of it, at least not in public. Well, she had her own ideas about that.

As soon as the service was over, Molly and Joy swarmed up the aisle with the others. The rest of the family seemed to have disappeared into the crowd. Molly tried to slip past Reuben Anthony, who stood shaking hands with churchgoers at the front door, but he waylaid her with a huge hand. "Could you stay for just a minute?" he asked. "There's something I want to tell you."

Molly only nodded as she looked around for the aunts. She remembered the last time she had waited alone at this church, and she didn't intend to be put in that situation again—daylight or not!

Iris waved to her from the parking lot where she and her sister stood talking in a cluster of people.

"Do you mind waiting a few minutes longer?" Molly asked. "I want to speak with Reuben." She left Joy standing with the group and smiled to see a tall, bony lady with a gold-headed cane and a hearing aid engage her daughter in conversation.

"It's about yesterday," the minister began after the last of the hangers-on had left. "I've thought about what you asked, and I feel a bit guilty about my answer." He led her by the arm to a narrow bench just inside the doorway. Molly was relieved to see that the double doors remained open.

Reuben Anthony stretched his great broad back against the wall and sighed. "How about letting me in on this? Why is Rowena Sterling's past love life so important?"

"I'm not sure it is," Molly told him. "But it could be. It might have something to do with her disappearance." She was glad to see two people still talking outside on the walk.

The minister laughed softly. "But you couldn't have been more than a child then! Did you know Rowena?"

Silently Molly shook her head.

"I thought not. If you did, you'd know how stubborn she was; headstrong. You say she disappeared, and so she did, but you can rest assured Rowena went of her own accord. She got her way, regardless of the consequences."

He looked so sad when he spoke that Molly wondered if he, too, had been in love with Rowena Sterling.

After a deep sigh he continued. "You asked if Rowena was seeing someone other than the fellow she ran off with, and I think she might have been." His robe billowed in a gust of wind, and Molly edged a little closer to the wall. "I did escort her to some parties," he said, "but it was only because she asked me to. Her father was very strict, and I was known as a safe date." He smiled. "She would start out with me and meet someone else later." Reuben shrugged. "She used me, of course; I knew that at the time. But I also knew it was probably the only chance I'd ever have to date somebody like Rowena Sterling." He threw his shaggy red head back and laughed. "And do you know what? I was right!"

Molly found herself laughing, too. "But you never learned who you were covering for?" she asked.

He shook his head, frowning. "I'd thought she was seeing Barlow Jones. Until one night after I'd taken Rowena to a party, I saw him coming out of the Honey Bee Café, and he was alone."

"Still, you think he was the one she ran off with?"

Reuben stood, towering over her. "She hung around him all the time, flirted like crazy. Her father was furious; that's one reason he fired him, I think. Besides, who else could it have been? The rest of us were still here after she left."

"Rowena might still be here, too," Molly said softly.

He walked with her to the door and stood on the top step watching after her. Molly waited for what she had said to sink in. When it did, she heard him mutter, "Oh, my God!" She didn't think he meant it as a prayer. But then again, maybe he did.

EVERYONE WAS especially glum during lunch. Asa had once again brought up the subject of the pearl pendant, and Emma Beth had once again denied knowing anything about it. With funereal expression, she retired to her room, and Ivalee spent the entire mealtime imploring her to come out. After staring at his plate in silence, Asa stalked from the house and tore out of the driveway in a squall of gravel. Joy only picked at her food. Molly could tell she was trying not to cry, and she wasn't far from tears herself. Each bite hit her stomach like a lump of clay.

"Why don't you go upstairs and call a friend from home?" Molly suggested. "Make it a credit-card call," she added for Iris's benefit.

Joy jumped up so fast, she almost knocked over her chair. "Really? Can I? Oh, thanks, Mom!"

"Just don't talk too long!" Molly called after her. She hadn't been specific as to whom her daughter was or was not to call. Just then she really didn't care.

"More coffee?" Iris asked from across the dining-room table.

Molly shook her head. She hadn't decided whether Ethan's Aunt Iris was reserved in nature or was so wrapped up in herself that she was unaware of what went on around her.

But she was aware of Tyrus Duncan. "I thought your friend might have lunch with us today," Iris said, leaning back in her chair while her coffee cooled.

"He's at the hospital with Jud," Molly said. If Iris had an ounce of sensitivity, she would understand that she didn't want to discuss Tyrus Duncan—if that was really his name—much less invite him to lunch.

Iris nodded solemnly. "I don't believe poor Zebina will pull through this one." She said it in the same tone one might say, "I don't believe I'll wear those earrings with that dress."

"That's awful!" Molly thought of the drab, sickly woman lying in a hospital bed while the whole town "poor-Zebinaed" her life away. She hoped Judson Horne's ailing wife would get well just for the hell of it. "Myrtis seemed better," she pointed out, trying for a more positive outlook. "I wonder what the doctor had to say."

"Myrt's as strong as a horse." Iris took a dainty sip from her cup. "She must have been sick if she saw a doctor. She was the only one of us who had perfect attendance all through high school."

Molly played with the parsley on her plate. "About how old was Myrtis when her sister ran away?"

"How did you know about that?" Iris didn't seem to know what to do with her napkin.

"Ethan was visiting when it happened," Molly said. "It caused such an uproar, he never forgot it."

"I see." Iris smoothed the napkin in her lap. "Well, I was in college then; we all were except for Jud. He was already working at Gideon's. We're all about the same age, so Myrt would've been about nineteen or twenty."

"Ethan thought Rowena was beautiful," Molly said. "She must have been popular with the men. Was she seeing anyone beside the poet she ran off with?"

Iris flushed. "I really don't remember. That's been a long time." She cut a thin slice of pound cake and slid the platter across to Molly. "If you ask me, she was too popular for her own good," she muttered. "But that's neither here nor there." Iris peered into her empty cup as if she could read a fortune there. "I remember Ethan's being here that Christmas," she said, looking across at Molly. "He and his friend Neil. Mama enjoyed them so."

Molly cut off a sliver of cake and tasted it. It would have been better if it were chocolate. "There was another friend named Gus," she said. "Gus Duncan—remember? It must

have been a lively Christmas that year with three ram-
bunctious boys underfoot.''

Iris put down her fork. ''Well, yes, we did have three
boys here when Asa was about, but I remember Augusta
Duncan, and a daintier little girl I never expect to see!''

SEVENTEEN

THE ENVELOPE! Molly suddenly remembered that Tyrus had the envelope. In all the commotion that had followed Iris's announcement about the skeleton, she had allowed him to leave with the message tucked inside his jacket. Molly started for the telephone, then thought better of it. She would have to think of another way to get it back, to pretend she didn't know—at least for a little while. But if Ty wasn't Ethan's friend Gus, then who was he and what did he want?

Molly helped Iris clear the table and wash the few dishes. Ivalee had given up on her granddaughter and was spooning the contents of a casserole into a foil pan. Molly smelled chicken and onions and a whiff of celery. Ivalee licked the spoon, frowned, and added a few shakes of pepper.

"For Jud," she explained. "He loves anything with chicken in it, and I know he isn't taking the time to eat right." Her eyes misted over. "This was my Beckworth's favorite supper."

"Oh, I expect that housekeeper—what's her name? Mrs. Larsen—will see that he's fed," Iris said, whipping out a clean dish towel. "Besides, I doubt if Jud's ready for such rich food after that bout with his stomach."

"I imagine it will freeze," Molly said, seeing Ivalee's stricken expression. "And it smells wonderful! Would you like me to take it over there for you?"

"Oh, would you?" Ivalee was already stretching foil over the pan. "Just tell him to bake it for about an hour.

Here, I'll set it in this cardboard box.'' She dashed about the kitchen ignoring her sister's silent objection and her not-so-silent rattling of silverware.

Molly smiled to herself as she slipped into her coat. This would give her a perfect excuse to get inside the Hornes' home, and she intended to find that envelope if she had to search Tyrus Duncan's room from wall to wall!

As she pulled into Jud's driveway, Molly saw his sister Jodean and her son Larry leaving by the back door. ''Is anyone at home?'' she called to them.

''Uncle Jud's still at the hospital, but that woman's in there,'' Larry said. ''I reckon she's still in the kitchen.''

''Eating,'' his mother answered, slamming the car door. Molly waved to them and started inside with Ivalee's casserole. She had the distinct impression that neither of them was fond of Undine Larsen.

Molly found the housekeeper putting away a hearty meal of German potato salad and some kind of fat sausages. Her starched white bosom rested heavily on the table, and her feet were planted firmly on the floor, as if to give her better leverage. A calico cat sat expectantly by her chair. Molly could have told her she was wasting her time. The woman didn't get up.

''I've brought a casserole from Mrs. Brown,'' Molly said, and took the liberty of sliding it into the refrigerator while giving the woman her aunt's baking directions. She noticed a loaf of bread, a chocolate cake, and a jar of home-canned soup stock on the kitchen counter and realized that Ivalee wasn't the only neighbor to think of Judson Horne's nutritional needs.

''I wonder...is Mr. Duncan still around?'' Molly backed toward the hallway. ''I didn't see his car.''

The woman waved with her fork. ''Went to the hospital this morning; ought to be back pretty soon.'' She cocked her head as if listening. "His room's just over the dining room, so I'm sure I would've heard him."

Molly nodded and thanked her. "My aunt lost a charm bracelet while we were caroling the other night," she lied. "We think the catch must have broken. Do you mind if I look around for it? It means a lot to her."

"Seems like I would've seen it, but no, go ahead."

"It could be anywhere," Molly said. "Maybe it slipped down under a cushion."

"Sure!" The housekeeper lit a cigarette and fanned out the match. "Hope you find it."

Molly tossed her coat over the banister and made a cursory search of the main floor, making a point to disturb a cushion here and there, then clomped heavily on the first few steps to the downstairs recreation room. After waiting a few minutes, she crept up the carpeted stairs to the room where Tyrus stayed. The door was closed, and after receiving no response to her inquiring little taps, Molly turned the knob and peeked inside to find a pleasant, airy corner room facing the front of the house. A brass bed, covered in a plum-colored comforter, stood in the far corner; white organdy curtains hung against fern-patterned wallpaper.

The drawer in the bedside table squeaked. There was nothing inside but a box of tissues. Molly eased it shut. The chest at the foot of the bed contained only blankets, and there was no place to hide anything on the corner bookcase by the fireplace. Molly checked under the pillows. A frilly throw cushion cross-stitched in a dainty floral design said: *Hearts that love are always in bloom.* Zebina. Poor Zebina.

The top drawer of the tall cherry bureau held an assortment of shirts and sweaters, most of them red. Tyrus's. The next revealed a jumbled pile of underwear. Molly hesitated only a second. It was disconcerting to search through something so personal, but it had to be done. The envelope wasn't there.

She had started across the room to the desk between the windows when she heard a footstep in the hall. Molly looked frantically about. The small cater-cornered closet hardly seemed large enough to hide her, and the bathroom was too far away. With two quick steps she reached the bed and rolled beneath, hoping the starched white dust ruffle would be opaque enough to conceal her.

Molly lay on her stomach with her head toward the head of the bed. Beneath the thick ruffles of organdy she saw the Chippendale feet of the small beside table and about two inches of green carpeted floor. Nothing else. She rested her face on her hands and listened as someone knocked on the door and entered, hesitating just inside the doorway. A floorboard groaned; a dresser drawer bumped and slammed, and someone switched on a lamp. Molly squinted to see the trespassing feet, but her range was severely limited. The closet door squealed open. Had she made this much noise?

The carpeting beneath the bed was dusty. Mrs. Larsen, or whoever was responsible for cleaning, had not vacuumed it lately. Molly's nose tickled and she pressed a finger under it to keep from sneezing. Was this person looking for the envelope, too? And how did they know who had it? She waited through another few minutes of secret little shuffling sounds. This was to be a thorough search, but not too thorough, she hoped.

A strand of her hair had become snagged in a bed spring over her head. Molly suffered in silence, afraid to budge. She heard a car move down the drive that circled the back of the house. The other snooper heard it, too.

A light snapped off; a door closed. She was alone.

One hair at a time, Molly disentangled the captured lock. She had a crick in her neck and a cramp in her foot. Leaving what felt like a good part of her scalp hanging from the spring, Molly elbowed her way from under the bed. Enough of this sneakiness! The envelope belonged to her; she would demand that he return it—if only she could get out of this blasted room!

Damn! Footsteps again. The space under the bed was becoming like a second home to her. This time she was more careful with her hair. Again the closet door opened—popular place, that closet. And since the person would undoubtedly have his back toward her, Molly risked a peek. Brown loafers in need of a shine. Red socks. Who else? Well, she would just have to wait him out.

The red socks walked over to the bed. The brown shoes came off, and the springs sagged within a half-inch of her face as Tyrus Duncan sat on the edge of the bed. A shoe sailed across the room and landed with a plop.

"Get outa here, cat!" Tyrus said. "Scat!"

The cat gave a frightened cry and darted under the bed. Molly looked up to see two bright green eyes staring into hers.

"Here kitty! Come on, kitty. You don't want to stay under there!" Tyrus stood and began coaxing the cat in a silly sweet voice. If she didn't act fast, he would bend over and look under the bed. Molly scooped the calico and thrust her out. The ungrateful animal scratched her.

"That's a good kitty. Come on now, I'll take you downstairs where you belong." The cat protested loudly as Tyrus picked it up. Molly heard him fumbling for his shoes. She rolled out from under the bed as soon as the door closed.

"You don't want to be in there anyway," Tyrus said from the other side of the door. "It's far too crowded under that bed." And then the key turned in the lock.

Molly's hand closed around the knob at the foot of the bed. It was smooth and cold—heavy enough to do some damage if she could unscrew it from the post. He had known she was there all along, and now he had locked her in! The knob refused to turn. Molly ran to the bathroom. She knew it adjoined the bedroom, and there was a chance the connecting door might be unlocked. But the heavy door was latched from the other side. It was a long drop to the ground even if the windows hadn't been painted shut. She was a prisoner.

Who was this man who had gained her confidence by pretending to be Ethan's friend—and hers? How long did he plan to keep her here? Something cold and hard seemed to be wedged in her chest. Three people had become ill at the caroling party, and now workers had exhumed a skeleton that might have been the beginning of it all. Did the key to it lie in Ethan's little treasure box?

Molly tiptoed to the bedroom door. She could hear him on the other side. Breathing. Well, she would have to take her chances. Somebody was bound to hear—the housekeeper, one of Jud Hornes' numerous relatives, somebody. "Open this door!" Molly screamed, shaking the knob with both hands. She hauled off and kicked the white painted wood as hard as she could. It left an ugly brown scuff mark. "Let me out of here!" Molly threatened. "Or I'll yell the whole place down!"

"My gosh, keep it quiet, will you? Jud's trying to sleep!" Tyrus scrambled to unlock the door. He stood in the hallway looking contrite and shaken and placed Ethan's envelope in her hands. "I assume you were looking for this."

"You assume right," Molly said, moving away from him. She looked inside the envelope. Everything was there.

"Look, I'm sorry. I didn't mean to scare you in there," he said. "I meant it as a joke."

"Well, I'm not laughing," Molly told him, "and I'm not fond of being locked in."

"And I'm not fond of having someone hiding in my room." Tyrus paused at the head of the stairs and spoke in a loud whisper. "If you wanted the envelope, all you had to do was ask."

Molly studied the scratch on her hand. "How did you know I was there?"

"There's a mirror on the back of the closet door." Tyrus smiled broadly. "I saw your skirt sticking out. What a surprise that was!" He touched her arm. "Why were you there, Molly?"

Molly hurried down the stairs and snatched up her coat from the banister. If Tyrus had known she was under the bed, then the first snooper had probably seen her, too. Molly's hands shook. The house was silent. The housekeeper had probably gone to her room to sleep off her midday meal, and if Judson Horne had returned, she had neither seen nor heard him. She didn't have the courage just then to face Tyrus Duncan—or whoever he was—alone.

But the man was not easily avoided. "You didn't answer my question," he said again from behind her. "Don't play games with me, Molly Stonehouse. Exactly what were you doing in my room?"

EIGHTEEN

MOLLY WHIRLED ABOUT. "You're a great one to be talk
ing about games, *Augusta Duncan*, unless you've had
sex-change operation!"

Tyrus turned suddenly pale. "Oh, I see," he said
grasping her arm. "Come on, we can't talk here." With
long strides, he propelled her through the kitchen toward
the back door.

"Hey, wait a minute!" Molly dug in her heels. "I'm no
going anywhere with you. I don't even know who you
are!" She looked around. Mrs. Larsen had gone and
huge wedge had been cut from the cake.

"Shh! Moby Dick might hear you," Ty whispered.

"Who?"

"You know—that great white whale of a woman with
the funny accent. I don't know that I trust her." He pushed
her, not ungently, into a kitchen chair.

"Well, I know I don't trust you. Just who are you, any
way?" Molly eyed the cake. She could smell the icing, dark
and rich. If this strange man was going to do away with he
anyway, what would it matter if she enjoyed one fina
pleasure?

Silently Ty took out his billfold and slapped a line of
plastic cards on the table before her: driver's license, credit
cards—even a Red Cross blood donor's record—all in the
name of Tyrus McClain Duncan. "Augusta is my sister,"
he said.

Molly smiled in spite of herself. "Tyrus and Augusta?
Your mother must have loved Latin!"

"My grandmother. She taught it for thirty-five years," he admitted. "And that's not all; we had a basset hound named Bacchus." Tyrus laughed. "He was a bit fond of the grape."

Molly frowned. "But why did you pretend—"

"That's what I want to explain—but not here." He looked at his watch. "Is there somewhere we can talk? How about that place we went before? The Greasy Spoon?"

She laughed. "The Cherokee Grill? Their coffee's not bad. Okay, I'll meet you there."

As she followed him out, Molly pinched off the tiniest crumb of frosting. It was a good as it looked.

She was still thinking about it when she met Ty at the restaurant a few minutes later.

"Do you want anything to eat?" he asked as they were seated.

Molly thought about the chocolate cake. "Just coffee," she said.

When the coffee came, Tyrus pushed his cup aside and folded his hands in front of him. "Augusta got a note from Neil Fry sometime last spring," he began. "It was a warning about something going on in Harmony, but she didn't realize it at the time. As you know, Neil was a great one for joking, and Gus stuck the letter away somewhere and forgot about it." Ty glanced up at her, his gray eyes thoughtful. "A few days later, he left a message on her answering machine, asking her to get in touch. She tried to call him several times, but no one was there. She finally gave up."

Molly nodded. "So she didn't know about Neil's death?"

"Or Ethan's. Not until she ran across that note from Neil while sending out her Christmas cards and decided to include him on her list. A week or so later she received a

letter from Neil's father explaining what had happened,"
Tyrus said. "It nearly frightened her out of her wits!
That's when she turned to me. Gus has two small children, plus a full-time job; since I have several weeks free
at Christmas, I agreed to come here and see for myself exactly what's going on." He leaned forward. "That's why
I don't want anyone learning who I am. Obviously whoever killed Ethan and Neil doesn't know how to find Augusta. Maybe he doesn't even know she existed—and I
want to keep it that way."

Molly felt a funny little shiver run through her. She
wanted to smile for no apparent reason. So it was Augusta that Ty had been whispering to over the phone yesterday! He was only protecting his sister.

The waitress hovered with the coffee pot, and Ty shook
his head. "But aren't you afraid someone here will remember you?" Molly asked as the woman moved away.

"I don't think so, but it's a chance I'll have to take. It
was a long time ago, and we didn't stay here long. Besides, that was the year I missed so much school with ton-
sillitis," he explained. "Finally, during Christmas vacation
that year my mother insisted the doctor take my tonsils
out. That's why I didn't get to know Ethan and Neil. I was
laid up at home eating Popsicles and milk toast!"

Molly smiled. "While Gus ran around having all the
fun."

"Yeah, and she told me all about it, too. I only wish
she'd told me more." Tyrus sighed. "She remembered the
airline tickets and some kind of message; she even remembered the arrowhead, but she forgot how the note was
signed."

"When we find our 'Christmas Mouse,' I think we'll
have our murderer," Molly said. "This morning Reuben

Anthony told me Rowena had been using him to cover for someone else.''

"So Barlow Jones wasn't the only man she was seeing?'' Tyrus studied the cooling coffee and decided against it. His fingers drummed on the red Formica table. "That skeleton they found . . . do you think it's Rowena's?''

"Yes, I do. I think somebody—maybe Barlow Jones— killed Rowena, buried her in that field behind her house, and went off with her money.'' She lowered her voice. "And whoever did it is here in Harmony. They know we have that envelope, Ty. I wasn't the only one poking about in your room today.''

He almost knocked over his cup. "What do you mean?''

"Someone came in before you did. You must have had the envelope with you because whoever it was made a pretty thorough search.''

"Not thorough enough!'' Ty's face flushed. "It was hanging in the closet in that jacket I wore yesterday. Do you have any idea who it was?''

Molly shook her head. "Couldn't see a thing. Could have been any of Jud's relatives, Undine Larsen, or even one of the neighbors. They've been parading in and out with food, and the house is unlocked.'' She shrugged. "It might have been Jud himself. You said he was at home resting.''

"He left the hospital when I did,'' Tyrus said. "He wasn't feeling well and said he was going home for a short nap.''

"Did he know you were coming straight back to his house?'' Molly asked.

"Well, no; I told him I'd probably stop by your aunts', which I did. They told me you'd gone to the Hornes'.''

"So it could have been Jud if he wasn't expecting you back,'' Molly said. "Funny, I didn't see his car.''

"Sometimes he parks it on the far end of the house and comes in another way," Ty said. "Their room's on that side, and they have their own entrance. Whoever it was, we're going to have to find a better place to keep the envelope. First they broke into the aunts', and now this. Somebody wants that in the worst way!"

Molly smiled. "Don't worry. I know the perfect hiding place for it—at least for a while." She looked out the window at the darkening street. "Ohmigosh! The pageant! What time is it?"

He looked at his watch. "Almost five. You aren't late, are you?"

"Not yet, but I'll have to hurry." Molly glanced at Ty's forlorn face and added, "Why don't you come with us? I know the aunts would like to have you."

"Are you sure it's okay? I really dread going back to Jud's. Poor man—when he's there, he's worried sick; and when he's not, there's nobody around but the housekeeper, and I can hardly understand a word she says."

It seemed unfair to Molly that Jud should have to come home to his beautiful, empty house in the season he seemed to love so much. Now, like a Christmas display in a magazine, it was void of human joy.

"It's a shame Jud won't be able to see the pageant," Iris said later as they drove to the church. "He always enjoys watching it after all the hard work."

Her sister sat beside her in the back seat, her lap piled with costumes that had needed last-minute alterations. Molly thought she looked tired. "Has anyone heard how Zebina is lately?" Ivalee asked.

"I called the house just a while ago," Ty told them. "The housekeeper said there's been no change."

The two aunts sighed simultaneously. "Poor Zebina!" they said.

MOLLY HAD LITTLE DOUBT that "poor" Zebina would have enjoyed the nativity play, and that Jud would have been justly proud of the production had they been there. From the moment the church grew dark and the organ prelude began until the star shone over the manger at the end, she was completely caught up in the experience. For a short time she forgot about the frightening things happening around her, her difficulties with Joy, and her mixed feelings for Tyrus Duncan. When the pageant was over, she stood in the close little room behind the choir loft as the congregation filed quietly out while Myrtis played "Silent Night." It seemed as if she had lived in Harmony forever.

Asa, already shedding his shepherd's robe, stuck his head in the doorway. His face was red and damp with perspiration, and his headgear sat crookedly askew. "Corrine and I are driving over to Cartersville for a movie," he said. "Would you and Ty like to come with us? If we hurry, we can catch the last show."

"I'll ask," Molly said, thinking how nice it would be to get away and lose herself in a fantasy world even for a while. Tyrus, too, seemed eager for a change of pace and even offered to drive, but they ended up using Molly's roomier car. It was not until they were on their way and Ty made some casual remark about her appearance that Molly realized that this could be considered a date.

"That color looks nice on you," he had said, noting her forest green sweater with obvious approval.

Molly thanked him, smiled stiffly at his dark profile, and wished she'd stayed at home. What was she supposed to say? How did one act on dates? She hadn't gone out socially with another man since she and Ethan had started seeing one another on a regular basis over fifteen years ago. She had forgotten the rules.

But Molly dismissed her anxieties during the movie, a comedy. How good it was to laugh, to hear other people laugh! And Ty bought her a chocolate bar without even asking. How did he know? She settled down in her seat. Maybe this wasn't going to be so bad after all.

On the return trip Molly turned the driving over to Ty so she could enjoy the Christmas lights, but the ride and the warmth of the car lulled her into drowsiness. She was searching for some lively music on the radio when Corrine noticed they were being followed. "That car seems to be keeping unusually close," she observed as headlights crept upon them once again. "They've been behind us since we left Cartersville. Why don't they go on and pass?"

"I don't know, but I'll certainly give them the opportunity," Ty said, swinging into the parking lot of an all-night truck stop. He pulled up next to the entrance and turned off the engine.

"Hey, what're you doing? I don't want to stop here!" Asa looked about him and frowned.

"Neither do I, but I want to give our friend a chance to pass," Ty said, watching over his shoulder as the dusty gray Pontiac dipped over the hill and out of sight. "Now we'll see if he means business."

Molly braced herself against the seat as he zoomed behind the building, threaded the car through a narrow alley, bumped across a side street, and came to rest between a large dumpster and a grocery store.

"Nice view," Asa quipped. "Come here often?"

Tyrus stared straight ahead at the main road. "Just wait," he said, "and watch." In less than a minute the gray car reappeared, coming slowly from the other direction.

"Look, it's turning in at the truck stop!" Corrine sat forward with her forehead pressed against the window. "He *was* following us! Why?"

Nobody answered because nobody knew. Molly reached out and found Ty's hand waiting for hers. Whatever this person was up to, it wasn't anything good.

"See if you can see the license plate," Asa whispered. But it was dark, and they were too far away.

When the driver of the car realized he had been tricked, he circled the truck stop and emerged through the alley, following Ty's route.

Corrine locked her door and buried her face in Asa's shoulder. "I'm scared. What if he sees us?" Her voice was somewhere between a squeal and a whisper.

Molly, who was also scared, giggled. "You don't have to whisper," she said. "They can't hear you." Still, no one spoke as they watched the red taillights out of sight on the road back to Harmony.

As soon as the gray car disappeared, Ty pulled out of his hiding place and eased up the side street in the other direction. "We'll go a back way," he said, turning onto a parallel road, "just in case." He gave Molly's hand a reassuring squeeze. "Don't worry. I'm almost sure I know where this comes out."

They didn't see the gray car again, but Corrine's eyes were red and her entire upper body was wrapped in the masculine security of Asa's arms when they drew up in front of her house. "I'm so scared, I'll never go to sleep," she said in a rose-petal voice inches from the helpless man's face. He offered to come in, of course. Only for a few minutes.

Molly giggled again as they drove away. "Well, I won't wait up for him," she said. The house with the reindeer on the roof and the blaring speakers (silent now) brought on another fit of laughter. She wiped her eyes with the back of her wrist. What was wrong with her?

"You're just nervous," Ty said as they pulled into the Stonehouse driveway. "And you've a good right to be."

"I'm not nervous," Molly said. "I'm just plain scared." She reached for the door handle. "It's late. I'll see myself in."

But Tyrus Duncan reached across and removed her hand from the door. Gripping it firmly, he drew her toward him. "Don't be in such a hurry," he said.

As his arms closed around her, Molly discovered there are some things you don't forget.

NINETEEN

"DID YOU GET A LOOK at whoever was following us tonight?" Molly asked against Ty's shoulder. The aunts had forgotten to turn on the porch light and only the Christmas-tree bulbs were reflected in the window.

He held her close against him and kissed the hollow just above her ear. "They were too far away, and I didn't recognize the car, either. I haven't seen it around here." Ty found her hands and sandwiched them in his. "Don't go anywhere alone, Molly. Promise me. I have a feeling all hell's about to break loose. We're coming down to the line now."

Molly leaned against the dusty porch column and closed her eyes. She felt as if she were wrapped in a cocoon of warmth with only her face exposed. "I'd better go in," she said finally. "There's a light on back in the kitchen, and someone's moving about downstairs. They'll wonder what we're doing out here."

Tyrus kissed her lightly. "I think they know," he said.

Molly smiled as she closed the door behind her. So what if Iris or Ivalee were to see us? she thought. We're all mature adults.

But it was Joy who stood on the bottom step in her long flannel gown. Like a life-size figurine, she leaned against the newel post with her arms crossed over her small breasts and her face turned away from the light. There was a fragile quality about her, a sad vulnerability. Molly thought of herself at thirteen.

Molly inhaled deeply and sighed. The whole house smelled of cedar, and a faint red glow came from the fireplace in the living room. "I could use some hot chocolate," she said. "How about you?"

Joy didn't look up. "I saw you," she said. "I saw you kissing that man."

Molly shrugged out of her coat and draped it over the deacon's bench by the door. There was no use denying it. "I guess I've been found out," she said.

"You must have been relieved to get rid of Dad," Joy said.

Molly's brain felt numb. She sat on the straight-backed bench and put her face in her hands while her daughter stood there bristling, her bare toes curled over the stair step.

"Where in the world did you get such an idea?" Molly asked wearily. She looked up at Joy whose narrow little chin was thrust forward and trembling. She had bathed this child, changed her diapers, kissed away her hurts. But she couldn't kiss this one away. "If you wanted to hurt me, you have."

Molly walked into the living room and unplugged the tree lights. She sensed, rather than heard, Joy padding along behind her. The tree stand was empty and she went to the kitchen for water, glad for something to do.

Joy slumped on the arm of the sofa. "Dad hasn't been dead a year yet. You sure didn't waste any time!"

Silently Molly poured water into the stand, testing the level with her finger.

"You certainly seemed to be enjoying it," Joy continued.

Molly sank to her knees by the tree. "Sometimes, Joy, I would dearly love to stuff a very dirty sock in your pink little mouth! Now get upstairs this minute before you catch cold. You don't have a thing on your feet!''

Joy jumped up and stumbled across the room toward the door, then stopped midway as a great sob tore from her. Molly reached her in one step.

Later, spent from crying, they sat together on the sofa and watched the last dull embers flicker and die. Molly tucked an afghan over Joy's bare feet. ''Your dad and I were having some problems,'' she admitted, ''but I still cared about him. I never imagined how difficult life would be without him.''

''I know.'' Joy squeezed her hand. ''Mom, I miss him so much.''

''Of course you do. I miss him, too. That's why I need you now—especially now.''

Joy put her head on her mother's shoulder and yawned. ''Is it too late for that hot chocolate?''

At this point Molly wanted nothing but sleep, but she rummaged up some instant cocoa mix and heated water in the kettle. They were sipping it when Tyrus called to tell them that Zebina Horne had died.

''Oh, no!'' Molly gripped the receiver tightly and asked the inevitable question, ''What can we do?'' as if there were a possibility of anyone bringing Zebina back from the dead. The aunts and Emma Beth hovered at the top of the stairs.

''Not much tonight,'' Ty said. ''I'm calling from the hospital. Jud's in there with her now. He's been here all night; poor guy's pretty broken up.''

''When...?'' Molly picked up a pine cone from a wicker basket on the hall table.

''About an hour ago.'' Ty sounded tired. ''I'm taking him home in a few minutes. The doctor has given him something to help him sleep." He yawned. "I'll call you in the morning."

"Myrt! Somebody should call Myrt!" Iris started down the stairs when Molly told them the news.

But Ivalee held her back. "Wait. What good will it do? Let her sleep. Tomorrow's soon enough."

Not one of them, Molly thought as she drifted off to sleep, had thought to ask what finally killed Zebina Horne.

"IT WAS DEFINITELY her heart," Ty said the next morning, "but the doctors seem to think it was brought on by an acute gastric attack. Maybe something she ate."

They waded through the friends and relatives who had dropped by the Hornes' to pay their respects. With all the food being left, Molly doubted if Undine Larsen would have to cook for a week. But with Zebina gone, she wondered if Judson Horne would have further use for the woman. How much of their lives were spent preparing food and eating it, she thought. Molly remembered Myrt's pale face. "*I've never been so sick I wanted to die,*" she had said. And Jud claimed to have eaten something that disagreed with him. Zebina had not been strong enough to withstand the assault. But what on earth had they eaten? And where? She thought back to the night of the caroling party. They had been offered food at every place they stopped. Why did only three people get sick?

"And that's not all," Ty whispered, leading her aside. "Wait till I show you what else I found."

"Where in the world are we going?" Molly asked as Tyrus herded her down the basement stairs. "You do have ultcrior motives, don't you?" she added in a whisper.

Tyrus laughed. "Is there any other kind?" He pulled her past the recreation room to a broom closet next to the laundry room. "See?" He jerked open the door and pointed.

"See what?"

"Why, the boots! They're right—" Tyrus shoved aside a dust mop and groaned. "They *were* right here and covered in mud—men's boots with that peculiar pinwheel design on the sole." He banged the door shut. "I was looking for a mop this morning. The florist's delivery boy tracked mud into the kitchen, and Moby Dick was nowhere to be seen. I should've taken the damned things when I found them!"

"Never mind; at least we know that whoever wore them has access to this house," Molly said.

"Oh, sure! Half the town!" Tyrus frowned.

"I wonder how long they were in there," she said.

"Probably since the night of the caroling party, when you heard them digging out by the gazebo," Ty said, jamming his hands into his pockets. "Well, we can be sure of one thing at least," he added. "It wasn't poor Zebina!"

TWENTY

"WE HAVE TO find out what happened to Barlow Jones,"
Molly said as she sat with Ty on the Hornes' kitchen steps.
The air was cold with a hint of dampness, but she was glad
to be away from the hot, stuffy house, the close smell of
funeral flowers. "Surely someone knows where he came
from!"

"What about Myrtis?" Ty suggested.

"She doesn't know. They tried to trace them after
Rowena disappeared." Molly shrugged. "She isn't even
sure Jones was his real name."

"There must be something—somebody!" Ty slammed
the wooden step. "I'd like to get that whole bunch together: Myrtis, Reuben Anthony, Iris—even Jud. I think
somebody's hiding something. Have they identified that
skeleton yet?"

"I haven't heard. Guess they haven't had time. I heard
it had long, dark hair—like Rowena's."

Ty shook his head. "Poor Myrtis!"

"Poor Myrtis, nothing! Poor Rowena!" Molly tried not
to laugh. Why was she developing this macabre sense of
humor? "Myrt stopped by here this morning with a huge
supply of paper plates; wouldn't come in," she said. "She
asked if I would do her a favor, so I'm going over there in
a few minutes. Come along if you like. Maybe you can get
her to remember something."

"What kind of favor?"

"She signed up at the church for the 'angel tree' to buy
Christmas gifts for a needy child and hasn't been able to

go shopping,'' Molly explained. "I told her I'd do it for her.'' She glanced in the kitchen window to see Undine Larsen biting into the last of Ivalee's good ham biscuits. Jud's sister Jodean was tossing dirty paper plates into a trash bag. "Let's go!" Molly said, starting for her car. She couldn't bear the thought of going back inside that house.

MYRTIS MET THEM at the door in her beige sweater and jeans with Colonel Sanders sticking close to her heels. "I can't thank you enough for doing this," she said. "Tomorrow is the deadline for these presents, and I haven't had time to buy one thing." She pulled a card from beneath the clock on the mantel. "My angel's name is Marcie and she's five. Here's a list of her sizes and colors." She smiled. "And she loves trucks."

"Trucks?" Ty lifted an eyebrow.

Molly looked at the list and laughed. "I'll get her a dump truck—a red one."

"I don't know where the time goes!" Myrt shouted from the kitchen. She snatched three mugs from a shelf with one hand. "My head looks like a stump full of spiders, and Willene said she'd work me in for a permanent at four." She clanked the mugs on the table. "You have time for a cup of tea, don't you? I have coffee if you'd rather have it, but I don't seem to have the stomach for it since I got so sick."

"Tea's fine," Molly said with a glance at Ty. She slid into a chair by the window. Colonel Sanders padded in and sat on her feet. It was getting darker outside. The sun seemed to have disappeared. "What did your doctor say about it? Was it a virus?" she asked Myrt.

Myrtis stood by the stove waiting for the kettle to boil. "He seems to think it was something I ate. I told him Jud was sick, too, and of course poor Zebina . . . but that must have been her heart.''

"Well, they're not sure about that," Ty said. "Do you have any idea what could have made you sick? It seems all we did was eat!''

Myrt poured boiling water into a bright red pot. "It was the fruitcake. I'm sure of it." She shuddered. "I'll never like fruitcake again!''

Molly watched as Myrt filled her cup with steaming amber liquid. "But which fruitcake? And where? Everybody served it.''

"And I ate it all!" Myrt joined them at the table and stirred sugar into her cup. "I even brought home a few samples—for later, you know. I wrapped what I couldn't eat in a paper napkin and tucked it into my pocketbook.'' She made a face. "Forgot all about it until the doc said he sure wished I'd saved some so he could have it analyzed.'' Myrt laughed. "I just dangled my purse in front of him and said, 'Here, help yourself. I can't even stand to smell it!' ''

Tyrus leaned forward. "So he took the cake for testing? Have you heard anything?''

"Not yet. But that was late Saturday, and I imagine the labs were closed.'' Myrt tasted the tea and added more sugar. "I can't believe Zebina's gone! Do they really think it could have been something other than her heart?'' She banged her spoon against the mug. "And Jud? How's he taking it? He doted on her so.'' Myrtis took a long swallow and sighed. "I'd rather fight a bear than go by there tonight, but I know I have to do it. Lord, this has been a most peculiar Christmas!''

"That's not all that's peculiar," Molly muttered partially to herself. "Myrt, is there anyone who might know where Barlow Jones was from?''

Myrtis picked up grains of sugar from the table with her finger and wiped it on her jeans. "He wasn't exactly a member of the crowd, although he did come to a few of our parties." She was silent for a moment. "I believe Reuben knew him a little better than most. They went to the same college, I think."

Molly turned to find Tyrus looking at her. Why hadn't the minister mentioned that to them before? Ty had pushed back his chair, obviously ready to move on, and Molly knew exactly where they were going.

"By the way," she said to Myrtis, stepping over the Colonel on her way out, "Do you remember anyone in your group having the nickname 'Mouse'?"

Myrt dug into her large canvas handbag for an envelope, which she handed to Molly. "Mouse? Hmm, I don't think so; could be, though. You know how kids label one another: names change from one week to the next."

Molly peeked into the envelope. It contained a one-hundred-dollar bill.

"If you'll buy the gifts at Gideon's, your money will go further," Myrt told her. "Jud gives us a twenty percent discount on all our 'angel' presents."

Molly tucked the bill, along with the card bearing the child's particulars, into her pocketbook. She would take the two girls to help her shop. It would be good for them to get their minds off their own problems, and she was glad for the chance to do something for Myrtis. Somehow she had the feeling that Myrt was afraid to go out alone.

"Hey, nice-looking boots! I wouldn't mind having some like these," Ty said, feigning interest in a sturdy tan pair behind the woodbox on Myrt's porch. "They look warm." He picked one up and examined the sole. Molly wasn't surprised to see it had a pinwheel design.

"Oh, they are!" Myrt laughed. "I wore them caroling the other night. They aren't too dainty, but they keep your feet nice and dry."

Ty frowned. "I think I've seen that style before."

"I don't doubt it," Myrtis said. "Just about everybody in Harmony has a pair. Jud had 'em on sale for half price last spring."

"Well, so much for the mysterious footprint, Dick Tracy!" Molly said as they turned onto Shake Rag Road toward town.

But Tyrus wasn't listening. "Things are getting curiouser and curiouser," he said, frowning at the road ahead. "Old Reuben knew that guy all along!" He whistled. "Fancy that!"

The minister's car was parked in front of the church office. "We'll have to be careful how we approach this," Molly warned him as they hurried up the walk. "We don't want to sound accusing, get his back up."

But the large, red-bearded minister looked up with a smile when they entered and shut off the tape recorder he had been using to dictate his sermon. He stood to greet them. "Don't tell me; let me guess. You have another question about Rowena Sterling." His eyes grew solemn. "Do you still believe that skeleton is hers?"

Molly sat in a leather-covered wing chair that was large enough for two. Tyrus settled for a window seat. "I think it could be," she told him. "After all, no one ever heard from her again."

"Or from the man she was supposed to have run away with," Tyrus added. "Was that his real name, Barlow Jones?"

Reuben rubbed at his beard. "I doubt it, but it's the only one I ever heard him use."

"Did you know him before he came here?" Molly pretended innocence.

Reuben nodded slowly. "Only slightly. We went to the same college for a while—a small school in Tennessee. He wrote a kind of rambling column for the school paper for a few months before he dropped out. I was news editor that year; and once in a while he'd fill in with our band. That's how I came to know him."

"And that's the name he wrote under, Barlow Jones?" Molly had to sit on the edge of her seat to make her feet touch the floor. "Surely he was registered there under his legal name. We could call the college!" And then she remembered that the college administration offices would be closed for the holidays, as hers were.

Tyrus stood abruptly, knocking over a stack of books on the floor. "The college annual! Maybe he's in there—if you still have one."

Reuben Anthony tramped across the room and poked about in a bookcase. "As a matter of fact," he said, pulling out a bronze padded volume, "I do." He began flipping through the pages. "But I doubt if Barlow's in here. He wasn't the type to show up for anything scheduled, such as classes or annual pictures."

Molly looked over his shoulder. "Are you sure this is the right year?"

"Positive." Reuben thumped the front of the book. "*The Plowman*, 1964; that was my junior year and the last one I worked on the newspaper. Barlow would've been a freshman, maybe a sophomore."

But Barlow Jones was not pictured with his classmates, nor was his name listed in the index in the back.

"Well...nice try!" Ty strolled to the window, but Reuben sat on the corner of his desk and thumbed through the glossy pages. "Wait a minute!" He held up a hand.

"Here's something." The snapshot showed a random group of student musicians performing at a campus gathering. Molly had no trouble recognizing Reuben and his guitar. Barlow Jones, he pointed out, was the thin, stringy-haired youth standing next to him. The caption identified them as The Metamorphics and listed their names and home towns. "Aha!" Reuben pounded the page with a beefy fist. "Barlow is from a place called Big Kettle, Wyoming! Or at least that's what this says."

"How in the world did he get down here?" Molly asked.

"Drifted, I guess," Reuben answered.

"Or he could have been running away from something," Ty said.

"A fat lot of good that does us!" Molly sighed, sinking back into the chair. "We still don't know his real name, and we—or I—certainly don't know anyone in Big Kettle, Wyoming!"

Ty grinned. "How big can a place like that be? Probably about the size of Harmony." He looked at Reuben. "If someone described Rowena to you—as she was when you knew her—but didn't use her name, would you know who they were talking about?"

The minister smiled broadly. "It's obvious that you never met Rowena Sterling! She'd be difficult to forget."

"I'm betting this guy would, too—for different reasons, of course." Tyrus examined the picture and frowned. "And if he wrote for one paper, maybe he wrote for another."

Reuben presented the telephone to him with an elegant sweep of his hand. "Be my guest," he said. "Let's just hope Big Kettle has a newspaper."

They did. The editor, a woman by the name of Temperance Brady, said *The Wagon Wheel* had been published weekly for eighty-seven years and she had been working there for thirty-six of them. Tyrus jotted, and as he talked his smile grew broader, his eyes brighter.

"He wrote up the high school news for them when he was a senior, using that same pen name," Ty said, hanging up the phone. "His family hasn't seen him since he left there in the sixties." Tyrus tore his scribbling from the pad. "This editor, Temperance Brady, says his father died a few years ago and his mother remarried and moved away." He gave the paper to Molly. "His name, by the way, is Eli Crump."

Molly threw her head back against the big chair and laughed. "No wonder he changed it!" she said. "I wonder if Rowena knew," she muttered as she drove Tyrus back to the Hornes'.

Ty sat low in his seat silent, thinking. "Knew what?" he asked without looking up.

"Knew that man's name was really Crump!" Molly giggled. "Can you imagine the fair Rowena running off with somebody with a name like that?" She let Tyrus off by the Hornes' back steps. The parking lot was filled with cars, and the kitchen with women. "I see Circle Number Four is here in full force," she said. "Aunt Ivalee told me they were feeding the family tonight." She smiled. It was obvious that he was reluctant to go inside. "You can eat with us if you like. The aunts might even take pity and let you sleep on the sofa."

Tyrus touched her chin as he swung out of the car. "That wasn't exactly what I had in mind," he whispered, leaning in the window. "You can't imagine how I dread eating, sleeping in this house, but I hate to run out on Jud since he asked me specifically to stay. I never knew Zebina well, and his family's so emotional! I guess he needs a good, steady shoulder." Briefly he reached inside and covered her hand with his. "Call me when you're ready to go shopping. I'm sure Jud can get along without me for an hour or so."

But Molly shook her head. "This time it's just the girls and me. We need this, Ty."

He frowned. "I don't think it's a good idea; at least take along one of the aunts or Asa." He gripped her fingers. "Promise?"

"I'll do my best," Molly said, waving as she pulled away.

And she did try. But Asa was out of town for the night; and it was a good thing, Molly thought, since he had come creeping home at two-thirty that morning just as they had all gone back to bed after Ty's startling call. And of course everyone was aware of where he'd been, especially Emma Beth.

Ivalee declined her invitation, saying her feet were killing her and there was a special program she wanted to watch on television; and Iris had volunteered to greet visitors that night at Jud's. Zebina's funeral had been scheduled for the next day, but the coroner had delayed releasing her body, so services would be held a day later.

As Molly and the girls passed Judson Horne's on their way to the store, she saw Iris, Myrtis, and Reuben Anthony huddled together on the front walk in animated conversation. Myrt, gesturing boldly, seemed to be trying to convince them of something, while Iris glared at her, arms folded like a shield. The minister planted his large bulk between them almost as if he were acting as referee. Molly wondered if Iris would pursue an interest in Judson, or vice versa, now that Zebina was out of the way. But somehow she didn't think they were discussing "poor" Zebina.

Main Street was crowded with shoppers. Molly circled the small parking lot behind Jud's store until she found an empty space, then hurried to keep up with the girls as they rushed inside. She was looking forward to shopping for Myrt's tree angel, but she couldn't rid herself of the nagging suspicion that the woman had sent her here to get her out of the way.

TWENTY-ONE

JOY AND Emma Beth would have spent Myrt's one hundred dollars ten times over if Molly hadn't kept a tight rein on the money. She allowed them to select a pretty dress for Marcie and used the rest of the bills to buy shoes, playclothes, and most important of all, a bright red dump truck. Molly was pleased when the two girls used some of their own allowances to buy the child a few toys.

The shoppers were beginning to drift away when they left the toy department and Molly looked at her watch. The stores would stay open for another half hour—just enough time for ice cream. Chocolate, of course. Hanging on to her shopping bag, she headed for the exit. "Come on, girls, it's dessert time. My treat!"

But the two cousins had discovered the jewelry counter, and she couldn't pry them away. "Hey, look, Mom!" Joy held up a pair of sparkling earrings about the size of hubcaps. "If you'd let me have my ears pierced, I could wear these! Aren't they adorable?"

"Will you look at that?" Emma Beth pointed to a pendant in the glass case. "That looks exactly like the one Dad bought for Corrine Harris." She caught the clerk's attention. "Could I have the price on that?"

The woman flipped over the price tag. "Three hundred dollars," she said, already moving away. She knew a "no sale" when she saw one.

"My gosh!" Emma Beth gasped. "I can't believe he spent that much money on that woman!" Her face turned red. "I just can't believe it."

Molly admired the delicate necklace. Tiny pearls had been set in gold to resemble a bunch of grapes. It was a beautiful piece of jewelry, one she knew Asa could not easily afford. "I thought you didn't know anything about that," she said. "Did you take that box from his room, Emma Beth?"

"Oh, who cares?" The girl shrugged. "It's not like they're going to get married or something!"

"That's an expensive piece of jewelry," Molly pointed out, urging the girls toward the door. "Your father paid for it, and it was his to do with as he liked. Besides, you don't know he meant it for Corrine."

"Ha! I'm not a baby, and I'm not blind, either!" Emma Beth shifted her packages from one arm to the other. "I know what goes on between them."

Molly stepped aside to avoid a fat woman carrying a table lamp in the shape of a fish. "If you're as grown up as you say, you'll have to accept the fact that your dad needs female company. He may even want to marry again someday."

"Not to that woman, I hope!" Emma Beth almost tripped over her own feet. "And she's not getting that necklace, either. Not ever!"

"You dummy!" Joy stamped her foot. "He bought that necklace for you!"

Emma Beth looked as if some high court had declared a permanent ban on pizza. Her eyes glazed over. "What do you mean? How do you know that?"

Joy walked faster. "Because he told me. He asked me to keep an eye out for it. It was supposed to be your big Christmas present!"

Emma Beth's round face went slack, and she sat down abruptly on a bench beside a display of mechanical elves. They made an interesting study in contrasts, Molly thought: Santa's helpers with expressions of perpetual glee, and Emma Beth's sad, drooping face.

OUTSIDE IN THE parking lot, the gray Pontiac waited. Molly saw it parked in the shadows between a recreational van and a pickup truck only two rows away from where she had left her car. She held out an arm to stop the girls, who trailed behind her. They were screened from view by the shrubbery on either side of the entrance, so there was a chance they hadn't been seen. The parking lot was emptying quickly, and the only people in shouting distance were a crowd of rowdy young men who had obviously had too much to drink. Molly turned and hurried the girls into the mall. She had seen a public telephone somewhere inside.

"What's wrong?" Joy asked. "Why are we going back inside? I'm tired! I want—"

"Hush! And wait right here while I call." Molly pointed to a lighted store window and ran to the phone booth across from it, digging into her purse for a quarter. Joy followed her. "What's the matter? Something's wrong! Why won't you tell me?"

"We may have a problem . . . Just wait!" Molly fumbled through the phone book for Judson Horne's number. She waited, twisting a short lock of hair into a tight knot while it rang three . . . four . . . five times. The voice that finally answered was familiar. Iris.

"I'm having a bit of a problem," Molly explained quickly. "Is Tyrus around?"

"He went to the funeral home with Jud," Iris said. "What's wrong?"

"The car won't start. Could you pick us up at the mall? We're at Gideon's. Oh, and come to the front entrance. We'll wait by the door." *Inside* the door, Molly thought as she replaced the receiver. She watched the two girls laughing over the antics of a kitten in the pet shop window across the mall. She was not going to let them out of her sight.

"THERE WERE A BUNCH of drunks hanging around my car out in the parking lot," Molly said on the way home. "I just didn't feel like going through the hassle—especially with the girls there."

"You did the right thing," Iris said. She sat ramrod straight as she drove. "They have no business being there! The police in this town ought to earn their salary and lock them up!" She glanced at Molly beside her. "I was ready to leave anyway. It's too late for people to be dropping by."

Molly looked out at the dark streets. She was ready to leave, too. She wondered how long the gray Pontiac would wait for her in the parking lot.

EMMA BETH WORE her discomfort like sackcloth. With a studied expression she silently wrapped the gifts, declined both the company and the popcorn Molly offered, and went upstairs to bed. Molly wondered what the girl had done with the pendant, but she didn't have the courage to ask.

After the others turned in, Molly sat curled in the armchair listening to carols on the stereo. Someone was playing "Silent Night" on a guitar, and the effect of the music and the soft tree lights was almost hypnotic in the dim room. From the table beside her, Ethan's young grandparents looked hopefully at the camera on their wedding day, preserved forever in a silver filigreed frame. Molly felt secure there, blending with the past.

Had the person in the gray Pontiac followed her here? Did they know where she was staying? Molly started to look out the window, but she was afraid she would see the car parked in front of the house. Waiting.

She heard a shower running upstairs. Probably Iris, as her sister had gone to bed earlier. Soft strains of "Ave Maria" filled the room. Beautiful! Molly yawned. She had never heard it played with such feeling on a guitar.

A guitar.

She found it where she had seen it earlier, in a far corner of the attic wrapped in a ragged quilt. Molly rubbed off the dust and held the instrument beneath the dim hanging lightbulb. The initials E.C. had been carved into the back of the guitar. *Eli Crump!*

Molly stiffened as she heard footsteps on the attic stairs, then hurried to rewrap the guitar in its tattered covering. She shivered, realizing for the first time that she was cold, regardless of her heavy sweater.

"What in the world are you doing up here at this hour?" Iris stood in the doorway, her dark hair in pink curlers, her face covered in white cream.

"Aunt Ivalee said I might find some things of Ethan's here," Molly said lightly. She turned instinctively to a trunk behind her and pushed up the heavy lid. Giving her husband's aunt a brief glance over her shoulder, she began to shuffle through the contents, sending up puffs of dust. The dry, musty scent was almost overpowering.

"Well, you won't find anything there." Iris waited. Molly knew she was standing there, arms folded, in her green quilted robe. "It's too dark to see up here, and too late besides. You'll wake the others." With a put-upon sigh, she clomped down the stairs.

Molly waited until the other woman had reached the floor below, then quietly followed her. Closing the door of her room firmly behind her, she began to undress in the dark, shivering in the cold room.

The pale light from the yard next door slanted directly across Joy's sleeping face, and Molly tiptoed to the window to pull down the shade. What she saw there made her freeze with her hand in midair, and it wasn't because of the cold.

Standing on the lawn beneath her, green shoes, holly, and all, was Sonny Earl Dinsmore. And he held a gun in his hand.

TWENTY-TWO

"Iris took it away from him," Molly told Ty the next morning. "She marched out there just as calmly as you please and said, 'Give me the gun, Sonny Earl.' And he did."

"Was it loaded?"

"Yes, but the safety was on—thank goodness!" Molly stuffed her gloved hands deeper into her coat pockets as they walked the oak-lined streets of Harmony. Although it was midmorning, the sun had not yet melted the frost in the shade, and there were still slick spots on the sidewalk.

"That was taking a chance," Tyrus said, skirting a puddle. "Sonny Earl seems harmless, but for all he knows, the thing is a toy! Why didn't you call me?"

"Because he doesn't know you. I was dialing Reuben's number when Iris stopped me. 'That's nonsense,' she said. 'We don't need Reuben. Besides, we don't have time to wait!' And she brushed right past me and went outside and dealt with him—bathrobe, house slippers, and all!" Molly looked behind her at the sound of a car, but it was only a pickup truck, and a red one at that. She remembered the presents waiting to be delivered to Myrt's "tree angel" and walked a little faster. Iris had taken the gifts by the church on her way to work, but in all the excitement, Molly had forgotten to tell Myrtis what she had bought with her money.

Tyrus easily kept pace with her, red plaid muffler trailing behind him. "Where do you suppose he found it? I can't imagine his mother leaving one lying around."

"She says it's not hers—never saw it before." Molly looked longingly at the chocolate glazed doughnuts in a bakery window. The thick, sweet smell wafted out to her. She held her breath until they passed. Discipline, that's all it took. Discipline and self-denial. She knew how the Puritans must have felt.

"Sonny Earl showed me where he found it," she told Tyrus. "It was out beside the gazebo. He said Santa brought it to him."

Tyrus took her arm as they crossed the street. An old-fashioned gesture; she liked it. "But when?" he asked.

"Sonny Earl doesn't know the meaning of *when*," Molly said. "But it's my guess he found it the night of the caroling party, the night I frightened someone away." She felt the warmth of Ty's arm tucked in hers as they waited for the light to change. "Sometimes I think he's smarter than he lets on to be. He must have hidden that gun from his mother or she'd have found it before now. Poor woman! We had to wake her in the middle of the night to let him back inside."

"What happened to the gun?" Tyrus asked.

"Aunt Iris said she'd take it by the police station," Molly said. "Now, maybe we can find out who was prowling around back there."

They walked through the small town square past a cannon from the War Between the States and a granite monument to World War I dead. Dry leaves tumbled in an empty fountain. "I saw our friend again last night," Molly said, and told him about the ominous gray car.

"Are you sure?" He gave her a puzzled smile. "There are a lot of gray Pontiacs. What makes you think it was that one?"

Molly didn't smile back. She didn't answer, either. A red-berried pyracantha bush with one-inch thorns clung to the brown stone wall at one end of the park. One good shove would send him sprawling. It would hurt. She walked quickly past, sorely tempted.

Ty hurried to catch up. "Sorry. Stupid question! I think we should report it to the police. Maybe they can find out whose car it is." He didn't try to take her arm again.

"Report what? We don't know the license number, and they haven't actually *done* anything." Molly slowed her pace, but only a little. "Besides, I have something even more interesting to tell. I found Barlow Jones's guitar!"

"What?" Ty sounded as if he didn't believe her. "Where?"

"In our attic—the aunts' attic—and it has his initials in it, his real initials: E.C." Molly shrugged. "Figure that out!"

"I wonder how it got there," Ty said as they started back toward Muscadine Hill. "And if his guitar is in the attic, then where is Barlow Jones?"

"I don't know; maybe it was an old one and Iris bought it from him secondhand." But Molly smiled as she spoke. She couldn't imagine Iris Stonehouse playing the guitar.

Tyrus walked along in silence. "Maybe your Aunt Iva-lee will know," he said as they reached sight of the house.

But Ivalee was waiting when they walked up the front steps. "Eula Dinsmore just called," she said from the doorway. "She wants you to come over so she can thank you properly for last night. Says she has something for you, Molly; Iris, too." Her aunt glanced in the direction of her neighbor's house. "My goodness, it's the first time she's asked one of us inside in fifteen years!"

Molly frowned. She didn't want to go calling on Sonny Earl's mother. "But I didn't do anything," she said.

"Well, you didn't call the police on him, and that's something," Ivalee reminded her. "Poor Eula! She has her hands full with that boy wandering off all the time." She lowered her voice. "There are people here who are frightened of him, you know."

Molly looked at Tyrus. "Would you go with me?"

"Sure," he said, grinning. " 'The Fall of the House of Usher' is one of my favorite stories."

"It does look a little Poe-ish," Molly observed as they passed through the hedge between the two yards. The shrubbery hadn't been pruned in years, and the trim needed paint, and one faded green shutter hung by a hinge from an upstairs window. "I'll bet it has a secret room and a revolving bookcase."

"That's probably how Sonny Earl gets out at night," Ty said without smiling. He looked at his watch. "At least we'll have an excuse to leave early. You can tell her your aunt's expecting you for lunch."

Lunch. Molly swallowed. She wasn't hungry. She twisted the doorbell. It was made of rusty brown metal and sounded like the one she had on her tricycle when she was five. It took a long time for Eula Dinsmore to come to the door. She was a small, white-haired woman with a slight hump, and she walked with the aid of a cane. "Thank you for coming," she said. "I've been waiting for you." Molly looked past her down the dark center hall. Sonny Earl was nowhere in sight.

They followed her past a massive mahogany staircase, through an archway, and into a large living room furnished in the style of the nineteen-forties. The doorway was decorated with a tarnished strand of silvery tinsel that looked as if it had seen better days, and a small pine tree trimmed with delicate antique ornaments stood in the far window. The house smelled of mildew and fried ham.

"This will be Sonny's last Christmas here at home, and I wanted to make it special." Eula Dinsmore spoke in a matter-of-fact way, but she kept her voice low. "I won't always be here to take care of him, and he has a chance to go into a supervised group where he can learn to live with others, perhaps learn a simple trade." She smiled at Molly, her frail hands crossed in her lap. "Sonny's good at some things, you know. He put that tree up for me, and he loves to run the sweeper and dust."

"I can tell," Molly said, noticing the gleaming furniture and polished brass at the grate. "Everything looks nice." A stuffed Coca-Cola Santa stood on the mantel next to a figurine clock, and a red and white stocking hung at one end of the fireplace.

"He wasn't always this way," Sonny Earl's mother said, passing them a framed photograph of a handsome, smiling schoolboy. "He was ten when this was made—the year before he was sick." She looked at her hands.

"He looks mischievous," Molly said. "I'll bet he kept his teachers hopping!"

Eula laughed softly. "He and Jud. Judson Horne. They were a pair. Some of the others didn't like for their children to play with Jud; he was from a tenant family, you see. But I've always been fond of him." She grasped the crook of her cane until her knuckles were white. "Even after the illness, he would come to see Sonny Earl. He was always kind—not like some of the others!"

Molly and Ty helped her bring tea from the kitchen, and they drank it from thin china cups with lemon cookies from a tin. "My niece sends them to me," Eula said. "She's the one who helped to get Sonny into the home." She reached for a shoebox full of well-worn papers on a table by the sofa, and Molly knew that she wanted to share them. "These are all I have of Sonny Earl as a boy," she said, ruffling through the stack. "These and memories." She laid a yellowing photograph on the table in front of them. "This was the class picture, made in the third grade. See, Sonny's making a face."

Molly smiled at the dark-haired boy on the back row with his tongue sticking out, fingers in his ears.

"Is that Jud beside him?" Tyrus asked, pointing to a plump child in overalls with a wide grin on his face.

Eula nodded. "And there's Myrtis Curtis. Her hair never would stay put!" She poked a finger at the child beside her. "And that Rowena! Fast as greased lightning and mean to boot. Look at her. Probably thinking of something nasty to say even then!"

Eula Dinsmore passed the tin of cookies again. "Shouldn't carry on like this, I know, but she said such cruel things to poor Sonny after he was so sick, when she knew he couldn't help being the way he was." She sighed, wadding a yellowing tea napkin into a ball. "Iris now, she's blunt like her mama—always was; and sometimes Sonny's a lot to put up with, but she's never been deliberately unkind." She unrolled several parchmentlike library certificates with the traditional gold star stickers. "These were for reading books in the summer program." Her eyes clouded over and she shook her head. "When I think of how that boy loved to read—what he could've been..."

"What's this?" Ty was reading a faded mimeographed bulletin from what appeared to be a school play. It was creased in the middle and brown around the edges.

"That's the program from a little Christmas play the children did in grammar school," Eula said proudly. Her hands trembled as she took it from him. "They took several children from each class; Sonny Earl was in the second grade then. He played a cow. I made his costume from brown pajamas!"

Molly laughed. "I'd like to have seen that. Was Iris in it, too?"

Mrs. Dinsmore nodded. "Yes, I believe she was . . . yes; she played a lamb. The little play was called *The Animals Celebrate Christmas*." She laughed. "I never shall forget Judson. He dressed as a tiny Christmas mouse and sang the cutest little song. Sonny used to tease him about it!"

"WELL, THAT ANSWERS that question," Molly said as she and Tyrus cut across the yard, stopping to wave to Eula Dinsmore in the window. Molly carried a hand-embroidered guest towel, slightly yellowed, wrapped in tissue paper, and a jar of pear preserves (with no date) for Iris.

"I still can't believe it," Tyrus said. "Judson Horne and Rowena! The two of them just don't go together."

"Obviously not. He's here and she isn't."

"Maybe she is. You said yourself you thought that was Rowena Sterling's skeleton they found behind Myrt's place."

"But Judson Horne!" Molly shook her head. "I don't think so, Tyrus."

He turned and faced her. "Molly, they're holding his wife's body because she died under rather suspicious circumstances. Murderers can be as jovial and as charming as your favorite uncle. You know that!"

Molly groaned. "What are we going to do?"

Tyrus frowned. "Zebina's funeral's tomorrow. By then, maybe we'll know whose skeleton they found." Ty pulled an aucuba leaf from the bush by the aunts' front porch and tore it down the middle. "I'd still like to talk with..." His face broke into a grin as Myrt veered into the driveway, jumped from the car, and ran headlong into the house.

"Hey! Here's just the person I wanted to see!" Tyrus started after her.

But Myrtis Curtis was crying. "The most awful thing has happened!" she said, falling into Ivalee's arms. "That fruitcake I ate was poisoned, and the police want samples from everyone at the party."

"Poisoned?" Ivalee held her at arm's length. "Oh, come now! Surely a little whiskey—"

Myrtis blew her nose. "No, no! I mean really poisoned! They found traces of it in Zebina's liver—kidneys, too. That fruitcake was loaded with mistletoe berries!"

TWENTY-THREE

THE BERRIES WERE FOUND only in the miniature cakes, Myrtis said. Two of the samples she had passed along to the doctor had contained the toxic fruits. Apparently there was a chance of higher concentration there, enough to kill someone with a weak heart and to make a healthy person very sick.

Ivalee's usually flushed face turned pale, and she looked at Molly with frightened eyes. Iris! Iris had made miniature fruitcakes, and Emma Beth had helped her. It was suspected in Harmony that Iris was in love with Judson Horne, and Emma Beth made no secret about her feelings for Myrtis. Molly remembered noting with surprise that the two of them had been unusually compatible in the kitchen, and that they wouldn't allow anyone else in!

"But wouldn't you taste it?" Tyrus asked. "They're bitter, aren't they?"

Molly shrugged. "So are citron and candied lemon peel, but most people soak the cake in whiskey or wine, so you don't notice the bitter taste too much." She almost smiled. "From now on, I'll take my liquor straight—thank you just the same!"

"And those cakes are so small, you can eat them in one or two bites," Molly remembered. "You could gulp one down almost before you tasted it." She sat next to Myrtis on the sofa. "You didn't notice anything peculiar? Didn't the seeds crunch or something?"

Myrtis held a handkerchief to her face and closed her eyes. "Not that I remember; besides, nuts crunch, don't they?'' She grabbed a magazine and fanned herself. ''Can we change the subject?''

Ivalee sat in the armchair by the window. She picked up a fallen icicle from the floor beneath the tree and wound it around her finger. ''Who could have done such a thing? And right here in Harmony!'' She shook her head. ''I just don't believe it!''

''Believe it,'' Myrtis said dully.

''But why would anyone want to make you sick? Or Zebina?'' Ivalee shuddered. ''I can't bear to think about it!''

''Do the police really think it will do any good to collect fruitcake samples?'' Tyrus asked. ''After all, no one would be stupid enough to keep poisoned fruitcake around.'' He stood and went to the door, pretending to show someone in. ''Oh, hello, officer! Poisoned fruitcake, you say? Well, of course! I just happen to have some left.'' He slammed his head with the heel of his hand. ''Gad! I meant to get rid of the evidence! Oh well, while you're here, can I interest you in a little arsenic tea?''

Molly laughed, but Ivalee didn't think it was funny. ''Well, we don't have any more of the fruitcake Iris made for the party. They ate it all—every crumb—and it didn't have any poison in it that I know of!''

''Let's try and remember who else served cake.'' Molly wrote Iris's name on the back of a Christmas card. ''What about Mrs. Dinsmore? We sang there first.''

''Just those lemon cookies,'' Ty said. ''But nobody wanted any because we'd just eaten so much here.''

''Agnes Tatum served some,'' Ivalee remembered, ''but it was sliced, not miniatures. And Ouida Kirkpatrick brought her usual mess. There oughta be a law against that ghastly stuff she makes, just on general principle!'' She frowned. ''And there were those little cakes Mildred Dobson brought. Obnoxious woman! Daughter sings in the choir. And she has it in for you, Myrtis. Remember how ugly she acted when you replaced Louann in the pageant?''

"And we don't know how many other cast members brought refreshments over here," Myrt reminded them.

"They served it at Zebina's too," Molly said. "Three different kinds." She sat with her head in her hands. She remembered someone passing her a paper plate containing several small individual fruitcakes, some cheese straws, nuts, and a Christmas cookie. She had eaten the cookie and set the plate aside and forgotten it while they were downstairs dancing. Throughout the evening a maid had passed around large platters of cake, but most people hadn't eaten any because they knew breakfast was being served.

"Zebina liked fruitcake." Myrtis spoke abruptly, staring at an empty chair as if she could see the frail woman sitting there. "The doctor didn't like for her to have it, but it was one of the few things she really enjoyed."

"How many people knew this?" Tyrus spoke quietly.

"You mean Judson, don't you? You think Jud poisoned Zebina." Myrtis smiled. "I'll admit that when Jud first married Zebina Murdock, I thought he'd married her for her money. And maybe he did. Jud was a sharecropper's son, and there were eight children in the family. Money is extremely important to him, but he wouldn't kill for it, and he really loved Zebina."

Ivalee nodded. "I think so, too. It's true her money enabled him to become the major stockholder in that department store. It's been a long, long time since he first went to work there as a stockroom boy." She sighed. "But I do believe Jud came to care for her. Anyone who knows him would tell you that."

Tyrus stood. "Speaking of Jud, I'd better get back over there, see if there's anything I can do."

Molly walked outside with him. "I wish Asa would come," she said. "I don't know what to do!"

"About Emma Beth?" Tyrus put an arm loosely around her.

She nodded. "About everything! Ty, you know she put syrup of ipecac in that boy's milk because he embarrassed her, and she as much as said she wished Myrt were dead."

"Do you really think Emma Beth would do that?"

"Not if she realized someone could die from it," Molly admitted. "But Emma Beth doesn't always think." She told him about the pearl pendant. "There's no telling what she did with that. Asa will probably never see it again."

Molly stood on the walk and watched him back into the street and drive away. Through the window she could see Myrtis pacing the living room, talking with her hands, while Ivalee sat and watched her. She wondered if the two of them would suddenly become quiet when she stepped back inside.

Molly hesitated with her hand on the doorknob. Should she take a chance and ask them about the guitar in the attic? About Jud's relationship with Rowena? She had to discuss it with someone other than Tyrus, someone who had known them all.

Reuben Anthony! He already knew she suspected something. Surely she could trust the minister!

After lunch Molly dropped Joy and Emma Beth off at the movies and drove to the Methodist church. The dark brick structure sat on a rise with evergreens partially concealing it from the street, and she was relieved to see three cars in the parking lot. At least she wouldn't be in the dark building alone.

Mildred Dobson glanced up from her typing and nodded curtly when Molly went inside, and she saw that Reuben's office door was open. She found the minister on his hands and knees trying to put together a tricycle.

He looked up and smiled when he saw her in the doorway. "For my tree angel," he said. "They're picking these things up in an hour, and I can't seem to find the thingamabob that goes across the back."

"You're sitting on it," Molly said, laughing.

"Oh. Well then, can you hand me those pliers over there?"

"I found Barlow Jones's guitar," Molly said, putting the tool in his hand. "It's in the aunts' attic covered with a quilt. I'm sure Iris put it there; I'm just not sure why."

Reuben was silent while he tightened a nut, his face taut in concentration. "I remember her trying to learn to play it," he said, giving the back wheels a spin, "but Iris didn't have the knack for it. She sang, too—not the kind of music Barlow sang, but they shared a common interest. He might've given the instrument to her before he left."

Molly thought his speech lacked conviction. She sat in the big red chair facing him and slowly removed a piece of cedar from her sweatpants. "I found out who was seeing Rowena," she said. "It was Judson Horne."

Reuben tightened a screw under the tricycle seat. He didn't look up. "I should be surprised..."

"But you're not. Why?"

Reuben set the tricycle on its wheels with a thump and rolled it across the room, pedals whirling. "Ah," he said, smiling, and sat across from her. "Why?" He scratched his bearded chin. "Well, I guess it's because they were always closer than the rest—best friends, in a way. Rowena's father didn't like it. I guess he was afraid of the inevitable—that they'd fall in love."

Molly frowned. "But why? What's wrong with that? Jud seems like a nice enough guy to me."

"Mr. Sterling was a bit of a snob," Reuben reminded her, "and Jud was a tenant farmer's son. He didn't want his only child marrying into that."

"Did you know this all along?" Molly asked.

"Of course not!" Reuben bent over and scooped up his tools. "It just makes sense. Rowena had me escort her around to give her father a false sense of security while she saw Judson Horne on the sly. She couldn't have used Barlow Jones; Clyde Sterling had a fit whenever she even spoke to the man!"

The phone rang, and Molly sat quietly while Reuben talked with someone about Zebina's funeral. "Services for Zebina Horne will be at eleven tomorrow," he said, making a note at his desk.

"You heard about the poisoning?" Molly stood and started for the door.

He nodded, rising with her.

"Well, what do you think? Could Jud have had anything to do with it?"

Reuben Anthony sighed and shook his head. "I'll let the police worry about that, and so should you, Molly. Right now I'm just trying to get through this mess one day at a time."

And so am I, Molly thought as she walked outside to her car. Mildred Dobson had left and locked the door to the office wing, so Molly had to wind her way through the Sunday school rooms to find an alternative exit.

The secretary's car was gone, and only Molly's and the minister's automobiles remained. She stood in the parking lot breathing the cold, brisk air, then checked the back seat before sliding under the wheel. After all that had happened, she wasn't taking any chances. Once inside, she quickly locked the doors before digging for her keys. Danger was there. The whole town throbbed with it, but she was determined to avoid it if she could.

It was impossible to avoid the note on the seat beside her.

> You'd better watch out,
> You'd better not cry.
> Or there won't be much doubt
> You'll be the next to die!

Beside it lay a shriveled sprig of mistletoe.

TWENTY-FOUR

THE FAMILIAR SONG ricocheted through her mind like a bouncing ball. A happy little childhood chant turned evil, it zigzagged behind her eyes in frantic patterns of red, yellow, and green: *Stop! Caution! Go*! Molly couldn't control it, couldn't block it out.

With shaking hands she dialed Judson Horne's number from the aunts' house. Tyrus would know what to do. Maybe he was right; it was time to go to the police. This time the killer had gone too far; he had put his threat in black and white!

After several rings, Judson's nephew Larry answered. Ty had gone to the church with Jud to discuss Zebina's service with the minister. She had just missed him!

Startled by footsteps in the aunts' otherwise quiet house, Molly quickly replaced the receiver. Ivalee came slowly down the stairs buttoning her old black coat. A bulging leather handbag swung from her arm. "Oh...Molly, I'm going to drop by the funeral home, sign the guest book and all, and I might stop at Jud's for a minute. Do you want to come with me?" A tousled lock of hair fell over her forehead, and Molly noticed that she still wore her house slippers.

"The girls will be out of the movie in an hour," Molly said. "I'd better stay here, Aunt Ivalee," she added softly, "Aren't you going to change your shoes?"

Ivalee Brown looked down at her feet. "Ye gods and little fishes! My Beckworth always told me I was absentminded!" She started back upstairs. "I don't know what in the world is going to become of us, Molly! I'll swear I don't.''

Molly reached up and covered the plump hand on the stair rail with her own. ''Don't worry, Aunt Ivalee, everything will be all right. I know it will.''

Sure it will, Molly, she told herself after her aunt had left. Everything will be just dandy fine! Some stern ancestor of Ethan's frowned at her from his dark portrait. He didn't seem optimistic, either. Molly glanced at herself in the hall mirror. She looked as if she had aged ten years. ''What a liar you are!'' she told herself. She walked through the empty rooms, rearranged cards on the mantel, straightened a picture on the wall. She had been followed, shot at, and now she had been warned. What else could happen?

Molly walked into the kitchen. Usually tidy, Ivalee had left the scant remainder of a Waldorf salad uncovered on the table. Molly dumped the contents and washed the bowl. She wiped fruitcake crumbs from the counter. The police had come, Ivalee said earlier, and had taken generous wedges from both the white and dark cakes. ''Enough for four or five desserts,'' her aunt grumbled. ''And probably the best they'll ever have!''

Molly looked at her watch. Only ten minutes had passed since she last checked the time. The girls would be getting out of the movies in a little while, but Ivalee had offered to pick them up. ''I'll be in that end of town anyway,'' she said. ''Besides, it will give me an excuse to get away from Jud's. I just can't help but feel like a third thumb at times like this!''

Molly switched on the television in the den. A chorus of white-robed choirboys sang ''What Child Is This?'' and Molly suddenly realized that Christmas was only four days away. She had risked her life and perhaps her daughter's by coming to Harmony for the holidays, and instead of learning the truth about her husband's death, she seemed to be sinking deeper into a dark mire of confusion and fear. According to the note found in the hollow tree, Rowena had been planning to run away with Judson Horne. There had been a fire in the Sterlings' stable, and Rowena had disappeared along with the recently dismissed farmhand, Barlow Jones.

Only the three children who discovered the note had the key to Judson's secret, and two of them were dead.

Now Molly and Tyrus knew, and Tyrus was with Jud! Molly had been reluctant to call Tyrus at the church, to disturb a meeting between Judson and his minister at such a sensitive time, but murder elbowed manners aside. She had her hand on the receiver when the telephone rang.

"Molly Stonehouse, please." The voice on the line was soft and feminine with a pleasant southern accent. At first she thought it was Asa's friend Corrine, but Corrine Harris had left the day before to spend Christmas with her parents and wasn't due back for a week.

The caller identified herself as Ty's sister Augusta. "I've been trying to locate Ty," she said. "I tried that number he gave me and they told me to call the church, but he'd already left there. Do you know where he is?"

The woman sounded frightened, almost hysterical. Molly knew how she felt.

"I'm sure he'll be back soon," Molly said. "If he stops by here, where can I have him call you?"

"I'm just on the edge of town," Augusta said, "and I'm frightened. Something has come up—something important—and I need to see him now!" Her voice trailed off. "It's about what happened to Rowena."

"What did happen?" Molly found herself whispering, too.

"I can't talk about it here! I've got—"

"Look, just drive on into Harmony and meet me here. You'll be all right. Please, Augusta. I'm Ethan's wife; your brother is a friend of mine. We'll wait for Ty together." Molly tried not to sound uneasy. "I don't think they even know who you are."

"I—I can't! Somebody knows...I was threatened!" The woman was crying now. "Could you come? Please?"

Molly looked through the leaded glass panels by the door, hoping to see one of the aunts return. Asa. Anybody! And where was Ty? "I don't know," she said. "Where are you?"

"There's a Gulf station—Willie's—about five miles north of town on Quimby's Mill Road. Turn left past Crane Eater School. I'll wait for you there—and hurry! Please hurry!"

The woman hung up without even waiting for her reply. Molly frowned. Quimby's Mill Road? Crane Eater School? She had never heard of either of them. She would have to ask someone how to get there.

A policeman directing traffic on a downtown corner gave her directions. Later, she wished she had told him specifically where she was going. But now, driving through town in the sparse traffic with one of those chummy down-home talk shows on the radio, she only wanted to reach Ty's sister as quickly as possible and try to convince her to come home with her.

Molly looked at the clock on her dashboard. It was half past four, and the sun had the peculiar late afternoon slant of pale winter light. Shadows stretched across the wide lawns on the street where Judson Horne lived. She drove past two young boys on scooters, and a stylish woman walking a sheepdog—or vice versa. Undine Larsen plodded down the street with a package under her arm—probably returning empty dishes to neighbors.

In some windows tree lights were already burning; a wreath hung from every door. What kind of wreath would adorn the Hornes' place now? Molly ignored the fluttering in her stomach. She had eaten little all day. She sighed. At last she had lost her appetite, and she couldn't even enjoy it.

Poor Jud! He had always loved Christmas, the aunts had said; always made it a point to celebrate in style. And now Zebina had died. Molly couldn't imagine Judson Horne poisoning his ailing wife—especially at Christmas. It was just too inconvenient. Zebina had been sitting next to her when Molly set her plate of refreshments aside to dance on the night of the party. Jud's wife had loved fruitcake; had she mistakenly nibbled from the wrong plate? Carried away with the revelry around her, she might have glanced at the plate beside her and eaten from it, thinking it was her own.

Who else had sat next to her? Molly remembered Reuben Anthony chatting with Zebina. She thought back to that night, saw again his dark blue sweater, the red stone in his class ring *as he handed her the plate*. The flutter in Molly's stomach became a throb. The car suddenly seemed close and hot. Had someone meant the poisoned cake for her? Had it been Reuben Anthony? He had admitted an interest in Rowena, and if he had hurried, he would have had enough time to put the note and the mistletoe in her car after she left his office. There were several exits to the parking lot. Had he made sure she would have to go the long way around?

She passed through the huge stone columns that marked what was once the city limits of Harmony and drove past a suburban area of modest brick homes, a small stone church with a nativity scene on the lawn. Molly pressed harder on the accelerator. Did Augusta Duncan really know what had happened to Rowena?

Farther on, Crane Eater School sat on a gentle hill surrounded by large cedars. Molly could barely glimpse its worn red brick through the foliage. It would be deserted now for the holidays. She turned left onto a narrow asphalt road that she supposed to be Quimby's Mill, but she couldn't be sure since there was no sign. Surely she had gone more than five miles!

Molly looked for signs of habitation as the road meandered through a brown patch of woods where bare limbs clawed at a bleak sky. The sun slid behind a hill as she crossed a bridge over a shallow creek. A rusty trailer sat in a clearing on the other side; tall grass grew around a leaning mailbox. No activity there, but somewhere on the hill behind it, smoke rose from a chimney.

She drove past a field of gray, withered cornstalks with a scarecrow still standing guard. Its faded red shirt flapped in the wind. Somebody had to plant and harvest the corn, Molly thought; human hands had fashioned the scarecrow. Surely she was not alone at the end of nowhere. Her mouth felt dry. Molly remembered the rural gas stations of her childhood, ancient red iceboxes full of frosty drinks. She would welcome one now.

Finally, around a sharp curve, she saw Willie's Service Station—or what was left of it. The gas pumps were long gone, windows were broken, and part of the roof had caved in. Bare vines clutched the crumbling stone walls. Molly slowed the car and crept over broken pavement where straggling weeds thrived. The name WILLIE'S in faded blue letters was still legible on a wooden sign over the door. She looked around. There was no one there; nothing moved. It was almost dark and here she was miles from anywhere, and no Augusta. Molly felt as if she were the last person on earth.

Had Ty's sister remembered the old filling station from her childhood and considered it a safe place to meet? Was she waiting somewhere out of sight for Molly to show up? Molly tapped on the steering wheel; she would give her five minutes and that was all. She had no intention of sticking around this desolate place!

She stiffened expectantly at the sound of a vehicle approaching from the opposite direction, but the truck lumbered on past and disappeared in the thickening shadows. At least someone else uses this godforsaken road, Molly thought.

Somewhere in that phantom area at the edge of peripheral vision she thought she saw something move. A pine bough stirred in the underbrush at the far corner of the building. Molly checked her doors. Locked. She reached for the ignition key, then she heard it; a soft cry for help. She opened the window a crack. Again, "Help! Help me, please!" This time there was no doubt about it. Someone was back there. Someone in trouble!

Molly tapped twice on the car horn. "I'm here," it said. "Let's get on with it!" She waited. Nothing. She put her mouth close to the window. "Gus? Augusta?" Only the cold air sliced through the opening. Could Augusta be lying there injured? Bleeding? She had seemed afraid over the phone. Someone had threatened her, she said. Molly blew the horn once again. She had been threatened, too.

A sharp cry ripped from the blackness. This time it sounded as if it came from the building itself. Cold silence followed.

Grabbing a flashlight from the glove compartment, Molly threw open the car door and ran for the building. The place smelled damp and moldy, and the decaying floor groaned under her feet. She cast a narrow beam of light over a tiny room filled with years of debris. "Augusta?" Her voice quaked as much as the ancient timbers beneath her. "Where are you? Answer me!" She couldn't see past the filthy boxlike counter at the end of the room. A rusty iron stove stood on a platform in a corner surrounded by empty cans. One of them clanked across the floor when Molly brushed it with her foot. Mice scampered in the walls.

Molly shivered convulsively and made her way to the back of the room. A small tree had grown through the yawning window behind the counter. Her flashlight beam picked up a gleam of broken glass on the floor. No one was there. Not Augusta, not anyone. She had been tricked!

Molly whirled about, expecting to see Reuben Anthony crouching behind her. Not the jovial minister she had watched putting together the tricycle, but a dark, fierce-eyed monster of a man who had killed Ethan and Neil and who knew how many others. She had made the mistake of telling him she would be alone that afternoon. He had probably used his secretary to lure her away from the house. Molly wouldn't be surprised to learn that Mildred Dobson had had a hand in it all along. Surely it was Reuben who had meant the poisoned fruitcake for her, had been plaguing her all along.

Darkness encircled her. Switching off her light, she stood just inside the doorway. The smell of the place sickened her and she felt trapped, surrounded by crumbling walls, yet Reuben, or whoever was out there, could be waiting, shrouded in shadows.

Molly took a long breath and listened. She had only the mice for company. She couldn't stay there all night. She would just have to make a break for it. She could see her cold breath in front of her. Her fingers were getting numb.

It was now or never! Molly jumped over the warped doorstep and ran. The cold metal of the car door handle was in her hand. Trembling, she slid under the wheel and reached for the ignition switch, but the keys were gone.

Molly scrambled for her pocketbook. She was sure she had left it on the seat beside her. But the handbag was gone, too. In the darkness her hand brushed something small and furry and very still. When she switched on the flashlight she knew: She had been led here for a purpose, and this time the killer meant business.

Molly refused to scream. It was not as if she hadn't been warned. On the seat beside her where her handbag had been lay a gruesome reminder: a tiny, gray mouse, stiff in death.

TWENTY-FIVE

MOLLY CROUCHED on the floorboard. She was helpless, completely at the mercy of this maniac playing cat and mouse with her life. The dead mouse remained on the seat. It was the least of her worries, but still she cried out sharply when her fingers touched something soft and cold. Gloves! Gratefully Molly pulled them on. They must have fallen to the floor when she slid from the seat to hunt for Augusta.

Stupid, stupid, stupid! Tyrus had warned her not to go out alone. Molly huddled with her head down, arms clutching her knees. What was she going to do now? Was Reuben going to abandon her, or would he move in for the kill? As if in answer, a gun fired close by. A bullet splintered the glass over her head and plunged into the padding in the back seat. She had to get out of there, quickly! Molly tensed, one hand on the door handle, the other clenching the flashlight. Slow, measured footsteps approached her; she heard the threatening crunch of hard soles on gravel, the click of a rifle being cocked... and something else: a low hum. A car was coming!

Molly threw open the door and ran toward the road screaming. "Stop! Wait, please!" She staggered down the slight incline without looking back. The car whizzed past in a burst of speed, a pale blur of frightened faces. They must have thought they were being pursued by the devil himself!

A stone rolled under her foot, and she stumbled into a shallow ditch by the road just as another bullet whined past. Closer this time, but the passing car had bought her precious seconds. Now the darkness was her friend. If she could cloak herself in it, deceive whoever was stalking her long enough to reach a house—a phone—she might have a chance.

A concrete culvert went underneath the road that turned into Willie's, its entrance curtained with weeds. Molly shoved them apart and crawled inside. Her head bumped the top, and she felt cold, wet goo seeping into her clothes. It wouldn't do to even think about what might be in there with her. She gritted her teeth to keep them from chattering and listened to the heavy tread pacing the bank, then crossing over her head. Molly remembered her dad reading the familiar animal fables from "Uncle Remus" *And Brer Rabbit, he lay low*.... If it worked for Brer Rabbit, maybe it would work for her.

The person above her turned suddenly and hurried back toward the gas station, and soon Molly understood why. Another car was coming. She used the noise of its passing to work her way to the other side of the pipe. She knew he was up there watching, waiting for her to make a move.

And then a small animal, a rabbit perhaps, rattled the dry leaves across the road and drew the hunter's fire. Molly realized she had been holding her breath. She would never eat wild game again! Once more footsteps tramped over her and crossed the road in long, purposeful strides. She heard someone moving, searching through the underbrush on the other side.

Blackberry bushes tore at Molly's coat, and broken glass cut into her knee as she crawled out of the culvert and crept along the side of the road using the ditch as a cover, but the pain in her knee was a victory, the sharp wind a blessing. She was still alive! Molly could make out the dark mass of trees just beyond. With luck she could lose herself in them, stall for time. She didn't count on the dead limb lying across her pathway.

The brittle wood cracked with a noise loud enough to wake the dead, and the fall sent Molly sprawling into a matted clump of honeysuckle vines. She heard her pursuer utter a short howl of surprise, and then the cold, deadly click as he cocked his rifle. Her groping fingers closed around an egg-shaped rock in the darkness, and as the rustle of footsteps drew nearer, Molly hurled the rock over her shoulder and ran for the blob of trees ahead. She heard the stone strike the broken cement of the driveway and skid into the grass and doubted if it fooled her follower for more than a second—if at all—but she was desperate enough to try anything now.

Once under the cover of trees, Molly didn't even try to be quiet but crashed through the thicket like a wounded animal. She smelled the dried pine needles, felt them slick and brittle under her feet, and blundered about with her fingers stretched out in front of her. She could distinguish the darker shapes of the trees, but the ground could fall away from beneath her before she would be aware of a drop-off. Somehow she had to get close enough to follow the road.

For the first frantic minutes of running, Molly had been aware of the person behind her echoing her noise. She pressed a hand against the sharp pain in her side as she ran uphill, slipping back one step for every two she advanced. A pine cone crunched beneath her, and a few yards behind her a limb creaked and broke. Molly struggled to breathe silently; she felt as if she were trapped in a giant bowl of rice cereal!

She couldn't run anymore. Molly squeezed between twin trees and hoped her shadow would merge with theirs. Gradually she became conscious of the stillness. Other than her breathing, there was a complete lack of noise. The hills were listening.

Who waited out there in the night? According to Eula Dinsmore, Judson Horne was the Christmas Mouse, but had his name been on the original message to Rowena Sterling? The desk had been in Reuben Anthony's possession for weeks, yet he had seemed strangely uninterested in its contents. Had he *wanted* them to find the note? Perhaps even put it there? And then she had a startling thought: On the night after the caroling party when she had heard someone trying to dig up the box, could they have been *putting it back in the ground*? But why would the minister want to throw suspicion on Judson Horne?

Molly pressed against the tree and waited. Had her tormentor given up, left her? Or was he waiting, too? A few yards away a car passed on Quimby's Mill Road; its headlights splashed the hillside in yellow. Molly closed her eyes. Could he see her now?

But the car rushed on and nothing happened. Her leg ached with a cold pain; her fingers grew stiff in damp gloves, but Molly was afraid to move. The slightest noise would give her away. How long would she have to wait?

Oh, to hell with it! Molly decided finally. If I stay here much longer, I'll die of pneumonia. With complete abandon, she started walking toward the road. She found herself on a slight hill only a few feet above the narrow winding lane. When bright beams again peeked over the hilltop, Molly waited, watching from behind a shaggy cedar as the car crept along, almost as if it were patrolling the area. There was something familiar about the shape of it that in her urgency to hide, Molly had failed to recognize: it was the gray Pontiac that had been following her, and now Reuben or Judson, or whoever was driving it, was going to keep a constant vigil on this stretch of Quimby's Mill Road until she showed herself.

Molly watched the taillights disappear, knowing the car would soon return. She had to get back to the road! There was no other way to cross the creek. In her hurry to meet Augusta, she had not thought to leave a note. No one would know where she was. And Tyrus? He had supposedly gone to the church with Jud . . . and then what? Had the killer gotten Tyrus out of the way before he set his trap for Molly? And who *had* she talked with on the phone? It had sounded like a woman's voice identifying herself as Augusta.

Molly made it all the way to the bottom of the hill before the headlights returned. The tattered cornstalks gave scant protection in the rough winter field, but she kept to the tall grass by the ditch and hoped the lights wouldn't pick up the deep green color of her coat. Surely the whole garment was mud-caked by now!

The car would have to go back at least as far as the old gas station in order to turn around, which should give her about two minutes to run. Molly tucked her scarf inside her coat as she sprinted for the square of light in the distance. She knew it came from the shabby mobile home with the crooked mailbox and wondered if she would find help there. A dog snarled and barked from a corner of the red clay clearing and sounded as if its one purpose in life was to kill and destroy. Molly's heart beat loud and fast as she hesitated at the edge of the field. The person in the gray car would hear the racket and find her if the dog didn't get to her first. She heard the rattle of a chain between growls and realized the animal must be tethered. "Oh, shut up, will you?" Molly was running out of time and patience, but the dog only barked louder.

The door of the trailer opened a fraction of an inch, thrusting a splinter of light into the blackness. "Hush, Queenie!" The woman's voice was tired, yet it had a hardiness about it. "Who's out there?" she said.

Molly caught a glimpse of a woman with graying hair wearing a faded pink robe. A small plastic holly wreath hung from the door by a length of red yarn. "Please help me!" she called. "Phone the police! Someone's trying to kill me!" She was so cold and frightened, she could hardly speak. Soon the menacing car would return and seek her out.

"I don't want no part of it," the woman said. "Go somewheres else—git away from here!" This was the voice of someone who had endured enough misery and wanted no more of it.

"Look, I won't hurt you, I promise! I'm freezing out here! Can't you at least call the police?" Molly bent over against the wind. Far away at the top of the hill she saw the two headlights, like demon's eyes in the night. "If you don't help me, they're going to kill me!" She was begging now, crying.

"Look, there's no phone here." The voice was less harsh now. "I can't let you in, but there's a house up the road a piece—the Holsombacks have a phone."

"Hurry! Shut the door!" Molly darted behind the trailer, avoiding the lighted windows. "Here he comes! He'll see me."

"Wait there," the woman said as she quietly closed the door, and Molly did. She stood stiffly behind the trailer, feeling the cold metal against her back, and waited for the car to complete its agonizing surveillance. Queenie, she noticed, had gone back into her overturned barrel house and forgotten her. For now. Was she going to die here in this red clay-patch place and be buried in a wilderness so deep no one would ever find her? Molly wanted to cry, but the tears were cold in her eyes.

"Miss?" The woman held a coat at arm's length through a slit in the doorway. "Put this on; maybe it'll help. I'm sorry I can't do more, but my daughter's workin' second shift, and it's just me here with the baby."

Molly thanked her with chattering teeth and wrapped the warm, dry coat about her, letting her slime-caked jacket slide to the ground.

"Don't leave that!" the woman warned her. "If he comes here, he'll know. Throw it in the woods somewheres." She hesitated. "Do you have a light?"

Molly nodded. "Is there another way across that creek? He's watching the bridge." She pulled the heavy coat collar up to her chin.

The woman nodded; her narrow face looked yellow in the dim light. "There's a footbridge down behind the house a ways; kids used to take that back path to school, but you'll need that light to see. You'll find the Holsombacks' place at the top of the hill across a little dirt road. You tell 'em Louvina sent you."

"You've probably saved my life," Molly said as she stumbled away. She didn't know how to thank her, and the wiry little woman didn't wait to be thanked. "Hurry now!" she said, and firmly closed the door. The dark circle of holly quivered with a cold, plastic rattle.

Evidently schoolchildren still used the path through the woods, Molly thought, as the way was clear and easy to follow. She had briefly switched on her flashlight in order to find the small bridge and had followed the hard-beaten trail deeper into the trees until she felt safe enough to use the light again.

The pathway emerged from the woods and twisted through an open field, which she guessed to be about a

half-mile from the road. Ahead Molly saw a small frame
house set in what appeared to be a pecan grove. She walked
faster. What if the Holsombacks had gone to bed? What
if they took a shot at her? She had no idea what time it
was, but it must be at least nine. Her stomach rumbled
hungrily. She hadn't eaten since noon. She winced as her
foot sank into a stumphole, and her knee was beginning to
throb. If this keeps up, Molly thought, I won't have a
square inch on my body that doesn't hurt!

Holding the rough cloth coat together, Molly hurried
across the dirt road, scattering pebbles in her way, and ran
up the circular drive that led to the house. She almost
didn't see the car lights turn onto the narrow road that in-
tersected Quimby's Mill. Just in time she threw herself
behind a large nandina bush at the edge of the lawn as the
gray car swept past and turned around in the field across
the road. Of course! This would be the most logical place
for the car to make its turn. Molly almost smiled. She
wondered how long Reuben Anthony—if it was Reuben
Anthony—would travel back and forth across the bridge
waiting for her to make a mistake.

From her position under the bush, Molly saw the bluish
glow of a television screen in a window at the side of the
house, and as she drew nearer, the firefly flickering of tiny
white tree lights winked at her from behind a magnolia.
The thick magnolia screened not only the living-room
window, she found, but a small front porch as well. Molly
felt secure there, if only for a minute, hidden from the
threat that haunted her.

Molly reached out woodenly and rang the bell, willing
her arm to move, her finger to press the small black button. She saw a large woman walk slowly toward the door.
It was an old-fashioned door with curtained glass in the
top, and someone—probably the large woman—had

gathered a spray of magnolia leaves and pine with a red plaid bow and suspended it in the center of the glass. The ribbon seemed to fade in upon itself as the woman opened the door and a surge of warmth rolled over the threshold.

"Louvina sent me," Molly blurted. "Oh, hurry...the car...please, call the police!"

She felt warm, soft arms around her, skin with a honey-and-almond smell. "Oh lord, Wiley, come here quick!" a voice shouted. "There's a woman out here who's in trouble, and I think she's about to faint!"

TWENTY-SIX

THE SMELL OF HOT COCOA revived her. "You're all right now," the woman said as she held the cup to Molly's lips. What a kind woman, Molly thought drowsily as she sat before a woodstove while wrapped in a soft, woolly blanket. Who could ask for more than this? She could stay here forever. And she curled up on the long corduroy sofa and went to sleep.

The Holsombacks did call the police, who notified the aunts, who had reported Molly missing. Her car, with key and pocketbook restored, was still parked in front of the ruined gas station, but there was no disguising the shattered windshield and the spent casing that had penetrated the back seat and emerged in the trunk. The police immediately put out an all-points bulletin for the gray Pontiac, but it seemed to have evaporated in the mist.

Molly slept soundly that night in her bed on Muscadine Hill with Joy's bear, Marjorie, nestled under her chin. When Ivalee woke her for breakfast the next morning, she swore she hadn't budged an inch all night. Molly barely remembered the ride home from the Holsombacks' the night before, snuggled into the back seat between Joy and Ivalee, with the rest of the family jammed into the front. Someone—Iris, she thought—had helped her bathe and dressed the cut on her knee.

She still wasn't sure what had happened to Tyrus, except that Ivalee had seen him briefly as he left the Hornes' the afternoon before. He had received a call from his sister, he had said, and would be in Atlanta for the night.

Whoever had telephoned her pretending to be Augusta, Molly thought, had probably called Ty to get him out of the way. But why had he not tried to get in touch with her after he reached Atlanta? Surely he realized he had been the victim of a hoax.

Molly and Joy dressed in companionable silence. Earlier, while Molly was brushing her teeth, her daughter had tackled her around the waist and cried. "Mom, I was so worried! I couldn't stand it if anything happened to you!" Joy's love made her feel as if she had survived for a reason. But Ty? What if Ty had not? Could he have returned to Jud's by now? She didn't even know his sister's married name. Surely someone would know how to get in touch with the real Augusta!

Molly pulled a navy sweater over her head. It matched the circles under her eyes. Her knee hurt when she walked and her head ached, but then, she hadn't eaten in almost twenty-four hours. Maybe breakfast would help.

Joy walked downstairs with her, one hand under her arm as if she were a fragile invalid. Molly was glad it was there. She heard the clinking of china and Asa's laughter from the kitchen. Joy sniffed. "Hmm, cinnamon! We're having sweet rolls." She hurried her mother along.

"Any word about the gray car?" a man's voice asked: not Asa's. "Are you sure Molly's all right?" It was a familiar voice. Tyrus!

He sat at the table with a coffee cup in one hand and a roll in the other, and when Molly pushed open the swinging door, he jumped up and kissed her in front of God and everybody.

Molly kissed him back. "They know about Gus," she whispered. "Is she all right?"

He nodded, never taking his eyes from her face. "She's fine for now; it's you they seem to want." Silently Ty took er hand and pressed each finger, as if he were counting them.

Iris tried not to smile. "He was waiting at the door before I even had my coffee," she said. "Would've waked the whole neighborhood if I hadn't let him in."

Tyrus grinned at Iris. "I called from Atlanta last night, but your matron here said you were asleep." His smile faded as he looked at Molly. "It must have been some night. You look like the devil!"

"Gee, thanks." Molly reached out for a mug of coffee and let the steam waft into her face. Someone put a cinnamon bun on a plate in front of her. "I guess you know it wasn't your sister who called," she said, staring back. "Somebody wanted you out of the way. I think it was Reuben Anthony or Judson Horne."

But Iris shook her head. "You're wrong, Molly. Why, Reuben Anthony's as gentle as a lamb. And why would he want to harm you? He'd never hurt anyone! And it couldn't have been Judson. I was with him until way past dark; Jodean, too. I think he just wanted someone there."

"Poor Jud!" Ivalee blinked. "They're burying Zebina this afternoon and the police think he might have poisoned her."

"What?" Emma Beth dropped her spoon into the cereal, spattering milk all around.

"Will somebody please tell me what's going on?" Asa stood and pushed back his chair. He looked from his mother to Emma Beth. "Poisoned her with what?"

"Mistletoe berries. In fruitcake," Ivalee said. "And they're not sure, but Myrtis thinks the samples she gave them came from Jud's. They were in those little foil cups; ours were pink paper."

"I'm still confused." Asa sat down so hard, the chair groaned. "Why would Jud poison poor Zebina? And why would anyone want to kill Molly?"

Molly and Tyrus looked at one another and Tyrus shrugged. "It's a long story," Molly said.

"A very long story," Tyrus added, pouring coffee all around.

Molly told them how Ethan and the others had found the message in the tree the day before Rowena disappeared and had buried the airline tickets and the note as part of a "time capsule." "For some reason," she said, "Ethan came here last spring, unearthed the box, and put the note and tickets in that old pine desk for safekeeping. Or at least, that's what Reuben Anthony wants us to think."

"What?" Tyrus looked at her and frowned. "What makes you think Reuben Anthony had anything to do with it?

"The note was signed, 'Your Christmas Mouse,'" he explained to the others, "and we learned from Reuben that Rowena was seeing somebody else besides Barlow Jones, someone she called 'Mouse'!"

"That's no surprise!" Iris scraped orange peels into the garbage disposal and turned on the switch. It filled the room with an awful thumping, grinding noise, but the whole kitchen smelled of oranges. "Rowena had many bedfellows."

"Iris! For all you know, the poor woman's been lying out there under that kudzu for all these years." Ivalee seemed to speak more out of duty than conviction.

"We found out yesterday," Tyrus went on, "that Judson played a mouse in the school Christmas play. Mrs. Dinsmore said Sonny used to tease him about it. Judson

Iorne left that note for Rowena. He was her Christmas Mouse."

"But how can we be sure the note we found was the same one Ethan and the others buried?" Molly asked.

Iris smiled. "I'd almost forgotten that little play. I was a lamb; remember, Iva?"

"This doesn't make any sense," Asa said. "Why would Jud plan to elope with Rowena, then kill her and set fire to he stable?"

"I don't know. Maybe she changed her mind, wouldn't go away with him—or maybe it wasn't Jud who killed her. I think Reuben Anthony was in love with her, too." Molly reached for Joy's hand. "All I know is that Ethan was killed for it; Ethan and Neil Fry, because they had seen the note." She looked at Tyrus and continued. "And somebody here in Harmony wants me dead, too, because now I'm a threat as well: I know where that note is."

"Oh? Where is it, dear?" Ivalee asked.

Joy's eyes filled with tears. "Oh, Mom! Do you really think—"

But Asa wasn't satisfied. "Why would Reuben or whoever it was wait all this time to kill Ethan and Neil when they've known this all along?"

"The killer didn't know they knew," Molly explained. "Neil met him at a convention or a vacation somewhere last winter and mentioned finding Rowena's message. Of course he didn't know he was speaking with the person who wrote the note."

"Even so," Ivalee said, "no one suspected Rowena was dead until the skeleton turned up. Everybody here just assumed she'd run off with that hippie."

"But Judson knew that field had been sold for a shopping center," Ty reminded them. "And so did Reuben. Whoever killed Rowena and buried her there knew 'them bones were gonna rise again' when they started grading the land."

Joy grasped her mother's hand. "Why would anybody do a thing like that?"

"That's ridiculous! Everyone knew about the shopping center." Ivalee rose and put her dishes in the sink. "It could have been anyone in this town! Why, I've known Judson and Reuben practically forever. It was that poet, that Jones man who killed Rowena. I've wondered about that all along, and now I feel sure of it!"

Tyrus spoke softly. "Barlow Jones never came home to Big Kettle, Wyoming. We talked to the woman who runs the newspaper there. His real name, by the way, was Eli Crump."

Emma Beth's eyes were huge. "Maybe he didn't come back because he was scared to, because he was on the run!"

"Oh, for heaven's sake, leave the poor man alone!" Iris dried her hands on a candy-striped dish towel. "Barlow Jones was the kindest person I ever knew!" She threw down the towel and looked at all of them for a minute before she left the room.

"Well, what was that all about?" Asa asked.

"You'll have to ask Aunt Iris about that," Molly said. "Only not just now." She lowered her voice. "Yesterday I found a warning note in my car. I seem to be next on the list." She told Asa and Ty about the threatening verse and the mistletoe she had found with it.

"What did you do with it?" Ty asked.

"Don't worry; it's in a safe place," Molly assured him. "I don't know what this person expects me to do, but he—or she—wants me out of the way." She frowned. "Ty, are you sure Augusta's okay?"

"Spending Christmas with her husband's folks in Texas," he told her. "I took them to the airport this morning."

Joy still sat at the table picking raisins from a bun. "Come on, honey, get your coat and we'll take a walk," Molly said. "That is, if someone will let me borrow a wrap. I'd like to have Louvina's coat cleaned for her today if I can. It's the least I can do."

"I'll take it by the cleaners," Asa offered. "Maybe they'll do a rush job on it."

"I'll go with you," Ty said with a knowing look at Molly. He knew she needed this time alone with Joy.

Together Molly and Joy strolled around the yard past the red oak by the back door, the row of holly trees screening the old garage, and sat for a while on the steps of the gazebo. Once Molly looked up and saw Sonny Earl Dinsmore, plastic greenery encircling his head, watching them from an upstairs window. She wondered if he knew he would soon be leaving.

"Mom, what makes you so sure Dad's death wasn't an accident?" Joy asked finally. Her eyes looked gray today, gray and sad. Molly put an arm around her as she told her of Neil Fry's note and of his hit-and-run death. "I didn't know Neil had been killed until I got a card from his family a few weeks ago," she said.

"But Daddy had probably forgotten what was in that note they found in the tree," Joy said. "I'll bet he didn't even remember who signed it." She crushed an acorn with her foot. "People don't remember silly things like that!"

"It wasn't silly to the person who wrote it," Molly reminded her. "And as long as that note was around, he was in danger of being found out."

"But how do you know it was the minister or Mr. Horne? Maybe it was that other guy—the one who disappeared?"

Molly looked up at the window of the house next door, but Sonny was no longer there. She stood and pulled Joy to her feet. "I don't know for sure, but we should find out soon," she said as they walked back to the house. She dug her hands for warmth into the pockets of the jacket Emma Beth had loaned her. Something brittle and dry crumbled in her fingers. Molly brought out a handful of shriveled mistletoe and let it fall to the ground. Don't let this mean what I think it means, she said to herself, and looked up to see a blue and white police car parked in the driveway.

A uniformed officer from the sheriff's department sat in the living room talking with the aunts and Emma Beth. With him was a young policeman from the city force. "We're working together on this one," the older man, a Sergeant Webster, explained as they introduced themselves. He waited until Molly and Joy were seated before continuing. "I'm afraid we've had no luck tracing the gray Pontiac. Without a license number there's not much to go on, and whoever owns it has it hidden away somewhere. But we did find out who that revolver belongs to that Sonny Earl found out back here. It was registered in the name of Clyde Sterling. 'Course he's been dead a good long time now."

Molly glanced at Iris, sitting across from her. "Rowena's father," she said.

The policeman nodded. "Right. But it was left to his stepdaughter, Miss Curtis; you know, the one who teaches math over at the high school. She hadn't even realized it was missing. Somebody obviously knew where she kept the key to the cabinet and helped themselves."

"They didn't take anything else?" Molly asked.

He shook his head. "No, just that old revolver, and it hadn't been fired." He pulled a pack of cigarettes from his pocket, then looked at Iris and stuffed it back inside. "Now, that woman in the trailer out on Quimby's Mill Road—Louvina Odom—she says that gray car pulled into her yard to turn around after you left there. Says it seemed to be guarding the bridge."

Molly nodded. "Louvina told me about another way to cross the creek. He was waiting for me. Watching."

Sergeant Webster laced his hands together, made a steeple with his fingers. "Well now, that's what I wanted to ask you, Mrs. Stonehouse: Did you get a good look at the person driving?"

Molly laid Emma Beth's jacket across the back of the chair. "I only heard his footsteps," she said, not daring to look up. "I was too busy running, trying to hide."

The sergeant plucked a fragment of tobacco from his lip. "The thing is," he said, "Louvina Odom got a right quick look from her front window while the car was turning around, and she's pretty sure it was a woman driving."

"A woman! But who?" Molly stared at him. She was glad when Joy came and sat on the arm of the chair and put a hand on her shoulder.

"That's right." Sergeant Webster studied his Masonic ring, straightened it on his finger. "Said it looked like a woman—a big woman—and she was wearing an orange hat."

"Like Miss Curtis wears!" Emma Beth's voice was shrill.

"You did say it was a woman's voice on the phone?" The sergeant looked up, steadying his glasses with one blunt finger.

"Well, it sounded like a woman's voice, but it could have been affected.... I'm just not sure!" Molly felt like a witness under questioning. She looked at Emma Beth who was examining the presents under the tree. "Look, it couldn't have been Miss Curtis! She left that hat at the Hornes' the night of the caroling party. I know it wasn't Myrtis!"

Emma Beth didn't look up, didn't say a word. Molly could have slapped her. Would the child never learn? "Emma Beth, how could you say such a thing? Why are you so vindictive? The woman's never done you any harm."

"She called my mother a tramp!" The girl glared at them through narrowed eyes. "I came to pageant rehearsal early one time; she didn't know I was there, and I heard her telling Aunt Iris it was a shame my daddy married that tramp! Said she'd sure messed up his life good and proper: meaning she had me."

Iris started toward her but stopped when Emma Beth turned away. "Oh no, Emma Beth, that's not what she meant at all. Why, you're the one good thing that came—" Iris Stonehouse flushed and sank silently back onto her chair, apparently embarrassed to be airing the family linen in front of strangers.

Sergeant Webster cleared his throat and looked longingly at his cigarettes. Molly sensed his discomfort. "Miss Curtis told us about losing the wraps," he said, "and several others have backed up her story." He turned to Emma Beth. "I believe you said the intruder who was here the night of the party was wearing that same hat?"

Emma Beth nodded, chipping away at her flamingo nail polish with a stubby fingernail.

The young policeman stood and looked down at Emma Beth. "From what Dr. Rosenberg says, Miss Curtis would've been too sick when she left the Hornes' that night to be prowling in anyone's house—hat or no hat." He turned to the aunts. "It looks as though someone's made good use of Miss Curtis's orange hat—if it's the same one."

"You mean someone wanted us to think it was Myrtis?" Molly asked.

"Don't look at me!" Emma Beth hugged her knees. "I can't even drive yet."

"We're still backtracking on that poisoned fruitcake," the policeman continued, "although Miss Curtis is pretty sure those samples she gave us came from the Hornes." He stood in the center of the room and shifted his weight from one foot to the other, nervously eyeing the aunts. "I do have to ask you: who made the cakes you served here?"

Iris drew herself up stiffly. "Why I did, and I ate some myself, and so did about everyone else here that night." She smiled at her sister. "As far as I know, I haven't killed anyone with my fruitcake yet."

"Why don't you tell him the truth, Aunt Iris?" Emma Beth asked. "I was in the kitchen with you. I helped to make those cakes." She glared at the policeman. "Aren't you going to ask me if I poisoned them?"

Molly felt sick. What was wrong with this child? "Oh, Emma Beth, you didn't—"

"No, I didn't, but I might as well have. Everybody will think I did!" Emma Beth put her head on her grandmother's knee while Ivalee stroked her bright hair.

"By the way," Molly said as the two men started to leave, "have they learned who that woman's skeleton was that they found the other day?"

The older man nodded. "Wasn't a woman, ma'am. It belonged to a man. We think it must be that guy who disappeared when Rowena Sterling ran away."

"Oh my God!" Iris moaned softly. "Oh, dear God, it's Barlow! Barlow Jones!"

TWENTY-SEVEN

MOLLY FOUND Emma Beth curled up in bed reading a paperback romance. "Thanks for the use of the jacket," she said, sitting at the foot of the bed.

"That's okay. Keep it as long as you like." Emma Beth turned a page without looking up. "I have another."

"I'm afraid your mistletoe fell apart," Molly said. "I threw it away."

"What mistletoe?" Emma Beth didn't blink.

"It was in your pocket."

She shrugged. "So?"

Molly told her about the note she had found in her car. "Did you put it there, Emma Beth?" she asked.

The girl slammed the book down beside her. "Why would I do that? Besides, I was at the movies." Her blue eyes were sullen. "You took me there yourself."

"But I heard you telling Joy to go ahead and get the tickets while you went in the dime store for candy. The church parking lot is just across from the dime store, Emma Beth." Molly looked at her young cousin and sighed. Emma Beth stared at the ceiling.

"I know you don't always realize some of the things you do can bring about...well, undesirable results," Molly went on. "But if you did leave that note there, I'd like to know why."

"Well, I didn't," Emma Beth said finally. "A boy gave me that mistletoe at school, and I stuck it in my pocket and forgot it."

"What boy?"

"I don't have to tell you that!" Emma Beth frowned. "Besides, you wouldn't know him." She picked up her book and pretended to read, but Molly wouldn't go away. "I found it," she muttered at last. "Somebody dropped it in the hall; and I didn't put that stupid note in your car, but I know who did because I saw her. It was Myrtis Curtis!"

Molly shook her head. "Oh, come on, Emma Beth! Ease up on the poor woman."

"I knew you wouldn't believe me, but it's true. I didn't know she was leaving a note, but I saw her put something in your car after you'd gone inside the church." Emma Beth's eyes blazed. "I'm not lying!"

Molly silently walked out and closed the door behind her. As far as she was concerned, Emma Beth Brown didn't even know how to tell the truth.

"I MUST HAVE BEEN blind!" Myrtis leaned on the stable-yard fence and fed Shortcake sugar from her hands. She had just come from Zebina's funeral and still wore what she called her "Sunday best" underneath her bulky coat. "Iris and Barlow Jones! I remember now how she used to wander off and talk with him whenever she was here. Iris was so quiet, so reserved, we never even knew what she was thinking." She stroked the mare's soft nose and sighed. "And all those years she thought he ran off with Rowena! It must be almost a relief for her to know."

"I don't think she ever stopped loving him." Molly told her about the guitar in the attic. "Iris said he had left it with her the night before he disappeared. She was learning to play and he wanted her to practice. And that peculiar shade of lipstick she uses..."

Myrtis smiled. "It's the only color I've ever seen her wear."

Molly spoke softly. "He—Barlow—said it suited her He liked seeing her wear it. I guess a lot of women gave up using makeup in the sixties."

Tyrus shielded his eyes against the afternoon sun. "Did she really think he set that fire and eloped with Rowena?"

"Don't underestimate Rowena's charms," Myrtis told him. "We were all used to having her take what she wanted, but even I had trouble believing Barlow set that fire. It wasn't like him."

"Then who did?" Molly asked, reaching out to pat the horse's flank. "And what happened to Rowena?"

"Somebody had to kill that man and bury him out there. If Rowena didn't do it, then who did?" Ty's words were relentless, chilling, but the time had come for answers.

Myrtis looked silently at the fields behind her house. "I'll be damned if I know," she said at last.

Molly waited, gripping the fence with both hands. "Reuben Anthony was dating her," she said, "but he claims he was covering for someone else. It might have been Jud." Slowly she told Myrtis about the message to Rowena and what had become of it.

"Jud." The name fell heavily from Myrt's lips, as if the word could fall to the ground and break. She shoved her hands into her pockets. "I don't know." Her voice was dull. "If Jud and Rowena were planning to go off together, I didn't know anything about it. They were always close—best friends really—but Daddy Clyde would have had a fit if he knew there was any more to it than that. Why, he didn't even like for Jud to take Rowena to parties!"

"That's why you never knew what was going on," Ty said softly. "They didn't mean for you to find out."

"Do the police know—about Jud and Rowena, I mean?" Myrtis looked at Molly and turned away, reaching for the horse's muzzle as if she needed to touch something warm.

"I told them about the note and the airline tickets," Molly said. "Of course he can deny it; most people around here have forgotten he was ever called 'Mouse.'" She watched Myrt's face, her eyes. She and Ty had not told her of their suspicions about Neil's and Ethan's deaths. The time wasn't right; not yet.

"I never will forget that little play," Myrt said. "Rowena and I were kittens." She smiled. "Isn't it funny how you remember things like that? The excitement of being on a real stage, being too scared to eat!" She chuckled. "Now, that's stage fright! Rowena, of course, took to it like a dog to a bone. They practically had to drag her offstage." She frowned. "I'd forgotten about Jud playing a mouse, though. That's been a few years!"

Myrtis shook her head. "But Rowena wouldn't forget, and she'd never let Jud forget, either." She took Molly's arm as she walked with them to the car. "I'm sorry you've been through such an ordeal, Molly. Please take care; you will, won't you?"

"WHICH SHOULD I give the Holsombacks?" Molly asked after they had collected Louvina's coat from the cleaners. "The chow-chow or the crabapple jelly?" They were on their way to the country to thank the people who had helped her the night before, and Ivalee had insisted on sending something from the pantry. Molly held the jars on her lap, a red bow on one, a green bow on the other.

"I don't know. From what you told me about Mrs. Holsomback, she probably has a whole cellar full of both, but I'll bet Louvina would like the jelly." He touched her hand lightly. "You aren't nervous, are you?"

"Just the thought of going down that road again makes me feel like somebody's having a pillow fight in my stomach," Molly said. "But if I see the place in daylight, maybe I won't have nightmares."

But Molly had no intention of going near the desolate gas station where she had come so close to death. The people from the garage had taken her car to replace the windshield, and she would have to have the seat reupholstered to cover the hole made by the bullet. Police had removed a casing from a 30-30 rifle from the trunk of the car but so far had been unable to trace the owner.

Mrs. Holsomback acted as if a jar of chow-chow were at the very top of her Christmas wish list. "Lord, I'm so glad to get it," she told Molly, clutching the jar with both hands. "My tomatoes just plumb dried up on me last summer! Didn't get hardly a one to can, much less make chow-chow!" Talking constantly, she bustled them into the small room with the tree that Molly remembered from the night before. The big cedar took up most of the window and a good part of the room, and Molly noticed that a lot of the decorations were at the bottom. "Our granddaughter did it," Mrs. Holsomback said, noticing Molly's curiosity. "Annette's four and excited to death about Santy Claus!"

What a lucky child Annette was, Molly thought, to have grandparents like this.

"Now, tell me how you're feeling, honey," the woman said after offers of refreshments were declined. "Law, you sure look a whole lot better than you did last night!" She looked solemnly at Tyrus. "It about scared me and Wiley to death! Shaking so she couldn't even hold a cup, and white as Grandma's bedsheets!"

"I'm fine now, thanks," Molly said. "A little stiff, but a hot bath worked wonders."

Mrs. Holsomback laughed. "Law, you sure needed one!" Then her face grew serious. "Have they caught that fool yet? The one who was after you?"

"Not yet, but soon we hope." Molly looked out the window. The shadows were growing longer, and she still had to go by Louvina's.

Tyrus got her message and stood. "I really hate to cut our visit short," he said, "but Molly wanted to see Louvina Odom, too."

"I'd like to thank you both for what you did for me last night," Molly told her. "I guess you know you saved my life; and here I come with a little jar of chow-chow!" She shrugged. "Not much of an exchange, is it?"

Mrs. Holsomback enveloped her in her soft embrace. "Well, my goodness, what else could we do?" she said almost in a whisper.

LOUVINA CAME to the door with a fat baby in her arms and circles under her eyes. She thanked Molly for the jelly and the coat but didn't ask them in. She had just gotten home from her shift at the carpet mill, she said, and was trying to get the baby down for a nap. She seemed embarrassed to see them. Molly glimpsed a small artificial Christmas tree on the counter behind the door.

"Have they caught her yet?" Louvina asked, peering down the road behind them.

Molly shook her head. "Are you sure it was a woman?"

Louvina shifted the baby to her other arm. "Could've been. Hard to say. I just got the feeling it was with that hat and all. 'Course the face was mostly hidden by a scarf." She closed the door as the baby began to cry.

Molly looked at Ty. "Merry Christmas," she said. She hoped Louvina would find the bills she had left in her coat pocket before too very long.

A FEW HANGERS-ON were still at Jud's as they turned into the now-familiar street. "Partaking of the funeral wines," Tyrus said, slowing the car.

"Ugh! Sounds disgusting!" Molly recognized Iris's car in the driveway, and Reuben Anthony stood on the porch talking with Judson's sister Jodean. As they drew nearer, she saw Mildred Dobson, Louann's mother, loading empty dishes into her car. She was almost certain that one of these people had something to do with Ethan's death. It could have been Judson or Reuben who had met Neil back in February and resurrected a long-buried secret. Iris had admitted that Jud attended a furniture show during that month, and Ivalee remembered Reuben taking a week off for a seminar on counseling.

"Can you imagine how I dread spending the night in that house again?" Tyrus looked as if he had swallowed a mouthful of vinegar.

"Then don't. You know you're welcome to stay with us," Molly offered.

"Can't. It would be like leaving a sinking ship." Tyrus sighed. "I wouldn't be surprised if the police arrested Judson Horne, and I don't think they're going to waste much time about it."

"For killing Zebina or for murdering Barlow Jones?"

"I don't know," he said. "Maybe both."

"But Jud didn't bake the fruitcake, did he?"

"He claims Zebina did, and she took credit for it," Ty said. "I ate some myself. It was good."

"You ate that fruitcake! You're lucky to be alive."

Ty started to move on. "I'm just lucky whoever was dispensing the poison didn't know who I really was." His smile was smug. "I guess you could say I didn't get my just desserts."

Molly cringed. "Tyrus Duncan, that's awful!"

He laughed, then stopped the car abruptly, swinging a red plaid arm across her in a protective gesture. "Oh my God, look! I was right, but somehow I didn't expect it this soon."

Molly followed his gaze. A police car was leaving the Hornes' driveway, and Judson Horne, pale and erect, was sitting alone in the back.

TWENTY-EIGHT

"I'LL HAVE TO GO in and see what happened," Tyrus said as they watched the car pull away. "Do you mind?"

Molly did mind. She didn't want to go inside that house again. It was like a box of wormy candy: when you opened the appealing container, you found decay inside. But Aunt Iris was there, and at least she wouldn't have to come face to face with Judson Horne.

"I'll be damned if I stay here and damned if I don't!" Ty said as he parked his car behind the house. "I don't want to run out on Jud if he wants me, but I'd think a stranger in the house is just about the last thing he needs right now."

"You really like Jud, don't you?" Molly followed him to the porch.

Ty looked thoughtful for a minute and nodded. "You know, I guess I do. I really do." He seemed surprised.

"Even if it turns out he's killed Ethan and the others?" Molly looked through the kitchen window at the people still milling about inside. They wore shocked, sad faces. Just about everybody liked Judson Horne. She had liked him, too, until she learned he might have left that note for Rowena. Had he left a warning note for her as well?

Tyrus stopped just outside the door and gently led her aside. "Look, Molly—I really don't believe Judson Horne's the bad guy in the black hat here; but I'm not certain he isn't, either. Until we find out for sure, I'm sticking close. I want this thing cleared up as much as you do, but I don't want a recurrence of last night!"

"Believe me, neither do I," Molly assured him as they went inside together. The house was oppressively stuffy with the smell of floral arrangements, which seemed out of place with the happy poinsettias lining the stairs. Why is it, Molly thought, that funeral flowers smell as if they're already dead?

Jodean Campbell sat with her son on the rose-brocaded sofa in the living room. She looked up as they came in. "They've taken him," she said. "They're putting my brother in jail." Her eyes were red and swollen, and she clasped a wad of tissues in her hand.

"I'm sorry," Ty said, pausing beside her.

Molly wasn't. At least one suspicious person was out of the way, and she felt a little safer.

"It's only for questioning, Jodean," Iris told her. "They probably won't even hold him overnight."

Larry Campbell got up and went to the window. "They can't. They don't have anything to hold him for. Everybody in Harmony knows Uncle Jud wouldn't kill Aunt Zebina!" His shoulders shook.

Iris crossed the room to stand behind him. "We'll just have to have the courage to face whatever comes, Larry. Your uncle's going to need you." She looked as if she wanted to touch him but didn't know quite how to go about it.

A tall man in a dark suit paced the hallway; Molly remembered meeting him at the caroling party. "They just came and took him away!" he said angrily, shaking his head. "Took Jud! I can't believe it. My God, I've known the man all my life!"

Molly recognized several members of the pageant cast she had met before. They hovered in small groups, murmured to one another, and stirred about the house like dark ghosts. Iris moved among them with whispery steps, pouring coffee and tea. Molly wondered what had happened to Undine Larsen.

"I'm going upstairs and pack a few things," Ty said aside to Molly. "I'm getting away from this place for tonight at least."

Molly sat on an uncomfortable Windsor chair away from the others. A silver bowl of chocolate-covered cherries sat on the table beside her. She could smell them. Everyone else ignored them. These people were grieving. What was wrong with her? Molly felt like slinking under the chair. She had craved chocolate even when Ethan died. The dark, sinful richness of it comforted her.

"Where's the housekeeper, Mrs. Larsen?" someone asked Iris. "Is she staying on?"

"I haven't seen her since the funeral," Iris said. "I think she went to bed with a sick headache." She fanned herself with a sympathy card. "There's a virus going around, you know."

But Molly saw a broad flash of white skirt disappearing from the kitchen as she left the house with Tyrus a few minutes later.

Tyrus saw it, too. "Oh, Mrs. Larsen!" he called. "I won't be staying here tonight after all." But the woman didn't answer. Her vast whiteness seemed to fill the hallway. Molly was glad she hadn't eaten the candy.

"Probably needed a little snack," Tyrus whispered when they got outside.

But Molly didn't answer. She was staring at the garage beneath the house. "Does that have a window?" she asked.

"I don't know. Why?"

"Because I want to look inside."

Tyrus laughed. "You think the gray car's in there, don't you? There's only room for two: Jud's Cadillac and whatever Zebina drove."

"I don't think Zebina drove," Molly said, hurrying around the side of the house. "I saw the Larsen woman chauffeuring her around in a shiny black car."

Tyrus peered through the window beside her. "A Volvo," he said. "Satisfied?"

"But where's the housekeeper's car?"

"Obviously she doesn't have one," Ty said, propping himself with one arm against the building. "She drove Zebina's."

Molly looked around. "Any other buildings around here big enough to hide a car?"

"See for yourself! Nothing!" Tyrus tugged at her hand. "Now can we go?"

"Huh! It has to be somewhere!" But Molly allowed herself to be led. Maybe Tyrus was right; maybe it wasn't Jud. Poor Jud. Poor Zebina. Everyone liked them. But when she thought about the gathering of close friends today, Molly gradually realized that Myrtis Curtis was conspicuously absent.

"Are you sure Jud was at home all last night?" Molly asked as they drove through the darkening streets of Harmony. "What makes you so certain he wasn't prowling around Quimby's Mill Road?"

"I haven't seen him except at the funeral," Ty said. "But when I left the house for Atlanta yesterday, he was upstairs resting."

"Yeah? How do you know he wasn't resting up for his little jaunt around the countryside?"

"Oh, Molly! The man had just come home from planning his wife's funeral. Besides, Iris and Jodean were there with him."

"Hmm. Did you actually see him when you left?" Molly yawned. She wanted to run, yell, kick something, but she was just too tired.

"Well, no. I didn't want to disturb him. I told Jodean I was leaving." Tyrus pulled into the aunts' driveway and kissed her cheek. "We both need some rest. I'm going to check into the motel tonight, and I'll see you early tomorrow; okay?"

Molly nodded. All she wanted was a hot shower and bed. "Tyrus," she asked as he opened the door, "the woman who called you last night—what did she sound like?"

Ty frowned. "I don't know. I didn't speak with her. When I got back from the church with Jud, there was a message that my sister had called."

"And you didn't call her back?"

"Of course I did, but no one answered, and that really scared me! Later I found out the whole family had gone to a Christmas program."

"You don't know who took the call?" Molly asked.

Tyrus slammed the door of the car behind her. "I didn't think to ask. The house was full of people and the phone was ringing constantly; it could've been anybody. The message said my sister needed me in Atlanta, and I was afraid whoever killed the others had found out where she was. I didn't wait around to ask questions."

He looked so remorseful, she wanted to hold him. Molly touched his lips with her fingers. "That's okay. Nobody would've admitted it anyway. Frankly, I doubt if anyone really called."

He caught her hand before she started up the walk. "This time promise me you won't go wandering off somewhere. I'd like to get a good night's sleep."

"Scout's honor," Molly said.

Tree lights gleamed from the window, and when she opened the door, the whole house smelled of cornbread. "Aunt Ivalee's baking it for the Christmas dressing," Joy said, looking up from a jigsaw puzzle. "Where've you been? It's almost dark."

"We were getting worried about you!" Ivalee came in from the kitchen wiping the steam from her glasses.

"The police have taken Judson Horne in for questioning," Molly told them. "I just came from there."

"Oh dear!" Ivalee stood transfixed in the doorway. "And right here at Christmas, too. Is Iris still there?"

"Yes, but she's coming." Molly tossed Emma Beth's purple jacket over a chair and remembered the morning's confrontation. "Where's Emma Beth?" she asked.

Joy added another piece to her puzzle. "Upstairs. She says she's gonna stay in her room until she starves."

Molly smiled. "That would be hard to do in this house."

Joy pointed to some letters on the table. "You got something in the mail—a Christmas card, I think."

Molly smiled as she read the card and message from their neighbor back home. Just now Charlotte, N.C., seemed a part of another dimension. She passed it along to Joy, noticing the opened cards that had come for the rest of the family. The one on top with a Currier and Ives scene caught her eye, and she picked it up with curiosity. It was a handwritten verse from Myrtis.

We've shared laughter, secrets, tears;
Made memories throughout the years.
And as the seasons come and go,
You're still the greatest gift I know—my friends!

The simple little rhyme brought a smile. How like Myrt to think of something like that. Molly remembered seeing the framed poem she had written as a child on the wall at her home. She had almost forgotten that Myrtis wrote verse. When the realization hit her, Molly dropped the card as if it were the dead mouse she had found in her car. The handwriting was the same as that in the warning note with the withered mistletoe.

TWENTY-NINE

EMMA BETH WOULD NOT come down for supper, and Molly felt so guilty about accusing her of the note that she could scarcely choke down her own food. Iris was silent and red-eyed throughout the meal. Molly didn't know if she was grieving for her friend Jud or for the long-absent Barlow Jones.

As she went upstairs for her shower, Molly knocked lightly on Emma Beth's door, intending to apologize, smooth ruffled feathers, but she got no response. Probably asleep, Molly thought; I'll talk with her in the morning.

But why, she wondered later as she lay in the darkness of her room, would Myrtis, who pretended to be her friend, leave such a vicious note? Was she trying to frighten her away, or did she intend to harm her?

Tomorrow morning, Molly decided, just before sleep crept in, tomorrow morning she would go to someone in authority and show them the warning note as well as the evidence she had hidden away.

But morning brought yet another surprise: Emma Beth was missing!

Her bed had apparently been slept in and she had draped her nightshirt across the foot as if she had dressed in a hurry, but she wasn't in the house or anywhere around it.

"I've called everybody I know," Ivalee said, hanging up the phone with a final sound. "All her friends, the neighbors, even some of her teachers. Nobody's seen her." She stood in the hall twirling the telephone cord around her fingers. "Where in the world can she be?"

"She's run off somewhere. I've looked all over town!" Asa jammed the car keys into his pocket and leaned his head on his arm as if he needed support from the wall "I'm calling the police," he said in a low, strained voice.

When a car pulled into the driveway, everyone dashed outside hoping for news of Emma Beth. Instead they greeted Tyrus coming up the walk with a puzzled look on his face. "Is this a reception committee or a lynch mob?" he asked. But his smile faded when he saw their faces. "What's wrong? I tried to call, but your line was tied up."

"Emma Beth's disappeared," Asa said. "The police are on their way."

They waited in the yard, spurning the confines of the warm house, and tensed at the passing of each car. "How long has she been gone?" Ty asked.

Asa had barely put out one cigarette before he lit another. He exhaled quickly. "Just since this morning...don't know when...I just hope she hasn't gone and done something stupid!" Asa paced to the end of the driveway, smoke trailing behind him.

"The police released Jud last night." Ty spoke with a warning look in his eyes. "They only wanted to question him; guess they didn't have enough to hold him."

"Yet," Molly said so only Ty could hear. "Have you been by there?"

"No. Myrt told me. She called this morning looking for you; wanted me to give you a message."

Molly sat on the cold cement step. "That's peculiar. Why didn't she just call me here?"

"I guess she couldn't get through—phone was busy," he said. "But it does seem strange. She sounded a little different—not quite like herself."

"I made it pretty clear I thought Jud might have had something to do with Rowena's disappearance," Molly said, "and I think Myrtis left that horrible rhymed message in my car the other day." She told him about finding the Christmas card in Myrt's handwriting. "It matches the note I found."

"Do you think she's warning you to protect Jud?" he asked.

Molly shivered and started inside just as the police turned into the driveway. "I don't know, but I plan to have a few words with Miss Myrtis Curtis *after* I've talked with the police. I'm tired of all this cloak-and-dagger stuff!" Molly's voice shook. She felt betrayed.

The officer, a plump, middle-aged man whom Molly hadn't seen before, didn't appear to be too concerned about Emma Beth's disappearance. "I don't want you folks to think I'm taking this lightly," he said. "We already have men patrolling the area; we'll find her. But kids can be foolish sometimes. They don't always think to let us know where they're going."

But Asa shook his head. "No. It's more than that. She's angry with herself—and with me."

"And with me, too, I'm afraid," Molly admitted. She looked at Asa. "I practically accused her of leaving a threatening note in my car. I was upset with her, but I was wrong. I know that now."

"What note is that, ma'am?" the officer wanted to know.

Downstairs Molly showed them the note and the crumbling mistletoe she had saved in an envelope. When the aunts were out of earshot, she quickly plucked Myrt's Christmas card from the array on the mantel and placed it alongside the other. "Does the handwriting look familiar?" she asked.

The policeman looked at it and frowned. "Does seem to be the same; of course, we'll have to have it examined by an expert." He put it in a folder with the menacing rhyme.

"Do you suppose Emma Beth went out to Myrt's?" Molly suggested with a hand to her mouth. "Maybe she got to feeling sorry for how she acted—wanted to apologize."

"That's a long way to walk," Asa said.

"No more than three or four miles," Tyrus reminded him.

"Then let's go!" Asa grabbed his coat, brushing past the policeman. "I'll take my car."

The man nodded. "Fine. I'll check the mall again."

"Go ahead; we'll follow," Molly told Asa. She wanted to talk with Myrtis, too, but first she had something else to do. "Wait!" she called as the officer started to leave. "I have something for you." She snatched a flat, gift-wrapped box from beneath the tree and shoved it into his hands.

The man was speechless. He looked at the present and frowned. "This is for me?" he said at last.

Molly smiled. "Well, not exactly. It has to do with Rowena Sterling's disappearance, and possibly with the skeleton they found."

"The note from the 'Christmas Mouse' and the plane tickets!" Tyrus was clearly impressed. "You hid them with the presents!"

Molly nodded. "Just give this to the detective in charge," she said. "These are the things my husband found twenty-three years ago, the day before Rowena Sterling left Harmony." She struggled to keep resentment form her voice. "Since then, several people may have been killed because of what's in this box. Please see that it gets there safely." She watched as the officer put the gift inside his jacket. "I hear you released Judson Horne last night," she said.

"Mr. Horne was never under arrest," the man told her. "We only wanted to ask him some questions."

"Poor Jud!" Iris stood behind them with her lean arms folded. "The Christmas parade is this afternoon, and this is the first time in years he'll not be able to play Santa."

"Oh, yes ma'am, he will," the policeman said, zipping his jacket over a bulging stomach. "He plans to ride in the parade same as usual. Said he didn't intend to disappoint these kids."

"What?" Ivalee caught her breath. "Why, they just buried his wife yesterday! I never heard of such a thing!"

"That's exactly what Jud would do." Iris nodded approvingly. "I'm not a bit surprised."

"Well, I don't think it's in very good taste," Ivalee muttered as she followed them to the door. She stood on the porch with a sweater around her, watching as they hurried to the car. "We'll wait here in case Emma Beth calls," she said. "Let us know as soon as you find her."

If we find her, Molly thought as Ty turned toward Shake Rag Road. The weathered gray barn and the large granite boulder in the field beyond were becoming familiar landmarks. She sat in silence watching the brown fields glide past. Now she was afraid of what they would find.

BUT AS IT TURNED OUT, they found nothing because Myrtis wasn't there.

"Her car must be in the garage," Asa said. "The door is shut."

But the doors to the house were locked and no lights shone from inside. Colonel Sanders followed them about, darting between their legs, fawning for affection. Molly stroked his shaggy brown head. "Where's Myrtis, boy?

Did she go off and leave you?'' But the dog only raced ec-statically in circles around them. They looked in the sta-ble. Shortcake had obviously been fed and everything seemed in order, but Molly checked every place where a person might hide or be hidden while Ty and Asa searched the area around the house, calling Myrt's name.

''Maybe she went to feed the neighbor's cats,'' Molly suggested, remembering the day she and Joy had cut the tree.

''Wouldn't the dog have followed her?'' Ty asked. Still, on the way home they drove up the narrow lane that led to the house next door, only to be greeted by silence.

''She probably went shopping,'' Molly said, thinking of the last-minute items she had yet to buy. ''I'll bet she's downtown at the mall.'' Or hiding somewhere, she thought. It was entirely possible that Myrt was afraid of someone, that she didn't want to answer their questions.

The closer they got to the sprawling white house on Muscadine Hill, the harder Molly prayed that Emma Beth would be there to greet them. At first she believed the girl had run off in a fit of pique to get her father's attention, but now she was frightened. When she saw Asa, who had gotten there before them, she knew the situation had not improved.

His face was white as he ran down the walk to meet them. ''Now your Joy's gone, too,'' he said, taking Mol-ly's hands in his. ''We can't find her anywhere!''

THIRTY

MOLLY LEANED AGAINST the heavy newel post and closed her eyes. She remembered one time when she and Ethan had gone white-water rafting and were headed for an especially rough spot on the river. She had been scared to death, but she knew she had to hold back the panic and do the right thing or risk the consequences. This situation wasn't so different, only this time Joy might be the one to suffer. She had to stay calm.

Ivalee hung up the telephone harder than usual. "People keep calling, tying up the line. They mean well, but what if one of the girls is trying to reach us?"

Iris put a hand on Molly's shoulder. "I'm sorry about Joy, Molly. We should've kept an eye on her."

"No, she's my responsibility. I should have kept an eye on her," Molly said. "It's not your fault."

"It's not anybody's fault," a small voice said, and Molly looked up to see her daughter slowly coming down the attic stairs. "Emma Beth has promised to come down in a minute if you'll all give your word not to jump all over her."

"Emma's in the attic?" Asa started up the steps, but Molly held him back. "She's been up there all this time?" His face was getting redder by the minute. "She must have heard us talking to the police!"

"How did you know she was there?" Ivalee asked.

Joy trailed one hand along the banister. "I thought I heard a noise—and she goes up there to sketch sometimes. It's quiet."

"Well, she's just about given every one of us a nervous breakdown!" Iris began, but Tyrus gave her a warning look as they heard Emma Beth's sluggish footsteps above them.

"Your daddy has been almost crazy with worry, Emma Beth Brown!" her grandmother said in an emotion-filled voice. "Why do you want to punish him this way? He didn't run off and leave you!"

Emma Beth stood motionless on the stairs looking down at them. "I threw away that necklace," she said in a low voice. "I'm sorry, Daddy."

When Asa opened his arms, she ran into them.

"MY EMMA BETH and me—we're a pair, aren't we?" Asa said over coffee in the kitchen. He took a long, slow drink from his cup and opened a fresh pack of cigarettes. "But we'll make out okay—damned if we won't!"

"Did anyone remember to call the police?" Molly asked. "They'll still be looking for her."

"I did," Ty said. He seemed to be trying to give her a message with his eyes. "And they still haven't located the gray Pontiac. Maybe we'll learn something from that rifle casing they found in the trunk."

"What if the gun's not registered?" Iris asked, slicing a loaf of her sister's homemade bread.

With her luck it probably wasn't, Molly thought. She wondered if the police had uncovered any more evidence on the murder of Barlow Jones and decided they would probably put it on hold until after Christmas. After all, the man had been dead for almost a quarter of a century. He wasn't going anywhere.

Molly set the table, using bright Santa plates to celebrate. She wondered if the Harmony police believed her story about the message in the tree. It sounded incredible, she knew, but now they had the actual papers to back it up; and the hole in her windshield would be hard to ignore.

"I'm worried about Myrtis," Iris said as she sat down to cooling soup. "I've tried to call her several times, and there's still no answer out there."

"You know where she keeps the extra house key," Ivalee reminded her. "If it'll make you feel better, why not go out and see for yourself?"

"I'll go right after lunch," Iris decided. "Don't want to run into that awful parade traffic."

Ty looked at his watch and then at Molly. "What time is the parade?" he asked.

"Starts around four," Asa said, "and then they light up that big spruce in the square. That's when Santa comes. With the band and the choral groups and all, I'd say the whole thing lasts about an hour—maybe a little longer."

"I think I'll walk downtown before the festivities start and pick up a few extra stocking-stuffers," Molly said.

"While you're at it, get a couple of cases of Grecian Formula for me," Asa said, running his hands through his hair. "I expect to be completely white by the time Emma Beth graduates from high school."

"If she graduates!" Joy giggled. The two girls sat at the kitchen table eating a late lunch. Emma Beth's red hair was knobby with curlers; Joy's was sheathed in a towel. Every few minutes they burst into laughter for apparently no reason at all. It sounded as if things were finally returning to normal, Molly thought, except, of course, for the killer who was still on the loose.

"I'll go shopping with you," Ty offered, reaching for his coat. "Until they find that lunatic running around out there, it's not safe for you to go anywhere alone."

"Okay," Molly said as they walked down the hill together. "What did you want to tell me?"

"Was it that obvious?" Tyrus put an arm through hers and pulled her closer. "I didn't want to take a chance on being overheard, but if Myrtis hasn't turned up by parade time, I'm checking out Jud's house from top to bottom."

"Jud's house? Why not Reuben's? It would have been easy for him to put that note in the desk and pretend he didn't know it was there. And that basement of his looks like a perfect place to keep somebody out of the way."

Ty shook his head. "Not with his mother there. I called before we left the house. Reuben's mother is here for the holidays. She answered the phone."

"But what makes you think Myrt's at Jud's?" Molly asked.

Ty shrugged. "To tell you the truth, I don't know where else to look. She may be perfectly safe, and for all I know, Jud might be the one in danger. I just don't feel good about it."

"All right then, I'll go with you," Molly said. "But what if someone's there—Mrs. Larsen or one of the Hornes' many kin?"

He frowned. "That is a possibility. We'll just have to wait until he leaves for the parade; since he's playing Santa, he'll have to go early. And surely that housekeeper has left by now! After all, Zebina is dead and it's almost Christmas. She must have a family somewhere."

"I hope so," Molly answered. "Undine Larsen doesn't seem the type for Christmas parades. But how do you plan to get inside?"

"Easy." Tyrus held up a key. "I conveniently forgot to give this back. Besides, I still have clothes over there. If I want to collect the rest of my things, that's not unreasonable, is it?"

"That person with a gun isn't in a reasonable mood, Tyrus," she reminded him.

But not only had Iris been unable to find Myrt, when Molly and Tyrus got back from town they found Sergeant Webster from the sheriff's department waiting for them in the living room. "I think we may have located that gray car, ma'am," he said. "Could you come next door for a minute and see if it's the one that's been following you?"

"Next door?" Molly frowned. "What's it doing there?"

"It's in the Dinsmores' garage," he explained. "Someone saw it turning into their drive the other night and called Mrs. Dinsmore. The car belongs to her, but she doesn't drive anymore."

"I've told Miss Eula to get rid of that car!" Ivalee said. "It doesn't do her a bit of good sitting in that shed, and she keeps a set of keys out there on a nail behind the door. Anyone could steal it."

"How many people know about these keys?" the sergeant asked.

Ivalee shrugged. "Just about everybody, I guess. At least everybody who lives around here. She's always done it."

The garage sat at the far end of the lot on the other side of the Dinsmore property and was hidden from the house by trees. The driveway came in from a side street, and since Eula Dinsmore slept on the other end of the house and was hard of hearing to boot, she might never notice the car was being used.

It took only one look to assure Molly that this was the sinister gray Pontiac of her recent nightmarish adventures. It looked so innocent in the old garage—a little old lady's ten-year-old car, probably used only for trips to church and the grocery store in the days when Eula Dinsmore drove. Still, Molly could barely stand to look at it without shuddering.

"I suppose whoever used it switched the headlights off before turning in," Sergeant Webster said. "You folks didn't see or hear anything, did you?"

Molly shook her head. She didn't want to look at the car anymore. "You don't suppose Sonny Earl . . . ?"

The officer drew in his breath. "I don't know, ma'am. We'll dust it for fingerprints and see what we come up with." But he didn't act as though he expected to find much.

MOLLY WAS RELIEVED when Joy chose to go to the parade with Emma Beth and a group of her friends that afternoon. At least she wouldn't have to make up an excuse about her whereabouts. The two aunts decided to walk downtown later. "I haven't missed a tree-lighting yet," Iris said. "I just hope they don't sing that silly 'Twelve Days of Christmas' song again! It's getting tiresome."

"Then I guess we'll see you there," Molly called as Tyrus prodded her out the door.

They were just in time to see Jud, plumped with pillows, opening the garage door in his jolly red suit.

"I almost hope he isn't the one," Ty said sadly as they watched 'Santa' drive away, crimson hat bobbing. "It takes a lot of courage to do what he's doing after all that man's been through."

The house seemed deserted. Molly couldn't resist a peek in the window as Tyrus rang the bell. The room that had been so festive only a short time before seemed to mock the season. The huge Christmas tree was gone, and a spray of white roses had replaced the bright wreath on the door. Molly squinted through the stiff lace curtains as Tyrus rang the bell again. Jud hadn't even left a light on to come home to.

"There's no one here," Ty said, inserting his key in the lock after a reasonable wait. "Come on—hurry!"

Molly felt as if the large taciturn housekeeper or the wispy gray ghost of Zebina Horne would suddenly appear at any minute as they walked boldly through the house. Tyrus clomped about poking into closets and dark corners while Molly padded after him. "You don't have to be so quiet," he reminded her, coming out of the laundry room. "Nobody's here but us."

Molly switched on a light in the garage, expecting to see Myrt's body bundled away somewhere, but only the sleek Volvo greeted her. Ty waited for her in the hall. "Let's look upstairs," he said. "I'll check Jud's room; you get the housekeeper's."

She hesitated with her hand on the knob, disliking to trespass in private quarters. The woman seemed so friendless, alone. Molly was reluctant to violate her sanctuary.

The bedroom was pink and frilly with pastoral prints on the walls—not at all the motif she would choose for the rigid Undine Larsen, whose crumpled uniform had been tossed over the back of a chair.

Molly stood in the center of the room and sniffed a peculiar odor, a strong, gluelike smell. On the dresser she found a bottle of spirit gum and several strands of false white hair. In the top drawer of the dresser she discovered a second set of blue-tinted contact lenses; and in a bag at the back of the closet were Myrt's orange hat and scarf.

"Tyrus!" she shouted. "Come here quick!"

THIRTY-ONE

TYRUS STOOD in the doorway with a stack of letters in his hand. "I think we've found Rowena," he said, making a fan of the envelopes. There were only about six in the lot. "I saw these in a sack in the trash can. He must have forgotten to get rid of them. They're all postmarked from different cities and were mailed in the first months after Rowena disappeared." He tore one from its envelope. "Look—notice the signature."

The note was written on pink paper. "Dear Mouse," the letter began, and it was signed "Rowena." Molly didn't read the contents. The woman's heavy perfume, the smell of the glue, and the horror of what they had found was making her sick. Rowena Sterling was the obese Undine Larsen! "If Rowena is playing Santa," she asked, "where in the devil is Jud?"

Ty stuffed the letters into his pocket. "Well, he's not here, unless he's become invisible. Do you think she's done something with him?"

Molly shoved him out of the room and closed the door behind them. "I don't know, but I want to call Myrt once again." She hurried into Jud's room and dialed, frowning as the ringing went unanswered.

"Why would Rowena pose as Jud in the parade?" she asked.

"To hide something? To give him an alibi?" He shrugged. "Maybe she wants to ride in a sleigh!"

Molly slammed down the receiver so hard, he jumped. "Tyrus, I think you're right!"

"About the sleigh?" He narrowed his eyes.

"No, silly! I think Rowena is giving Jud an alibi and covering for him, just like he's been covering for her. I think they're in this together!" Again she picked up the phone. "I'm calling the police!"

"But what if we're wrong about Jud?" he asked, as Molly dialed.

"Then I'll say I'm sorry!" She waited. "Yes, I want to report a possible—*Don't cut me off*!" Molly hit the button with her finger. "Damn! Can you believe it? They've put me on hold!"

"Call Asa, Reuben—anybody!" Ty paced the room behind her.

But it seemed that everyone had gone to the parade. Molly turned to face him. "I have the most horrible feeling that history is going to repeat itself if we don't do something to stop it." She grabbed his hand. "Let's get out of here! We've got to get to Myrt's. I just hope we're not too late."

"Will you please explain?" Ty said as they skidded into the street. "You don't really think Jud would harm Myrt, do you? They're almost like brother and sister."

"Maybe so, but Jud's gone too far to turn back now. I think the stable fire was a screen for Barlow Jones's murder," Molly said, "and I wouldn't be surprised if they used the same scheme again today." She leaned forward in her seat. "Can't you drive any faster?"

From a few blocks away Molly heard the choral strains of "Lo, How a Rose" being broadcast from a speaker. It was one of her favorite Christmas songs, and she wished she could stay and listen. Parked cars lined each side of the street, and she saw what looked like the entire population of Harmony milling in the square.

"There's a policeman," Ty said, slowing. "Maybe he can help."

The man was directing traffic around the closed-off area. "You can't go through here," he told Ty. "We're lighting the tree. You'll have to go around."

Molly leaned toward him. "This is an emergency," she said. "Someone we know is in danger. She needs help fast!"

He waved a car past. "Who? What kind of danger?"

"It's Myrtis Curtis out on Shake Rag Road. I think somebody's trying to kill her. Could you please get someone to follow us?" Molly yelled over the sounds of a flute ensemble playing "Winter Wonderland."

"Lady, if I left this post, all hell would break loose! What makes you so sure about this?"

"Would you just call it in? I don't have time to argue!" As they drove away, Molly caught a glimpse of familiar red hair and yelled, "Wait a minute! There's Emma Beth!"

Her young cousin was coming from the drugstore with a large drink in her hand. She smiled broadly when she saw them.

"Em, you've got to do something for us," Molly said as Ty brought the car to a stop. "Myrtis is in trouble, bad trouble! Go back into the drugstore and call the police. Don't let them put you on hold, and tell them to get out there *now*!"

Emma Beth stared at her open-mouthed with the beginning of a smile on her face. "Oh, come on, Molly!" she said.

"She's not joking," Tyrus told her.

"Hurry!" Molly shouted as her cousin still hesitated. "We're counting on you.

"Watch it!" she cautioned Ty as two little girls and a dog ran in front of the car. "We'll have to go several blocks

ut of the way to get around this crowd.'' She covered her
ace with her hands. ''I'm afraid we're not going to get
here in time!''

''Calm down, will you?'' Tyrus turned back onto the
main road. ''We'll get there when we get there. I can't go
my faster.'' He reached for her hand at the traffic light.
Sing something . . . recite a poem. . . .''

Molly squeezed his fingers. '' 'Twas the night before
Christmas...''' she began, counting off each landmark as
they passed: the stone columns, the old barn, the boulder
in the field. Was Myrtis already dead? She knew Jud—or
someone—had kept her hidden all day. But how? And
where?

''I don't see a car,'' Ty said as they approached the
house. ''I don't see anybody.''

''Rowena would have driven him here earlier,'' Molly
said. ''He can't take a chance on somebody seeing his car.''
She looked at the stable. It seemed strangely silent; then
she noticed Shortcake grazing in the stableyard. ''Somebody's let the horse out.'' She had the door open even before the car stopped. She could hear the Colonel barking
inside the house.

''Hold it! Don't be in such a hurry.'' Ty grabbed the
back of her jacket. ''We don't know who's out there or
what he might do. Go slow here, Molly.''

Molly pulled herself free. ''We don't have time to be
careful. He's going to kill her, Ty. He may have already
done it.''

Shortcake whinnied and trotted over to greet them, but
Molly climbed over the fence and ran quietly to the back
of the stable. She could hear Ty's footsteps behind her.
They leaned against the rough brown wall and listened.
Someone was moving around inside. Their eyes met, and

Molly knew they were both thinking the same thing: *Wh*
if he has a gun?

Molly tensed as she heard the low rumble of a man
voice and Myrt's familiar throaty tones. Her words we
dark and deep, full of despair, like a judge pronouncing
sentence.

"No, I won't do it," Myrtis was saying. "Why should
make things easier for you by writing a note when you'
planning to kill me anyway?"

"Well, it would make it easier, I'll admit," Jud said
"but it isn't essential." He paused. "Myrt, you know
don't like doing this. I've always been fond of you. I'
truly sorry."

"Huh! And I reckon you're sorry about poisoning poo
Zebina, too!"

Molly smiled to hear the pluck in Myrt's voice. He
friend hadn't given up yet.

"That was a mistake!" he snapped. "I wouldn't hur
Zebina. Rowena meant that cake for Ethan's prying littl
wife. Ethan! He's the one who started all this! If thos
brats hadn't taken that message, they'd still be alive to
day."

"Daddy Clyde was right! You and Rowena don't mak
a very nice twosome." Myrtis sighed. "That fruitcake wa
supposed to put an end to me, too—right? But yo
weren't really sick, were you?"

Jud laughed. "The doctor thought I was." He sounded
almost apologetic. "You were beginning to suspect Un
dine Larsen. Remember the night of the caroling party
when we were at Iris's? You said she reminded you o
Rowena. I tried to convince you otherwise, but Rowena
said we'd never really be safe because you'd always wonder. It wasn't my idea, believe me."

"Of course not," Myrt said. "And it wasn't your idea to take pot shots at Molly either. My God, Judson, I can't believe you're the same person I grew up with!"

"I only did it to frighten her, make her give up and go away. Why, I wasn't even trying to hurt her." He talked as if he were a sorely put-upon parent whose patience was being strained. "I don't enjoy killing people, Myrtis."

"Silly me! I keep forgetting. What about that bullet hole in Molly's windshield? Went clean through the back of the car, I hear. A harmless game, I guess?"

"That was Rowena. She took a shorter route to Quimy's Mill Road and was waiting for her there... Rowena does rather enjoy it, I'm afraid."

"And she seems fond of wearing my orange hat and scarf, too. Funny, it really isn't her color." Myrt laughed dryly. "Rowena must have broken some kind of record getting back to your house after searching Molly's room the night we went caroling. But then, she always was fast on her feet—and such big feet, too!"

Molly glanced at Ty, who had worked his way to the end of the building. Myrtis was stalling for time, she knew. But time was running out.

Scrap lumber had been stacked near the stable, and Ty grabbed a section of plank while motioning for her to throw some stones toward the front. Molly looked at her watch. The lighting of the tree should be over. Santa would be coming soon.

"You know I always enjoy our little conversations, Myrt," she heard Jud say, "but it's about time for the parade to be over, so I'll have to move right along now."

"Jud, this is crazy! People aren't going to believe I killed myself." Molly heard the movement of their feet, the rustle of straw.

"Think about it, Myrtis. Weren't you always a litt
jealous of Rowena? They'll think you killed her and h
hippie lover in a fit of jealousy and buried them in sep
rate graves. Rowena's, of course, will never be found."

"Everyone knows me better than that! And what earth
reason would I have to kill Zebina?"

"Jealousy again." Jud sighed. "Really Myrtis, yc
should have learned to control your passions. Your su
cide will only serve to confirm your guilt," he continued
"Of course, I couldn't possibly have had anything to c
with it since I am at this very minute shouting 'Ho! Hc
Ho!' and tossing candy to the kiddies. People will assun
you couldn't live with your conscience now that that poc
boy's skeleton has surfaced, so you set fire to the stab
and shot yourself. The gun, you see, will be found in yo
hand."

Molly heard Myrtis gasp. "Like hell it will, you piou
hog-eyed hypocrite!" And something slammed into th
stable wall.

"Now!" Tyrus whispered, and Molly sent a ston
skimming over the stableyard, where it pinged against th
watering trough. The second one bounced off the gate.

"Somebody's out there!" Jud said in a low voice. "Sta
here and keep still. Another trick like that and I'll shov
this gun right down your throat, Myrt. I swear I will!"

Molly heard him creeping toward the door and let fl
with another rock.

"Rowena?" Jud called. "Is that you?"

He didn't see Ty waiting behind the open stable door
He didn't see the approach of the shiny blue Cadillac witl
Rowena at the wheel or the patrol car closing in in the dis
tance. When Tyrus slammed down with the heavy piece o
wood, Judson Horne fell to his knees with a scream and

the gun skidded across the hard-packed earth, where Molly snatched it up.

"Don't move!" Ty stood over him, the wood still in his hand. "Don't you dare move."

Jud lay on the ground whimpering until he saw Rowena, and then he attempted to get to his feet. "Help me, 'Ena!" he cried. "Please! Don't leave me here!"

But Rowena—"Undine Larsen"—had seen the police car behind her and was desperately trying to circle and evade them. It didn't do her any good. Emma Beth had finally come through.

"He didn't hurt you, did he?" Molly asked as she walked with Myrtis from the stable.

Myrt looked down on Jud as Sergeant Webster hurried through the gate, leaving his partner to deal with Rowena, who still wore the trousers and boots of her Santa suit; little tufts of white clung to her face.

"No, but he had serious intentions." Myrt shook her head slowly. Her hair, Molly noticed, didn't look any different than usual. "Judson," she said, "I'm right disappointed in you."

"If your husband hadn't been so greedy, things wouldn't have gone this far," Jud said to Molly as the two men pulled him to his feet. His face was streaked with dirt, and his blue eyes looked as cold as the blood in his veins.

"My husband! What are you talking about?" Molly felt Myrt's hand close over her own.

"His greed, that's what I'm talking about." His face was only inches away. She could feel his warm breath. "He wanted to *sell* me that note, the tickets they'd found. When Ethan realized how important they were, he expected me to *pay* for them!" His voice rose. "Those things were put there for Rowena, and they took them, and then after all this time, he had the nerve to threaten me with them! How was I to know I could trust any of them after that?"

"And so you killed them?" Molly's voice trembled. "You killed Ethan and Neil!" But Judson Horne didn't answer. She looked at Ty. This was why Ethan had ordered that expensive leisure boat. Her husband had been a blackmailer! Molly turned away so Jud wouldn't see her cry. She hoped Joy would never find out.

"WHERE IN THE WORLD did he hide you?" Molly asked Myrt as they sat in front of her fire. "We turned this place upside down looking for you."

Myrtis mopped at her tear-streaked face. "They had me over at Jessie's; you know, my neighbor who's out of town. Jud followed me there when I went to feed the cats this morning—locked me in the closet." She reached for another cookie. "I'm starving! Haven't eaten a thing since breakfast!"

The police had taken Jud and Rowena away, and Iris and Ivalee arrived soon after. Ty sat close to Molly, his shoulder pressed against hers, and held her hand in both of his. She was glad for the nearness of him.

"You knew something was wrong when you called me this morning, didn't you?" Ty asked Myrt.

She nodded. "I was afraid for Molly. Actually, I suspected something a long time before that. I just couldn't come to accept it. He called early this morning wanting to know if he could come by for a cup of coffee. He never calls first; he always just comes, so I knew something was bad wrong then . . . and, well, you know the rest." Myrtis went to the window. "I guess poor Colonel Sanders is still running around out there," she said, staring into the dark. "He's been shut up in this house all afternoon."

Molly had to ask. "Myrt, you left that note in my car, didn't you? The one with the mistletoe."

"Yes. I was frightened for you. I wanted to scare you enough to send you home." Myrtis smiled. "Forgive me, but I knew a gentle nudge wouldn't do it. Things have been brewing around here for longer than you know."

Jud and Rowena had been planning this since Molly's arrival, she told them. They thought they had taken care of everything once they had the two men out of the way, and then she came along and they assumed she meant to blackmail them with the letter. Apparently they didn't learn about Gus until later. "Jud told me he met Neil Fry at a civic convention back in the winter," Myrtis said. "That's when he heard about the note. Of course, Neil didn't suspect until later that Jud was the one who wrote it."

"And he knew there was a good chance that boy's skeleton would come to light when they started clearing land for the shopping center," Ivalee said with a sad smile for her sister.

"Right; then when Jud learned you were coming, Molly, he panicked and called in Rowena to pose as his house-keeper," Myrt said. "That's when I became suspicious. You can't live in the same house as sisters as long as Rowena and I did and not get to know somebody. There was just something about her!" She sighed. "Anyway, she and Jud were in this together till the end."

"Tell us about the beginning," Iris said softly.

Myrtis nodded. "After all this time I only learned the truth today," she said. "It seems that Jud and Rowena had planned to elope that Christmas," she told them. "Rowena was halfway through her second year in college and wasn't interested in continuing, but her father insisted, and he hated Jud."

A few days before, Myrt continued, Rowena took her mother's jewelry, withdrew all her money from savings—which was quite a bit at the time—and hid them in the stable until they could get away to make a new start. Jud, meanwhile, made plane reservations under those fictitious names, and they agreed to meet at a prearranged place.

Rowena's father, however, had noticed the jewelry was missing and accused the hired man of taking it. Barlow Jones, of course, denied it and the two men got in a heated argument. That was when he was fired—or quit.

"That's why everyone thought he burned down the stable," Myrt explained.

Iris smiled. "Not everyone," she said.

"But why did they kill him?" Molly asked with a cautious eye on Iris.

"He happened to be in the stable that night when Rowena came to collect her things. He was going to tell her father and clear his name, and she killed him."

"How?" Iris looked up. Her voice was hardly more than a whisper.

"With a pitchfork," Myrtis said, covering her eyes with a hand. "Jud buried him in the field out there and they burned the stable because they couldn't get rid of the blood." She looked at Iris with only the sound of the fire crackling in the quiet room. "I'm so sorry," she said.

"He was a sweet man, and so gentle...." Iris smiled sadly. "I wonder..."

"Rowena decided to leave that night as planned," Myrt said. "Jud was to follow in the summer when things calmed down. She went as far north as her money would take her and took an assumed name. And at Jud's insistence, she gave him a part of her savings to keep quiet about the murder. That's how he was able to begin buying stock in the store. Then Rowena got involved in the theater up there and fell for some actor; I don't think they stayed together very long.

"Meanwhile, Jud was moving up at Gideon's, and he eventually latched on to Zebina and her money and did all right for himself here." Myrt slowly peeled an apple, making a thin corkscrew of red.

"But they kept in touch," Ty said.

"Oh, yes, Jud told me that for a while they fully intended to get back together." The fire hissed as she threw the peelings into the flames. "After that, I think they only kept tabs because they didn't trust each other!"

Which of them had killed Ethan and Neil? Molly wondered. She might never know. She wasn't sure she wanted to.

Everyone looked up at the sound of tires in the driveway, and seconds later a blast of cold air hit them as Reuben Anthony burst through the kitchen doorway with the Colonel at his heels. "I just heard about it!" he said, throwing his huge coat in the direction of a chair. "I've been out of town all afternoon." He reached Myrtis in two strides. "What a relief to see you, to know you're all right!" He captured her hand in his as she made room for his sizable bulk beside her. "They tell me you had a close call."

Myrtis smiled. "Well, preacher, this seems to be the season for miracles in a stable."